BETRAYED
MY BODY IS KILLING ME

By: DAVID J. BROWN

Copyright © December 10, 2022
DAVID J. BROWN BOOKS

PUBLISHED BY:
DAVID J. BROWN BOOKS, LLC

WEBSITE:
davidjbrownbooks.com

PRINTED IN:
The United States of America

GOD BLESS AMERICA

DAVID J. BROWN

This book may not be reproduced, transmitted, or be stored in whole or in part by any means, including graphic, electronic or mechanical without the express written consent of the publisher except in the case of brief quotations embodied in critical articles and reviews.

This is David Brown's eighth book, the seventh in his series of novels

Each book is a stand-alone novel but runs in a loose series with many of the primary characters moving through each book.

As in all of my other books, I am donating this book to:

The United States National Library Service for the Blind and Physically Handicapped.

BETRAYED

MY BODY IS KILLING ME

By: DAVID J. BROWN

www.davidjbrownbooks.com

Proudly printed in the
United States of America

DAVID J. BROWN

Never let anyone tell you that you can't do it.

Never tell yourself that you can't do it.

Dreams are worth dreaming

Dare to dream my friends

and

DREAM BIG!

A note to my loyal readers:

    This final book of eight, ends my ride of a lifetime. Due to my medical condition and the cruelty of aging, I no longer have the ability to do what I love to do. There is much more life in this old boy, just not this part. Weep not for me as I found a passion and a purpose in my later years like I've never known before.

Be true to yourself and take chances. There may be day's when faith is all you may have left and know that faith for that day is all that you will need.

Celebrate your blessings and speak of them often!

Within all fiction, lies a bit of the truth.
Within all truths, lies a bit of fiction.
Our perceptions are the deciding factors.

David J. Brown

This story is a work of fiction. It is inspired in part by true life events. In certain cases, locations, incidents, characters and timelines have been changed for dramatic purposes. Certain characters may be composites or entirely fictitious.

This novel is dedicated In loving memory and honor of:

Leslie Baker

Leslie was from the North East of England and was an Emergency Care Assistant which is the (equivalent of an EMT) with the North East Ambulance Service. Leslie was also a medic in the British Army and saw active service in Kosovo, Afghanistan and Iraq. At the beginning of last year Leslie was diagnosed with stage 4 Breast Cancer and she spent the next 6 months fighting her illness and fundraising for crucial, life-saving community defibrillators. The day after her passing, one of her defibrillators saved the life of a 17-year old boy.

Leslie was a mother, a wife, a warrior, a healer, a comedian and a lifesaver. The North of England is a significantly less interesting place without her.

Submitted by Kevin Cudbertson
Paramedic Sedgwick Uk

Readers praise and reviews of David's eight book titles.

DEEPLY TOUCHING

    Buy this book, "DADDY HAD TO SAY GOODBYE." This is the most honest and gut-wrenching piece of work I've ever read. Your courage in writing this will help so many people suffering from addictions and self-doubt. The Cottonwood tree story and Pops words hit me like a brick. It was so beautiful it had me in tears. Great book, thank you for sharing your life story. Your writing is raw and real, you just don't mince words and I deeply respect this. Finding the will to survive through interfaith really is the "Story of Hope." There are a lot of self-help books on the market, but the majority are written by licensed psychologists, psychiatrists, PHD's, etc. That's fine, but they're not written from the perspective of someone who has personally experienced childhood abuse, neglect, addiction, or PTSD. We can either wallow in our sorrows or we can fight the Demons by choosing a different path. "Know that hope is all you will need each day." -David J. Brown

I will finish with this; Ernest Hemingway wrote: There is nothing to writing, all you do is sit down at a typewriter and bleed. Well sir, you've gone above and beyond in that measure. It's incredible how good of a writer you are.

- Jan Swanson Kalligher   Duluth, Mn USA

THE REAL DEAL

I first became aware of David J. Brown about eight years ago when he was about to publish his first book, "Daddy Had to Say Goodbye." As a Paramedic, I'm always interested in books written by and about member's of the emergency services, so I contacted David and bought myself a copy. Now full disclosure, I may be initially interested and whilst I often start these books, I don't always read them however. Any hint of embellishment or lack of authenticity and I'm out. This did not happen with, "Daddy Had to Say Goodbye." I not only finished it but I absolutely loved it! It's the book that the great Charles Bukowski would have written had he been a First Responder and not a Postal Worker. I've told David this and whilst he's very polite and modest about it, I don't think he really buys it. Apparently there is quite a group of self-deprecating bunch from Minnesota, so maybe this was to be expected.

David could have written this book again (he certainly has the material) but every one of his books that have followed are quite different. There is a medical mystery, a mentor's handbook, a tribute to a most missed and loved friend but all of these books have one common thread in my opinion and that's optimism. David along with being a brilliant writer is a very optimistic one and in these troubled times a bit of optimism is a precious thing. Read a David J. Brown book, you'll be glad you did!

- Kevin Cudbertson, Paramedic,
  North of England, UK

GIFTED

David has the gift of walking you through his experience and while doing so, making you think about your own. Moments of madness can turn the highs with the right attitude and a plan to make changes. David J. Brown shows you how he has done that while making you believe you can too. Hope, encouragement and a sense of direction are only a few of the life lessons you will pull from his words.

Reading David J. Brown's books makes you blatantly aware that.... finding your balance in day-to-day living is a lifetime journey.

I encourage you to read his books one by one and let him show you how that can be accomplished.

- Lisa Burke, Southern Florida, USA
-
-

BRILLIANT

David was a guest on my UpTalk podcast show. As a man, as a writer and as a First Responder, I found him to be uncomfortably perfect! He tells it like it is for the many men and women who can't speak of it.

- Sean Conohan former Paramedic, Producer/Host at UpTalk Podcast for mental health issues for First Responders, Halifax, Nova Scotia

Introduction

The word 'betray' is a stand-alone word which conjures up a simple thought for most people but the word 'betrayed' enlists an entirely different emotion, in most all people. The word betray is simply a word, the word betrayed is in fact, an act that most all of us have suffered, at some point in our lives. In many cases, several times in our lives. Funny how a simple eight letter word can invoke such overwhelming emotions from our past.

Interesting that a simple, eight letter word out of the 171,476 words that are in current use in the English language (according to my pals at the Oxford English dictionary) can carry such paralyzing power. Although I've been at this writing gig for quite a span of time now, I must admit to myself and others that I don't always know the definition of all words. Oh I assume I do but do I? Do you? To avoid embarrassing myself and offending my readers, I realize that I have to lean on Google to give me the actual true definitions. Again, not what I think they are, but what they truly are, well this time is no different. So I enlisted my pals at Google and I was a bit relieved to know that I actually understood the meaning of the word betrayed, which is pretty cool.

Of course with all things to do with any Google search, you get slammed with advertisements from supposed expert professionals. The mental health industry is no different. There are sidebar writers with all these elaborate definitions that range from suicidal ideations to why your kitty-cat hisses. These are private stand-alone companies that want to explain to you what you're feeling and how they're going to fix you. All you really need to do is; read all of their bullet points, subscribe to their monthly magazine and of course, for a paltry fee you may buy their books as well as their workbooks and attend their multi-day conferences, where they provide a sack lunch for only $50.00 and working dinners for $150.00. After the four day seminar you paid the equivalent of six months of your home mortgage. Add the cost of their recommended discount travel and lodging packages, (which they get a kick back from) and you will miraculously come to a better way of life and heal all of your many ills.

How about if we are just honest with ourselves? Perhaps we should try that first? Betrayal comes in many forms, perhaps hundreds of forms, much the same as the definition of the word 'fear' does. Most betrayal comes from people who are not strangers. Most of these people are people that we trusted. We trust them with our secrets, we trust them with our dreams and many times we trust them with our very lives. Right up until that fateful day when we realize we meant nothing to them, when they meant the world to us. Yep, that's the heartbreak of betrayal. Oftentimes the greatest of all betrayals comes from our immediate family.

Back to these private organizations who offer to help us. It is nothing more than an elaborate sales pitch. They list the many signs and symptoms of depression, repressed memory, infidelity and emotional infidelity, conditional love, emotional withdrawal and the list just goes on and on. What they're trying to sell you of course, is your dreams coming true and making your emotional 'ouchies' disappear. They all have the best life lasting solutions. Let's not forget that they are trying to sell you their program that will cost you the price of a full time second job if you sign up for their continuing, 'After Care' programs.

In my personal life, betrayal has been the norm for many, many years starting from my earliest memories of my childhood.

No child should be beaten or starved, but that happened to me on a very regular basis. Truth be told, it happened each and every day of my young life. The why's of it are really of no value. It's simply just what happened, yes I've gone through many years of working through it all and my realization is that my parents were sick people. At one point I realized that I had to forgive them, not for their benefit but for mine, it's the only way I could have my own life. There are probably as many definitions for betrayal as there are for the word fear. Interesting how those two words seem to walk together, almost hand-in-hand. I have been betrayed by all of my five former wife's, by employers and sadly by each of my three brothers. They all turned out to be other than what they once appeared. It's a lonely place when you get honest

DAVID J. BROWN

with your hidden truths because we don't want to believe that our parents would want to harm us, we don't want to believe that our siblings would cheat, lie and steal from us. We don't want to believe that our spouses would cheat, lie and steal but yes, that happens in life, more often than most are willing to admit. The reason being is that we don't want to feel that pain they injected us with, so we overlook it but that pain stays with us and at some point, either we confront that pain or that pain will confront us.

Out of all the many betrayals that I've experienced, the greatest one that stands out in my mind and in my heart is that of my youngest brother and only living relative. All of my family is gone except for him but in my mind he is gone too! I had to tell myself that he's dead to me, so I could survive because I just can't believe what he did. Not just to me but the way he dishonored our mother, both during her life and after her death.

When my mother passed away, my brother was supposedly the executor of her will. My mother, who I spoke to every Sunday evening on the phone for more than the forty years that I have lived in the Western States and who I visited every few years. She always told me (on each Sunday) that she had two safety deposit boxes at Bank One bank. One was for my brother and one was for me, she told me that she had put money away for us from her house sale (before marrying my step dad) and stock sales that she inherited from her mother. Those stock certificates were the first issued from the 3M company, June 13th 1902! Yes, an absolute fortune! She also put money away every month from her social security. I simply said, "Mom, that's not necessary, spend your money, don't put it aside for us guys, it's your money, use it your way."

What I didn't tell my mother was that my brother (her loving and trusted son) was just another fucking coke head and degenerate gambling addict! My mother gave my brother the money every month to put in the bank. She had him set up the safety deposit boxes and make the deposits as she was fearful of riding in a car. She had not left the house for the last nine years before her death except for medical appointments. She was under the impression that my brother was putting that money and the stock certificates in two different accounts. I knew that there would be no money in any Security Box for me. I didn't have the heart to tell my mother however, she wanted to believe that her youngest son was an upstanding young man, who is actually nothing more than a slime ball junkie who played a hell of a good game as most junkies do.

When my mother passed, I of course came from Colorado for my mother's funeral service and to attend to my stepdad. I was there for ten days. At the end of the 6th day and after mother's service, I said to my brother, "I guess we need to go to the bank and clear out those Safety Deposit boxes and look at mother's will."

My puke brother, being the asshole that he is, gave me this most innocent look as he said, "David, there's no safety deposit boxes, there's no money, Mother never had a will." We were in a restaurant at the time having breakfast. I took a final sip of my coffee as I stood up. I looked at my loser brother as I said, "I'm done with you, we will never speak again, enjoy your miserable life." From that day to this, I have never spoken to him. But I would be remiss with not speaking of my brother's shenanigans with my step dad's passing, one year after my mother passed.

I had left Colorado and moved to Duluth to be with Heather and to look after my stepdad, as he was falling into dementia at the time. Both of his kids lived out of the area as well as my brother. I was the only one to look-in on him every day to make sure he ate, bathed and was dressed. I cleaned his house, took him to his medical appointments and grocery shopping. Heather made him dinner twice a week at our home and sent him home with frozen meals to carry him through the week. I spent countless hours sitting on his back deck listening to his life story everyday. All I could do was nod my head and act surprised as he repeated the same stories, day after day.

My step dad told everyone in the family that I would get his three rifles and the ownership of the house would be split equally amongst his two adult children and my brother and myself upon his passing. One day my step dad called me and asked me to come to his house and take him to the bank. He was going to put the title of his house in my, my brothers and his two kids names as he did not trust the lawyers or the bank that were holding his will. When I arrived at his house (twenty minutes after he called) he was not there. He often times walks to one of the neighbors houses for coffee, he didn't have a cell phone so I sat on the back deck and waited for him to return. An hour later, his daughter and my brother pulled into the driveway with my step dad in the back seat. He got out of the car with a large manila envelope, stepped up on the deck without greeting or looking at me, went into the door and I heard him latch the deadbolt. His daughter and my brother (who both live three hours away) drove away without a greeting or a wave. Yep, they fucked me again!

At my step dad's passing (4 months later) I found that he willed his house and all of his possessions to my brother and to his daughter and son. I was willed nothing, I was given nothing. Obviously no one thought I deserved anything.

At my step dad's funeral my brother said, "You should come by the house, most everything is out but you might find something you'd like. When I arrived, there sat a construction size, roll-off dumpster. It was probably four feet deep with what appeared to be my mother's and my stepdad's possessions that obviously neither my brother or his kids valued or wanted. I spent five hours wading through the debris in that roll-off container, looking for some small memories of my life. The only things that I found after emptying the entire dumpster which were of great value to me were my mother's, my dads and my stepdad's AA literature. Their 'Big Books' with their names written (in their handwriting) their 12 X 12's, "As Bill Sees It" and several other books of AA conference approved literature. That's the total sum of what I walked away with, that's the entirety of my life's memories with my mother, my dad and with my stepdad. All three of my parents were alcoholics in recovery. They had sponsored hundreds of alcoholics throughout their combined 106 years of sobriety. AA was their life, they lived a life of service to the fellowship of AA and their fellow alcoholics.

If that doesn't describe what betrayal and betrayed is and if it doesn't twist a knot in your guts, then you should put this book down

CHAPTER 1
As the Bile Rises

What drives an established writer to continue writing? Is it passion, financial gain, greater fame or do they just need more attention? Or simply, is it just for status or are they pathetically struggling to not be forgotten?

Of course, many readers wonder that, or perhaps none at all. Where does the author get their story lines? How do they come up with a title for their book? How do they come up with the vision and the artwork for their book cover that must tell a story in and of itself? It all has to come from somewhere, does it come from the 'heavy-hitters' staff members? Remember that some (if not many) of these famous authors don't always write their entire books. They pay ghost writers but sell it as their own work. Which of course brings me back to having to listen to celebrities hawk their pals, 'supposed' self-written books. As much as I enjoy Hannity on FOX, he too is a media bitch artist. In almost every nightly show he has to make mention of his martial arts training and the number of years he's dedicated to it. So what he is doing is that he is sending out a subliminal message to people that may want to attack and harm him or his family. His message is that he is prepared. Of course, he also mentions that he carries a firearm. Well, that's cute, I know a lot of people who carry firearms that have no idea what it's like to have incoming rounds screaming at you. Do these people train in foul weather, at night or just on sunny days with a light breeze to keep the bugs away? Everyone seems to think that if they go to a gun range and they hit their target (most of the time) that they are ready for intense combat. But what if that target is shooting back? What if there are multiple aggressors? What if you are out-gunned? What if that target or targets are holding high ground? What if that target is highly trained and accomplished? What if that target is holding a hostage? What if those hostages are one of your children or your spouse? Are you still as bad-ass as you think you are?

No, you're just another dead dummy who thought, "I got this shit" when you have reinvented yourself as the ultimate warrior and family protector all because you bought a gun. Now you are nothing and now, you are nothing because now you're dead. Hannity is a fool in that he just told his enemies that they should not take him head on. Professional enemies study their target and pick the time and place to fulfill the contract.

I have another point of contention with Hannity. In almost every show, he introduces a new best selling book about to be released by one of his friends or fellow network pals. How in the fuck are these best selling books when they have yet to be printed or released? Well, it's quite simple to understand. The "New York Times" sells the authors and the 'big five' publishing houses a slot on the bestseller list. The top twenty, top ten and #1 best seller all goes to the highest bidder, long before they're released. Oftentimes the best sellers are total crap! It's all about marketing and it's all about money and nothing more.

So where do I stand in the mix of the New York Times "Best Authors list?" I don't, I can tell you this much however, I'm not for sale. I can't and will not be influenced by anyone. My life experiences and observations are my own, nobody tells me what or how to write. That is of course with one exception, the only true love of my life, Heather.

This is my eighth and final book and I'm writing this out of protest. A mild protest but a protest nonetheless. She has an agenda that I don't share. I know what she is doing and I don't like it. You see, we both have a dirty little secret and neither of us can find the courage to discuss it for fear of upsetting the other. That dirty little shared but not spoken of secret is that I am mentally and physically failing.

I am seventy-four years old and Heather is seventeen years my junior. She is a very attractive, slim, fifty-seven year old gal who is whip-snap smart. She owns our home and it is paid for in full, no mortgage of any kind. No one helped her pick out this house, the only help she got to finance this house was from her bank. She paid off the loan last month, eleven years early. Of course I am proud of her resolve to do it all by herself. My true comfort is in knowing that she will always have a home and the memories we built together in this home when I'm gone.

CHAPTER 2
Dirty Loving Secrets

Heather has been twisting my arm and other body parts to write an eighth book. There are two stories behind her arm twisting. She likes to remind me that eight is her favorite number. That's the day of the month that she was born. Number eight was also the number that was affixed to all of her sports jerseys throughout her many years of school sports and adult recreation league softball and volleyball. I have been enjoying watching her playing softball for the last ten years.

She started playing competitive softball and volleyball at a very young age and of course, all these teams had to have sponsor jersey's and she always insisted on having the number 8 on her jersey. As time went on, and as she played through the years, well into her adulthood, everyone knew that she held the number 8. She has a drawer or two, jam packed with #8 jerseys. I have threatened to have a quilt made of all of her #8 jerseys as we don't have the wall space (three-bedroom home with a full finished basement) to put them in those glass frame jersey cases to display them on our walls. But it would sure be fun to do that!

She has always played first base. She is an incredible ball player, she can scoop a ground ball out of the dirt better than most any male ball player. They call her "Stretch" because she could do the splits to snag a ball and keep her foot on the bag at the same time. She played in a competitive co-ed league. Most of these guys were beasts and powerful but they never held back throwing to her at first base. They all knew that she could handle a 'heater' coming at her. They threw with their full might from their base, whether it was from third, shortstop or 2nd base, it didn't matter. That ball was coming and she was going to catch it and make the play! So that is the reason for this eighth book. One day I jokingly told her that I was going to title my new book:

EIGHT
BECAUSE SHE TOLD ME TO!

But I fully know her other dirty little secret. She is far too humble to be that excited for me to showcase her athletic abilities. Her true desire for me to author another book is glaringly obvious to me. Heather wants me to keep writing for the sole purpose of me keeping my mind fresh. She also knows of my hidden dirty little secret. She's witnessed many times in the last few months that I'm not the man I once was, just a few short months ago.

There are times I find myself standing up from the couch and not knowing where I'm going. I just stand there without knowing why I stood up as I search my mind for the reason. I can no longer walk in the straight line. Either I stagger or I stumble and in six short steps I unintentionally start to veer to my left. I have seen cattle and deer with 'Mad Cow Disease' doing that same circle thing. I have severe arthritis In my hips, my spine and my hands. I have a problem with balance as well. There were a number of times that if I wouldn't have had a wall to lean on, I would have fallen to the floor. If I look down at my feet, I see the ground moving in front of me and I get dizzy. I have to keep staring at the horizon to keep my balance. But that's not the most glaring indicator that I might be falling into dementia.

My symptoms are the same for many aging adults. The worst (for me at least) is that during a general conversation and without using any big words, I find myself searching for the simplest of words just to complete a sentence. I find myself searching for people's names, people I have personally known for many years. In a few cases that I do know their names, I just don't know how to pronounce them. It's very embarrassing for me, so what I do is, I avoid people so as not to embarrass them or myself. I have watched it over the years when people were trying to rescue other people that are 'word stuck' and that is a cruel son of a bitch to live with. I know that I have that problem and it pisses me off. Now I understand why older people sit in silence and smile when in a family or group setting. I can talk for hours about the betrayal I've lived with throughout my lifetime but there's no greater betrayal than your own mind and body working against you. I am currently waiting for a doctors appointment which is still three weeks away.

CHAPTER 3
The Inquest

We had only been home from the "lock down" at the Corker Hotel for twenty minutes.

I made a fresh pot of coffee to enjoy out on the deck. I couldn't help but smile as I noticed through the sliding glass door, that someone had brought up our deck furniture from the storage shed where they were stored for the winter. There sat our oversized oval glass deck table, six new metal framed high backed swivel/rocking chairs, a new table umbrella along with two new love seats that to my knowledge, we did not own before this day, but it was a damn nice touch! The table was positioned in the exact location that it was last year before we had to clear the deck for winter. So that meant somebody had to photograph our deck furniture from last year! That ment that we were under surveillance all that time and I had no idea! These security pricks are slick alright and I'm grateful to have them watching out for us. God love em but I'm not gonna pay anybody for those loveseats and chairs, they can all kiss my ass!

As I sat on the deck enjoying a cup of Folgers coffee I can almost feel my outer layer slipping off of me, kind of like a snake shedding its skin. Heather couldn't have been any more right about my needing to take my life back and of course that meant walking away from, "The Company." It was bittersweet at best but necessary, without question. I'm sure that in time when all the dust settles I'll learn how to breathe again. I have been mentally, emotionally and spiritually gasping for air for several months now. I'm ready to be done with all the cloak-and-dagger and book bullshit. I don't know where the normal people find freedom or where it comes from. It feels damn good to retire from the team, I will miss the people but not the darkness that few civilians will ever know of. Who knows, perhaps I'll even retire from writing. Both of those ventures have greatly worn on me and I'm feeling a bit weak. I can't simply entertain the idea that all of this is finally over however, I know better. If the call comes, I know I will want to answer the call to duty. The truth is that I will have to decline all future assignments due to my new broken me. As much as I might want to, I can not accept an assignment, I am not whole, I am and will be forever less. I could not live with the idea or reality that I may cost my friends their lives, because I couldn't be honest with myself or them. I know that I have to reach out to, "The Company." I must tell them my truths, hell knowing them, they probably already know but I have to put it on the table. I'm sure Heather will be on guard for any backsliding on anyone's part, she has set the rules and she will enforce them, she's not one to trifle with!

I had to smile when I heard the almost silent rustle of feet in the grass but I couldn't see them or any other movement. Yeah these fuckers are slick all right. I watched a car pull into the alley and into the parking spot of the Airbnb. Three men got out of the black windowed SUV wearing somewhat inconspicuous tourist clothing. What gave them away was their three, long hard cases as luggage, a tactical looking duffel bag for each and the dead giveaway with the, 'in-transit" license plate. Half of me just wanted to go up and ask if they'd like me to order them a pizza, the other part of me said, "No, stay out of their way, they have a job to do." It pissed me off a bit to see them arrive but I was grateful at the same time to know that we were being looked after. Then came the shadows from above the house which was obviously a drone. I guess they were flying an air dome. That meant that the two girls, Norbs and Cat, were about to arrive along with their 'two each person' security detail allowed by Heather. I called Cat and said, "Babe you two dolls better shag your ass up here, your security team is already in place and waiting for you." Cat started to laugh as she said, "They're not there to protect us, they're there to protect you because you're such an asshole, we'll be right there."

The ladies arrived and it was hugs and smiles all around, the dog's couldn't get enough pets.

Me: Alright you two, we're going outside and leave my dogs alone and you better have something to talk about. And one other thing, if you put any of your people up in my large cottonwood tree, tell them to dig out the limb cutters from the shed. I've got a few dead branches I want pruned.

So, what in the actual fuck are you two after this fine afternoon? Remember ladies, Heather ain't playing when she told you two about not keeping me up all night. And further, keep in mind also, that you're out of here at 2pm tomorrow and not a minute later. Whatever your game is, you best bring it hard, fast and dirty and it damn well better be good. Whose first?

Norbs: David I'm here to study you. I want to absorb everything about you. I've decided that I'm going back to writing but I want to be a better writer. I want to be my best and I know that I can learn from you. You have an incredibly unique way of threading a sentence together with enough information that it reads like a complete paragraph. No one does that. No one other than you and I want to learn from you. You don't have to teach me, I just want to listen, fair enough? Even my friends say that they have to reread paragraphs, pages and even chapters to fully absorb what you're saying because you move so quickly. You just dropped the bomb and you fired the next, how are you so wickedly fast? I desperately want to learn that and I want you to teach me, you are a true original.

    Me: Cute, now how about you Cat, you're here for a reason, you're not just hanging with the world's greatest author, our sweet sister Norbs. What's your game babes?

    Cat: David you have a texture about you, you have the ability to describe water evaporating into the air to the point that we can almost see it, at least we do feel it. Your voice control is incredible, you have such a unique way of snapping people awake without raising your voice. Your voice is commanding as well as your physical presence that exudes extreme power that demands respect. That's a power that I long for.

    Me: Oh so I guess you wanna do what, mimic me? You wanna be a little David J. Brown but in the female form? Honey, your power cannot come from me, you already own your power, it exists within you.

All you have to do is have the courage to release the beast, easy-peasy baby dollface.

Cat: There you go again! You use words that no other author would dare to use. You still call women Babe, Honey and Sweetheart and somehow that flows for you. In this day and age with all the woke bullshit and self-identifying you are just a huge breeze of fresh air. My most favorite one-line sentence in both your life and in all of your books is...."Still love me Babe?" How the fuck do you pull that off? You get away with snarky, snide and condescending remarks and people like it. They like it so much that they even ask for more.

Before I could respond to Cat, I heard the doorbell ring and feet shuffling, I heard Heather give a warm and inviting greeting to whoever it was that just came in. It has to be somebody I know as I'm sure that the outer perimeter security detail checked them out as they attempted to enter the property. Before Heather opened the sliding screen door she said, "Sweetheart, you have two visitors and believe me, they are going to be the last, I assure you."

Out on the deck stepped Tim (the doorman) and Ann (the night nurse). Yes, my pal Tim that opened doors for me for sixteen months held a bit of a secret. "Doorman Tim" was also an undercover Secret Service Agent, who Heather had blessed him with ownership of my private suite and office on the top floor of the Corker Hotel. Ann, my former night nurse, who I was led to believe was planning my demise and who was jailed for it. However, she was not jailed, she was a bonafide Critical Care RN who just so happened to also be an undercover agent who thwarted a kidnapping attempt on yours truly. I felt kind of guilty because when we were reunited at the FBO at the airport I promised her we would have dinner together. We haven't done that yet, so I felt a little ashamed. I stood and smiled as I gave them both hugs and pointed to the new chairs and invited them to have a seat. I excused myself and went to put on another pot of coffee. When the coffee was ready, Heather brought out a fresh carafe and a large snack tray of cheese, meats and fruits.

    I smiled as I asked Tim, "What are you doing hanging out with this old doll? Tim smiled back and said, "This old doll next to me, is actually my mother. That's right David, my friend Ann is my mother. This is how I found my way into, "The Company" and by the way, I tendered my resignation with, "The Company." My wife and two kids absolutely love your suite. The kids want us to sell our house and move in there."

    Me: Just a fuckin minute pal. Your wife and your kids? Are you shitting me? I thought you were twenty-four or five years old and working on your masters degree. How the fuck old are you?

Tim: David, I'm 31. My wife and two girls all want to meet you at some point, if you're willing. They want to meet the nice man who gave them all those computer systems, they love all the games!

Me: Norbs, get a hold of your systems people, do it now, I'm assuming that they can remotely take care of the computers. I want them scrubbed clean, I don't want any of that shit I've written on there for the children to see. Just children's games, can you do that for me sweetheart?

Norbs: I'm doing it now as she walked away to the far end of the deck, she talked for just a few moments, came back and said, "It's done."

Me: So what is your deal in being here today, Tim and Tim's mom?

Ann: I love you too sweetie, but keep in mind Buster, that I saw you naked. I bathed your parts, all of your parts, nightly! I just wanted to know what you look like wearing clothes, although I do prefer the former view. You clean up quite nicely!

Me: Cute Annie girl, I'll get back to you in a minute. So what's the deal Tim, you are resigning your position with, "The Company" or are you just on leave?

Tim: David, I could go back to the company anytime I'd like. I don't know if I'd ever like to do that again, after all, as the lady said earlier, "You are one of a kind, you are truly an original." I don't think I can keep up with you.

Me: Wait a fucking minute, these two ladies said that just twenty minutes ago and before you two arrived. So now my fucking deck is bugged? You two were listening to my conversation with the girls before you arrived? You spooks better knock this shit off and do it in a hurry! So Timmy boy, what are you going to do with your time now that you're retired at what, the ripe old age of thirty-one?

Tim: David, I don't want to take up a lot of your time today. This is for the ladies, but I want to continue a friendship with you. I want us to be pals, I like you for who you are, not just for what you do but for who you are. A man could use a friend like you. I want to learn how to develop a kind and loving heart and smooth my jagged edges. I've become hard and untrusting. I don't want to be that kind of man any longer. You somehow have mastered the ability to display kindness and recrute cooperation from some people that most others would cast off, if not outright destroy.

Me: What you are talking about is a simple matter of balance. Yes, I can embrace a person and lend comfort as I push off of them and send a bullet screaming into their forehead, all with one motion. Tim, answer my fucking question! What are you going to do with yourself?

Before you answer that pal, if you're angling to become another Ken (my nurse anesthesiologist) you're way out of your league. Ken has an ability to look into his own soul and to make the changes necessary, all I did was bump him a few times but with you? You're like the turtle in a foot race from the next county over, you never get to where you need to be. You're too guarded, you're too rigid and packed full of emotional fear. Say what you need to say, when you need to say it! There's no penalty for being human. Now you may continue and don't try to fuckin snow me.

Tim: Well, Lake Superior is of course the largest freshwater lake in the world and one of the truest gifts from god as far as I am concerned. There are approximately three hundred streams and rivers that spill into Lake Superior and they deliver a whole bunch of driftwood during the spring ice breakup. Most all boaters see driftwood as floating debris that could damage their boats. I see driftwood as a painter's blank canvas. The best driftwood comes from boat docks and pilings that have been adrift for hundreds of years that come ashore after a big storm. David I love working with wood, I'm learning how to make bowls out of cherry, maple and black walnut. I prefer to use burlwood but it's far out of my price range. I want to learn to be a cabinet maker using driftwood. My wife and girl's have a keen eye in searching the shorelines on both the North and South shores. I see driftwood as one of a kind much like yourself. It's God's artwork, there are no two alike and you can't replicate any two, it's impossible. We have found floating slab wood near the shoreline that has to be hundreds and hundreds of years old. It's actually worn from the wave action. I've made some very interesting coffee tables and some day I hope to make a fine dining room table. I have redone all the wood sashes in my home and door frames with driftwood. Better Homes and Gardens have approached me for a photo shoot of my home. I turned them down because this is strictly for my pleasure and no one else's. Although I'd love to show it to you and Heather someday, if you can find the time.

    Me: Slow your roll sport. I know all I need to know about Lake Superior. So it's 1.1 or 1.2 billion years old and has something to do with the North American Rift and its max depth is 1,332 feet. So now you're comparing me to water soaked, slick mossy waste wood? How fuckin kind of you! All that water wood is swell buddy but you have yet to mention just how you intend to pay your bills, now that you're unemployed or as you like to say, 'retired'.

Tim: David, "The Company" pays quite well. I received a modest inheritance from my grandparents when I turned 21 years of age. My hobby as a young child was studying Wall Street and how to make a fortune. I bought stocks and bonds with my inheritance, mostly in utilities. My family and I are set for life and for a few lives thereafter.

I called Heather out to the deck and asked her, "Baby have we received payment from, "The Company?" She smiled and said, "Do you remember the hotel suite with all the goodies to go with it?"

Me: Oh honey, are you talking about the private suite that I owned on the top floor of the Corker Hotel with the multi-million dollar view that you gave to my friend here, Tim? Is that the one?

Heather smiled as she gave me the finger as she continued with, "Let me finish, do you remember paying any hospital bills from your injury? How about all the personal protection, do you remember all of the free airfare on some of the most sophisticated private jets in the world? The shooting range downstairs, all the top of the line to die for two dozen dream guns and the six pallets of ammunition have all slipped your mind? Oh how soon we forget, shut your pie hole my love, we have plenty of money."

Ann: David this might sound strange, but I've only received your first two books, I do not have the other five you've written, can I ask you for the other five copies to be signed please. I will pay for them.

Heather smiled and said, "Darling I'll be right back." Heather brought out the other five books along with an ink pen. I smiled and I wept a bit as I signed them, thinking of this wonderful woman who kept me safe and alive both as a professional bodyguard and a critical care nurse. My blessings are many.

I turned back to Norb's and I said, "Are you ever going to get to it? You still haven't told me what you want or how you want it. Let's have it babes, I might need a nap if you don't pick up your speed."

Norbs: I've been puzzled with you, but for now, all I really want to do is listen. I want to hear the cadence of your voice and your breathing patterns that are so uniquely you. Your voice structure, your voice tone is also unique. The way you use words and form a sentence. Your colorful slang and profanity are also enticing. Just the sound of your voice speaks volumes. You have a deep country soul singer's voice with a sharp Chicago accent. I have watched you command the attention of several hundred people in a room without you even raising your voice and without any cheesy props. So here's what I've come up with.

    We're all going to remain quiet. What I think could be interesting is if we sit on this deck and listen to you describe your neighborhood. I'm looking at the four houses above the alley from you. I want to hear you describe the people in each of those homes and your interaction with them. If that's not enough, how about the few houses on the avenue and then you have the gravel street below you? I'd like to know about all of those people. I would like to know what your perception is of these people. Can we start with the modest but large yellow house at the end of the dead-end alley? I Love how you put your observations to words, no one I know can describe what you see, no one could even come close to matching those skills. In your life, everything has a story and in that story there's always a back story. You have an incredible mind and personality. Now I want to be done talking, I want to spend the time we have together simply listening, can we do that please?

Me: So now, I'm Mister fucking Rogers and you want me to welcome you all to my neighborhood? This neighborhood sucks, the people in this neighborhood suck! This is hard core democratic, liberal territory and believe me they're all stupid and they all suck. The only decent two people are the young couple in the yellow house that you asked me to describe. Ok, so here you go.

But hold on for a minute, I have something for Tim. Timmy boy, you are off the mark, far off, now listen to me. So you have used salvaged driftwood for encasing doorways in your home, I'm guessing you did the same with cabinets, vanities and a few bookshelves. No good my friend, you forgot to think. Sell the house and all is lost. Unless you think a few pictures of something you once owned will excite the young minds of your great grandchildren. Think tangible, let them feel your presence, give them something to touch, feel and hold. You mentioned that you wanted something in the way that I did with Ken. Ken did something life lasting for generations to come with planting those trees with his grandparents, parents and children that will be enjoyed and respected for many generations. All you did was doll up an old house with driftwood that didn't somehow find its way to a beach-party bonfire. Do this or don't, it's all on you. Build memories with your art. Use your beloved drift wood to make jewelry boxes, toy boxes, wooden toys, rocking horses, pull toys, wagons and maybe toboggans and a few sleds. Develop a brand, as in a branding iron that ranchers use to brand livestock. If you don't know how to make a branding iron, have a blacksmith make a branding iron for your signature. A brand, your brand, burnt into wood will last many years longer than a 'sharpie marker' signature. Got it sport?

CHAPTER 4
A Spin Around the Block

Now back to you Norbs. Maybe it's just a thing in this part of the country, maybe it's just my thing, I don't know but I always name people's homes like the yellow house by the former owners names. I refer to the yellow house as the Anderson house that the young couple live in now. The Anderson's son sold the house about four years ago. The Anderson's were quite elderly. He always waved when he drove through the alley. Ms. Anderson always had a permanent, constipated bitch face. She never spoke to or even looked at me for the eight years that I have lived here, right up until she was put away. Except on one occasion shortly after I moved in, when she walked down the alley with a small paper plate of cookies. She had a hard challenging look on her face as she said, "These cookies are for Heather and only Heather. I don't approve of you two living in sin, you should leave, if you two are not going to be married." I remember smiling as I said, "I suggest you take your religion and these cookies and cram them up your already deeply impacted ass."

That afternoon Mr. Anderson slowly drove down the alley. He waved like a little kid at a parade with a huge grin on his face. Obviously she told her husband of our exchange and he was showing approval of my comments. The next month the police visited their house three times in one week. A neighbor told us that Mr. Anderson had to call the police because she was beating him up. She was locked up in a nursing home memory care unit. It was less than three weeks and they were both gone. I don't know what happened to him. The Anderson's son sold the place in just a few days after listing it.

A nice young couple bought the house and have made a ton of upgrades on it. We speak on occasion but nothing with any depth. They have two beautiful golden retrievers, they walk the dogs through the alley daily. The female dog is a total lover and much older than the male. The male dog is a rescue and was beaten by the previous male owner. So that dog doesn't like men and shies away when men are nearby.

The interesting thing about the people in the homes all around us (excluding the young couple) is that everyone loves to gossip. Nobody has a life, their only thing in life is to talk about the other neighbors, hopefully that's just a Minnesota thing but I've seen that bullshit in other parts of the country too, but these people here are especially different. Heather used to bake a hundred and forty-four dozen cookies for Christmas every year and she being the sweetheart she is, gave out her cookies to some of the neighbors but most of her baked goods were confiscated by her stepdad and mother and they had her ship them all over the world and of course they took full credit as they were the 'bakers' of their personal gifts, with no mention of Heather baking them.

Now that I think of it, there was one other time when Mrs. Anderson, being one of the community snoops, found a way to bring over some fresh baked cookies to introduce herself. She had more questions than I had time. At that time she wanted to know if I was her dad or maybe her older brother. I smiled as I said, "No, I'm just the guy that sleeps with her!"

One of the other common traits of this community is this entire city, maybe even this entire region, is that people are locked into their old time religion and they are judgmental as hell. Well after that brief one sided first conversation with Mrs. Anderson she stopped with the cookies, and she stopped waving as she drove through the alley way. I guess Heather has now been declared a sinner. I really enjoyed Mr. Anderson, I think he worked at the steel mill before he retired. His garage door was always open and you could hear power tools. He loved woodworking and made shadow boxes, cutting boards and trivets. He sold them at craft fairs. I think that was his way of getting away from the Mrs. and from what I saw of her, I sure as shit can't blame him!

This hillside that you're looking at rivals the steepness of San Francisco's steep hills. Our back yard is inundated with a lot of water that rolls down the hill. There are a number of underground natural springs above us. The contractors keep opening up these springs while building new homes. Part of our back yard is usually saturated with runoff. When I mow it, I get mud splashing back on my feet and legs. One day we had a straight-line wind and of course with having heavy clay soil that prevents deep rooting, our trees are not as stable as they should be. At that time we had three mature, gorgeous weeping willow trees in that moist area. In two months time, all three of those trees were blown over and of course I had to dig them out down to the root system. There's no joy in trying to hand dig through clay soil. It seemed like there was no end to those roots and I was chopping my ass off with an ax, trying to get the roots free. Of course the root holes filled in with groundwater and the splash back had me wearing goggles and after each ax swing, I had to stop and wipe the muddy goggles and my face. Mr. Anderson came down the alley and handed me a reciprocating, battery powered saw and said, "Use this, it should take care of it." The hole was so deep and so full of water that I was fearful of damaging his saw. Mr. Anderson said, "Go ahead, I've got a couple more of them in my garage." Well it took care of those roots in no time at all. He was a nice man. I wish I could have spent some time with him but he pretty much kept to himself and his woodworking projects.

Now back to the new couple that live in the Anderson home. He works for a mining company up on the North Shore in the Silver Bay area. I think he must be a millwright as this cat is handy as hell. He works his ass off on that house. He's rebuilt a major portion of it including a new deck. As you can see, they are repainting the garage and house with an attractive modern gray color and it's going to cover over the ugly, chalky and faded yellow of the house itself. It will make it look much more modern and it definitely needs fresh paint. With the strong winds and the rain and snow as part of hillside living, a fresh paint job is only good for about six years. The girlfriend who is actually the homeowner, works side by side with him. We met her at a city council meeting because the house right next to them was applying for an Airbnb license. The Airbnb was built just ten years ago. All the city lots in Duluth can be no smaller than 25 ft by a 125 ft lots. Those pricks used every inch of their narrow lot and were shoulder to shoulder with the homes on each side. Worse than that, the Airbnb entrance and patio looked directly onto our back yard and elevated deck. The city council meeting was about approving his license for an Airbnb and it was a total fucking joke. The committee holding this hearing had already decided to approve the application. There were seven neighbors that showed up and spoke opposing the permit due to lack of privacy including ourselves. The young lady in the yellow house was very emotional, she testified that this was her first dream home that she's ever owned. Other people had other good arguments against it, but the leader of this committee said, "The applicant has already submitted all of the licensing fees and taxes so we're going to approve his request." That speaks loudly of Duluth and it's internal politics, it's all and only about the money, fuck the neighbors and their privacy! It's no different than this house right next to us, it's a group home for mentally challenged women. But in this matter there was no hearing about putting in a group home of unbalanced if not dangerous women living right next door to you, is that not fucking charming? We've had a lot of screaming and profanity with the women threatening each other and several police visits to that property next door because of the clients or residents whatever the fuck you wanna call them, for acting out. So who is the owner of this group home? It is the former Mayor of Duluth! So let's get back to that Airbnb. As you can see this is a single track dirt alley that only serves four homes and dead ends at the Andersons garage. Last winter on five different occasions, renters from the Airbnb slid off the road and down onto my lawn. It's a rather steep hill, and each time the drivers thought they could hit the gas and drive their way out of it but got high centered and all they accomplished was to tear up my lawn and it pisses me off. Of those five times that I know of when I was home, each of those vehicles had to call for a wrecker. You know how big and loud heavy-haul diesel trucks are, then add the flood lights mounted on the back of the cab, the flashing amber and red lights mounted on the roof of the cab that light up the entire neighborhood and ask yourself if that would be acceptable in your neighborhood. Well, the prick face that owns the Airbnb lives directly upstairs with nothing but glass facing towards the alley. Somehow and for some reason, he never heard the loud diesel engine noise of the wreckers or saw the flood lights on the back of the wrecker or the flashing lights mounted on the roof. He never heard the engine noises of the cars spinning their tires as they were ripping ruts into my lawn. That asshole never came out to help any of those five people that he was renting to. He is just pretty much one of those, "Fuck you, I got mine, I don't care about you" kind of people. Yeah and sadly, our world is full of them, well here's something else about this charming piece of shit. He's also a pervert and a predator.

His house faces directly behind the group home right across from here and again the whole face of that house is glass and has three stories. He lives on the upper two stories and has two separate deck levels. One summer day and towards the early evening, we saw him open the blinds of his sliding glass door which appears to be his bedroom. He smeared himself up against the glass naked and was gyrating to some kind of weird music. Another time he was obviously high or drunk or probably both when he went into the yard of that group home, with the four women sitting on their deck and and brought his little white dog and said to the girls, "My dog just loves you all, she thinks you girls are so wonderful and so pretty that she just can't wait for you to pet her!" That piece of trash weaseled his way from the alley which is the divider of properties, to their yard close to their deck. Suddenly he's up on the deck holding his dog and passing out cigarettes to the women while saying, "Take all you like, I have a lot more in my house, you girls are welcome to stop over anytime for a cigarette!"

Heather and I sat in disbelief for a moment, I started to get up from my chair to go down our stairs and confront him, Heather grabbed my shirt sleeve and said, "They have staff there to deal with him, we both know what he is, you'll beat his ass and you will end up in jail."

In the next few minutes he was actually in their home. Now again, understand these women have severe mental and emotional challenges. Well the group home is monitored twenty-four hours a day by staff and obviously the staff member didn't know what was going on. After him being in that house for ten minutes or so, we suddenly heard the staff member say in a rather excited and angry voice, "You can't be in this house, there's no males allowed here, you have to leave now or I will call the police!" He left while blowing them kisses and saying, "Sadie and I love you girls, come over and see us tomorrow."

The next day we noticed that two of the girls had crossed over the alley and were standing in the perverts lawn smoking as he was passing them packs of cigarettes. A couple hours later they were sitting up on the edge of his driveway smoking cigarettes with him. So what do you think happened? He repulsed Heather to the point that she had her 380 caliber pistol in her pocket. She said, "If he puts one hand on those girls or if they go into his house, I will kick his fucking door down and blow his balls off and stand there giggling as he bleeds out!" Hell, I just wanted to tap dance on his skull for a little while. Well enough about that flesh eating garbage.

The house next to the perves also has an interesting story. The guy in that little white house, is also an anti-social freak, or let me correct myself, was an anti-social freak. He was married to a strange acting woman much like himself. The wife had an oversized German Shepherd and that dog was a hateful son-of-a-bitch too! That dog hated everything and everyone. I don't recall the dog's name but it was stupid name for a dog. I know, I do remember, it was called Liberty. I'm guessing maybe that they rescued it from a shelter. The dog was so damn aggressive that I could see why it was in a shelter and probably soon to be put down. The dog was totally uncontrollable, it attacked and bit a Mailman, a Police Officer, the neighbor next to them and the neighbor's dog, he also took down a bicyclist. All of those attacks were unprovoked. One summer evening Heather and I were sitting on the back deck and we heard a loud crash of glass like it was probably a glass dining room table and the guy was screaming at the dog at the top of his lungs and the dog was whining and crying. It sounded like he was beating the dog.

    They were at the city council meeting about the Airbnb license. They were both very unkept and obviously neither of them bathed on a regular basis. Neither one of them spoke during that hearing and I think everyone in the room was grateful for that. The next time we actually met them was when they came into our yard to inform us that Bud (the guy that lives three doors down the avenue) has been stealing their mail. The entire neighborhood knew that Bud was well into dementia and Bud was out walking everyday and he watched for the Mailman and when the mail truck goes away, he goes to the homes and takes the mail out of their mailboxes that are at the curb. Our mailbox was affixed to our house and Bud never came on our property. This white house wife told us that they went down to Bud's house and retrieved their missing mail from Bud's wife. They were trying to inform us that if we're missing any mail that we were expecting, that we may want to check with Bud's wife. In my opinion Bud was kind of a cool guy. He would walk up the avenue every day, sometimes three times a day. If I were out in the driveway or doing something in the lawn I would wave and greet him with, "Hello Bud." Bud would wave back and grin but not say anything, the next morning I would find a tennis ball in my driveway and I knew or at least I suspected that it came from Bud. I would always take the tennis ball and I would roll it down the hill towards his house, about a half a block away. The following morning there was the tennis ball, back in my driveway. It got to be a fun game for about two weeks and then Bud decided to switch up the rules and put the tennis ball in the bed of my pickup truck which I park out in the driveway. So every morning, I'd go out and look in the bed of my pickup truck and sure enough, there was the tennis ball. This game went on for almost a month. Oftentimes I would see Bud walk up the avenue with his hands free and a half hour later, Bud would come strolling back down the avenue with a sweater or a jacket or a pair of shoes in his hands, so obviously, Bud was not just taking mail from mailboxes, he was also taking items from people's unlocked vehicles. Now understand that Bud was maybe in his late seventies, early eighties and was a big beefy guy. I'm certain that Bud could tear a car door clean off a car, back in his younger years. One time I did actually see Bud open the front door of my neighbors car and at the same time the neighbor hollered at him to leave their car alone. Bud responded with a heavy voiced, "Go fuck yourself." The police came and when the police officer confronted Bud about stealing mail and entering vehicles, sweet ole Bud did the only thing that came to his mind, he punched the cop. Well, Bud didn't go to jail that day because the cop understood Bud's mental health condition but I do think Bud stopped stealing mail and swinging at the cops. A week or so after the 'cop punch' we don't see Bud again. We found out a few days later that his wife had to put him into a nursing home, with a secured unit where Bud couldn't run around and cause mischief. I miss my ole pal Bud, we may have never spoken but we understood and respected each other.

So let's get back to that white house and the crazy dog. We heard the husband and wife arguing on a regular basis and there were a lot of angry, threatening words exchanged.

Whenever he walked his dog which was two or three times a day, the dog would pull heavily against him. He never had full control of his dog. It was obvious to us that the dog hated him. The guy would short chain him and hold the dog off its hind feet by the choke chain. Heather and I both hoped the dog would lunge at him and tear his throat out. That poor dog was just full of fear and rage. Sadly, I understand that kind of wild behavior.

I felt that dog was extremely dangerous. I was fearful that someday, I would have to shoot the dog and the son of a bitch who mistreated him. It got to the point where I carried my gun while I was mowing the lawn because of that damn dog. The guy would stand in the alley and let his dog bark and growl at me for several minutes in his sissy attempt to intimidate me. I told the owner repeatedly that if he released his dog and it came anywhere near me that I was going kill it, and if he took exception to it, I'd be more than happy to kill him too.

Well one day, just a few weeks later the neighbor next to him on the corner tells us that the crazy guy's wife had left him and moved to another city, several hundred miles away and gratefully, she took the dog with her.

Now here's something that you may find quite interesting. This guy worked nights at that large facility for unstable children that I wrote about in my last book, "The System is Guilty." You know the one that had the riots with rumors of physical and sexual assaults on children by staff members? It closed and released all those children into the wind! Well just before that facility closed, that crazy neighbor with the crazy dog hung himself in his home after his wife and dog left him. I took a great sigh of relief because I was very much afraid, really afraid actually, that I was going to have to kill him and his dog. So the question now begs to be asked, did he kill himself because he was under investigation or indictment and he couldn't take the heat? Hell, who knows. I'm just damn glad that he's gone.

Now onto the next neighbor in the corner house. She's a real piece of work. Her name is Lillianna, she's an uppity retired college professor and a screaming liberal. If homely was a picture it would be her. She is a shapeless sack of flesh who probably lives off of kale and birdseed. Get a load of this shit. She is a precinct election judge. She fills her yard with democratic party election signs. She also has gay pride flags and a number of BLM signs. Her car is plastered with Biden bullshit stickers, her rear bumper, windows and even the painted surfaces are smattered with gay rainbows and coexist stickers. When Heather and I are in the yard she tries to engage in conversation with Heather. On more than one occasion, several occasions actually, she would position herself to lead Heather away from my line of sight for a private conversation. It looked to me to be the textbook maneuvering of a sexual predator. Hell, she may have been the one that wrote that textbook. When I first moved in, she of course questioned Heather as to who I was and where I came from. One day when Heather was at work, Lillianna asked me if I was still involved in law enforcement. (neither of us told her of my personal or work history). I saw it as a wonderful opportunity to fuck with her head. My answer was, "Yes, at times, I usually just observe and report activities having to do with same sex, sexual harassment and sexual assults. Some special assignment cop's don't work scheduled shifts, wear uniforms or drive marked units."

That broad couldn't dance away fast enough. I suspect that ole Lil got the message. On another occasion she and a neighbor from the corner house across the avenue (I'll get to her next) came into my driveway as I was washing my truck. Lil said, "We just found out (oh the power of the web and neighborhood gossips) that you are a published author, I am also a published author!"

I smelled where this conversation was going. I set down the hose and lit a cigarette. Like most every other college professor, they throw away the standard college textbooks that pertain to their course of teaching and write their own textbooks which are mandatory for their class that they are teaching. The students must buy the professors textbooks from the university bookstore to take their class and the slimy pricks books are not resellable. The student must turn their books back into the bookstore (to be destroyed) to receive their final grade. Ain't that some kinda bullshit! The university turns their head because they are the celebrated all-time, premier extortionists.

Lil went on to tell me that she is enjoying her retirement and that she might write another book, strictly for pleasure and profit. Lil grinned as she said, "I hate writing educational text, it's dull and time consuming, but it has paid for my annual six week trips to Paris and Amsterdam for the last twenty-three years. I also go to Africa every three years, where do you vacation?"

Me: Lil honey, you left out the part where you buy a new car every two years and pass the old one down to your son, all on your former students dime from you extorting them to buy your books, if they want to pass your mandatory class. Now that you're retired and have lost your cash-cow I'm guessing that you slicked your replacement to continue with using your books with a sweetheart 60/40 split. The new Prof doesn't have to write any text and pockets 40% of your book sales for their class. It's time for my nap now and I think your wide-eyed friend here has a few questions for you and about your illustrious career.

Lil lives alone, she claims to have had an ex-husband who was some kind of, "Dean of Bullshit" at another university, who edited her books along with some other prune juice swilling geek of higher education. She was angry at both of them because she didn't like the way they insulted her with their red ink pens. I smiled as I said, "No one tells me how or what to write, but then again my books are for sale, I am not for sale. Just my books are for sale, nobody owns me. Money is not my god nor are exotic travel destinations my bitch. I write what I want, the way I want, I'm nobody's whore."

She got the drift of what I was telling her and she didn't talk to me for a couple of weeks, which was just swell with me. Lil is one of those neighborhood daily walking people like the many other snoops and gossips of the neighborhood. They can oftentimes be seen standing in the street in tight huddles spewing their bullshit.

I think you'll find this interesting, Heather and I went to vote at our local precinct for the Midterms on November 6th 2018. Of course, there sat sweet sister Lil checking ID's and handing out voting forms. Of course we were fully aware of the thinly veiled hostility towards us damn republicans voting in the core of the democratic stronghold.

When we finished voting at the table, we walked to insert our ballots into the scanner. We were stopped by an election official who said, "Our scanner is not working, there is a man on his way to fix it. You can slide your ballets into this secured slot. After it is fixed we will scan your ballet for you." I smiled as I responded with, "The fuck you will. We will sit here and wait for fifteen minutes. If it's not fixed so we can scan our ballots in that time period, it will be media and police time and I will shut this shit down."

I was told to leave. I gave her an easy smile and said, "Make me, perhaps you should call the police? Perhaps I will." Out of nowhere came a guy in a suit, jingled a large ring of keys and opened the face of the scanning unit. He pushed a button and closed the scanner. He then put a key in the "secured ballot tray" to be scanned. He pulled out a few completed ballots and reached over to put them on a table. I blocked him and gave him a less than easy smile (much less) as I said, "Sport, you don't have a choice, scan those ballets now or be fitted for an orange jump-suit!"

There was a crowd of two dozen or more voters standing in line waiting to scan their ballots. Several people were laughing over my exchange with the keyring clown. One rather large fellow stepped alongside of me and leaned forward (inches from the keyring clowns face) and said, "Scan those now or you are about to learn what the true meaning of, 'Fuck Around-Find Out' is all about."

This election official was shaking like Barney Fife, trying to draw his gun. He scanned the ballets and slithered away. After we scanned our ballots I gave the election judges table a salute and said, "Nice try" as several others laughed on their way out. Heather told me on the drive home from voting that she heard one of the male election judges sitting at the table of six to say, "We need to throw that guy out." Heather heard Lil say, "He's a cop and he always carries a gun. Keep your seat"

I guess that I'm probably no longer on her Christmas card list!

CHAPTER 5
Keeping My Power

Well kids, Midterms are just thirty-two days away and if you look at Lillianna's yard you may want to call me a liar. You will not see a political yard sign of any kind, no bumper stickers and no window clings. Word on the street has it that a rather inquisitive American Patriot, contacted the city, county, state and even the feds as to the rules that govern a sworn election judge. I guess that sweet ole Lil was innocently (or perhaps not) violating her sworn oath of office. Well, I'll be damned!

Let's move on, the two story tan-beige house across the avenue on the corner once belonged to a retired local firefighter who when he heard of my writings was interested in reading one of my books. I gifted him a copy of my first novel, "Daddy Had To Say Goodbye." He raved about the book to neighbors and told me that everybody in the fire department knew about the book and they all bought it. Well that's a whole bunch of bullshit. There are approx. one hundred and forty one uniformed firefighters with nine fire stations and one rescue/fire boat. I can instantly check my website and Amazon for an up-to-the-minute sales report of my books and where they were shipped to. Nobody in the Duluth area bought that book during that time period, so he was just another big blow-hard. I guess he must have been lonely and was looking for a new friend to hangout with and someone that would pay him some attention. If you read my books, he's the guy that had the garage sale before they moved. He had my book (that I signed and gifted him) on a $5 table, which was moved to a $1 table on day two of his garage sale, the following day it went to a 25 cent table. That's the guy and his wife where I picked up my book and said, "Oh, this looks interesting but it's probably not worth two bits," as I threw it back on the table and walked away. That was the 2nd to the last time I spoke to those prickheads.

The new people (three years ago) that bought that house have never spoken to us. She was the gal that was with Lil in my driveway when I gave her the dressing down of her calling herself a published author. She too is a walker and part of the neighborhood gossip crew. She appears to be in her mid-sixties. During the warm weather months, I open my garage door and put my gun cleaning table in the open doorway for better lighting and ventilation. It seems that if I'm not shooting, I'm cleaning guns. I never put away a dirty gun. The cleaning chemicals get to me in a closed environment. Well, this gals name is Violet or something like that. I always say hello when she walks bye but she never looks over or returns the greeting.

The gentleman she lives with is quite elderly, I don't know if it's the woman's dad or husband but then again, I guess when people look at Heather and me together they almost think the same thing. In one conversation with Heather, Lil told Heather that he is a retired minister of some kind. The poor guy is very unstable on his feet (I guess him and I do have something in common) so that's why she walks their dog up-and-down the avenue alone on a very regular basis. Suddenly, one morning she waved and returned my greeting. The next day she waved and extended her greeting before I could, with a big smile to follow. My first thought was, "Shit, she either want's something or is on a mission for the neighborhood snoops. She must have not had the nerve to approach me on her own as that afternoon, here she comes with Lil on a direct path down my driveway. "Well fuck me!"

I knew there was some kind of a hustle in the works so as usual, I lit a cigarette and waited for the con job. Lil spoke first and introduced me to Violet. Violet shook my hand and got right down to business.

"David, you do know that the city has been tearing up the street in front of our house for several miles while replacing the underground utility service lines. Our driveways will be inaccessible for almost three weeks, we can't park on the street either. Starting Sunday evening, we will have nowhere to park except on the avenue. We can't see the avenue from our house. I know that you stay up late every night, would you mind looking after our cars and if you see any funny business please call us and the police?"

    I stood in silence as she handed me an index card with her home phone number and both of their cell numbers and their names along with (you will fuckin love this) "Duluth Police–911." I almost pissed myself laughing. They both looked at me in shock as I said, "Thank you for listing the Duluth Police Department's 911 phone number. I'll try to remember that number." I assured her that if I saw any "funny business" that I will let them know. They both left as I was blowing smoke rings into the still air.

    That certainly explains her sudden friendliness and sweet smile. This is the same woman who could never wave or say hello and now she walks up to me and says, "Here's my husband and mine's cell phone numbers, please call us if you see anything that looks funny?" I said I certainly would. Truth is, I could give a shit less, especially after I found out that he is a retired minister who is rumored to have a lustful attraction for money. Neither of them self-righteous sweethearts approve of smokers or people living in sin. Yeah you fuckers judge me and ignore my greetings but now you want me to be your security guard for your vehicles? Yeah, here's a whole bunch of kiss, my entire ass right there! If I saw anyone doing 'funny business' like stealing their tires or car batteries I think I would pour myself another cup of Folgers and sit back and enjoy the show. If the 'funny business' people bring in an engine hoist I will try to find her index card and look for the secret phone number to call the Duluth Police Department.

Now on the avenue here, directly across from us is Billy's house. Billy has since moved. The house was on the market for several months. The house was bought by an investor who is known in the city as a half-assd contractor and house flipper. I have heard on more than one occasion that he was stuffing the pockets of a few building inspectors in the city. He and his family restored it and sold it to the current pukes that reside there, but let's get back to Billy.

Billy was an interesting cat. Billy was in his late forties and was injured in some type of industrial accident that he received a full medical disability retirement along with a rather hefty settlement from workers comp. He had noticeable difficulties with walking. Billy and I got to be morning coffee buddies, almost every morning. I'd usually go over to his place. What I shortly found out is that Billy was a drunk and a pill head. Whether or not his addictions derived from his injuries, the poor guy would drink his breakfast as soon as his wife left for work. Billy would be bottled-up before nine o'clock in the morning and he would sit there and drink beer along with shots of whiskey all day, which were not in a shot glass but in a half filled water glass. In the period of time that I sat with him and drank three cups of coffee he could barely move. Billy was a nice guy but he had some strange ways about him. He could barely walk but went golfing and played eighteen holes each week. We get a lot of snow here and of course (like many folks in our area, excluding me) Billy owned an ATV with oversized tires and chains. He had a snowplow mounted on the front of his ATV and he would push the snow out of his driveway which was just dirt. He would then drive at that wind-packed snow at full speed and blast it into the snow banks. Each time, he all but put himself over the front handle grips of the ATV. One day I suggested that he install a seat belt on there so he didn't launch himself head first into his garage. The next week Billy called me and said come on over and check out my new seat belts. He had somebody install 5 point racing seat belts on his ATV so he didn't have to eat any part of a building when it came to such an abrupt stop. Well that made me deeply question his spinal problems with the way he rode that ATV and slammed into the frozen snow banks. Billy had this thing about driving his cars and trucks far faster than the posted speed limits. He would tell me, "I'm afraid of getting into a wreck and hurting my back even worse than it is, so I go fast to get there and back home again. The less time I travel, the less time I'm at risk!"

Now there's some twisted logic that gives me a headache. Understand that he's out of his mind with both his medication and whatever drugs he comes up with as well as his alcohol. His wife would go to bed at night and Billy would sit up all night watching TV because he was so strung out.

For whatever reason, Billy liked to watch these very late night infomercials. Like his meds and booze, he got hooked on purchasing things late at night. He bought all kinds of shit every night that he didn't remember he ordered even when they arrived a few days later. Billy developed a romantic relationship with some kind of 'Green Frying Pan' that ran loop programming all night long. He enjoyed these channels so much that he bought eight of those same Green fry pans, he ordered three of the same size in one night! When his wife found out, she took away his credit card. Billy never remembered that he bought one of them, let alone all eight, that's how stoned he was. Good ole Billy was not to be outdone by his wife.

He just picked up another credit card and did his thing as always with his late night shopping. Billy phoned me one day (now get this) this is the guy with such a severe back injury that he can no longer work for the rest of his life. He called me when he was out golfing one day saying, "It's such a nice day we are going to stay and play thirty-six holes, UPS should be dropping off a package this afternoon, please grab it as soon as they drop it off. I don't want my wife to see it, just bring it into your house and I'll pick it up tomorrow."

Tomorrow came and Billy came over and got his package and he said, "Wait till you see this nice Green Fry Pan I just bought."

Well Billy and I had a bit of a falling out. Oh wait, let me backup a minute. Billy and his wife had an above ground swimming pool, the kind you just blow up and put together yourself and fill it with a garden hose. It was substantially larger than most because they were both extra large people, they floated in it on air mattresses. They put it right in their front yard just ten or so feet from the avenue. I thought that was extremely weird, why wouldn't they have put it in their backyard or their side yard for privacy? But no, right in front of the fucking street, they floted and waved at the cars as they drove by! Yep, that's weird. Now back to my falling out with Billy. His wife had her daughter and husband come and live with them for several months while the son-in-law was finishing up some kind of studies for a PHD in psychology. The wife never mentioned to Billy that they were coming or staying. Billy hated both the step daughter and her husband, Billy would come over (with a bottle in hand) and tell me how this twenty-six year old shit head guy, would try to analyze him and tell him, "Here is what I think you are trying to say" and other clinical voodoo bullshit to show his superior intelligence.

I wondered why the son-in-law just didn't tell him that, "You're a drunk and a junkie" and leave it at that.

I think Billy had to bite his tongue because his wife was truly the breadwinner and she pretty much owned him. Or perhaps when he received his injury settlement she might have put it where he couldn't get to it. That made plenty of sense with his out of control late night shopping. One fine day I went out to mow my lawn and there's a car parked on my lawn. We don't have any curbs here so my lawn borders the street. They didn't just have a tire on the edge of my lawn, no this car was fully parked on my fucking lawn! Who does that shit? I went over to Billy's house to see if they might have a visitor whose car it was. The stepdaughter answered the door and I inquired if she had a house guest that owned the vehicle across the street parked on my fucking lawn. She said, "Oh yeah, do you want her to move it?" I could see and smell heavy marijuana smoke coming out the door. I stepped back to avoid a contact high and asked, "What the fuck do you think honey? Why don't have your visitor drive up my fucking stairs and park next to my god damn mail box?"

Billy and his wife never spoke to either of us again, suddenly they decided to move. No goodbye, go to hell or kiss my ass. Here's an interesting thing, they had been gone for three months when Billy's wife sends me a text and follows it up with a phone call like an hour later, she is giving me instructions on how to open the realtor's lockbox to get the key to let myself in because they left a small dining room table that they were using for 'staging'. Some college student had bought it for forty bucks and he was going to come by and pick it up and she wanted to know if I would let him in and then help him load the table into his car and collect the money. Well, I still have a liking for Billy so I said yeah, "Sure, I'll do it." So the guy came, I let him in, helped him load his table and collected the forty bucks and off he went. I called Billy's wife and said, "The guy came by and picked up the table and I've got your forty bucks, give me an address so I can mail it to you." She said, "No, would you give it to the retired fireman who lives up on the corner as he's been mowing our lawn since we've left, just give it to him for gas money for his riding lawn mower."

Well that's the end of the Billy story but it's not the end of that yellow piece of shit house. The people that bought it clearly came straight out of, 'Asshole Acres Trailer Park and Meth Lab Emporium'. From the very first day that they moved in, that place instantly turned into a back corner trailer park, trash dump site. There is one forty year oldish woman (wheelchair bound) and three adult males in their late twenties to early thirties with an average weight of about three hundred and fifty pounds plus. They all have multi-colored hair and she has a spiked, eight inch high Mohawk haircut with closely shaved sides of her head. If you want to see a bunch of shit, just look over there right now. They mow the lawn maybe two times a year. Hell, a full grown deer could be standing in their lawn and you'd never see it! Then again, they have no lawn, they have let everything go to weeds. They don't treat the lawn to prevent or at least control the weeds, so of course, we get weeds. The only color in the lawn is from the Canadian thistle that is damn near three feet high, maybe even higher! They have two non-running cars just sitting around along with old washers, dryers, stoves and BBQ grills. They don't use trash bags, they just throw their trash into the trash bin and never close the lid and let it blow to the four winds. I'm damn tired of picking up their trash out of my yard or watching it blow down the avenue. I'm sure the other neighbors aren't too excited about them either. They also have an out of control large dog that's on a heavy metal chain in the driveway. It snarls and barks and lunges at people as they walk the avenue. Postal carriers have refused delivery because of that dog and I sure as hell don't blame them, it's a vicious acting son of a bitch. Both Heather and I have said hello to them and waved on many occasions. But there is never any response from any of them. At first we thought that they may be deaf or mute. But we hear them talking amongst each other so we know they're not without voices or ears. Now these dirtbags have lived there for almost three years and have made no repairs to the broken patio door or the storm door that somehow came off and is laying in the tall weeds. Their favorite trick to do in the winter is that they'll move their wheeled trash bins out into the street when snow is forecasted, so when the snowplow comes by, they lift the blade and swing further onto my side of the street to avoid the trash bins. These dinks do that for the sole reason so that they don't have a big snow bank in their driveway to deal with. Where does the snow go? Of course, it all gets pushed over into our driveway. They don't own a snowblower and are far to fucking lazy to shovel their driveway. When they get stuck in their driveway after a moderate snow they don't try to shovel their way out. They just gun their engines and repeatedly slam the transmission in forward and reverse to rock the cars out. I have to guess that those two non-running cars parked in the grass had met their untimely demise due to three lazy fat pricks gunning their engines.

OK, enough of those butt clowns. Now the white corner two story house with the six gables and all the ivy that reaches to the roof, is owned by a very nice woman who lives alone. She had young daughters living with her until obviously they became old enough to strike out on their own. She mows her own lawn with a walk behind vintage mower and she removes her snow with a shovel without any help. I understand that she also has two sons. I don't know if her kids live in the area but none of them have ever come by to help her with her lawn or snow removal. Our neighborhood has a generous smattering of crab apple trees and wild strawberries along with some blueberries. The homeowner's name is Connie, but we call her grandma. Not out of disrespect but because she wears older women's clothes and has no airs about her. She looks like a simple woman who enjoys the simple ways. She works in her lawn from morning to sundown. She works a sizable vegetable garden and tends to the strawberries with watering and pruning of both. We have never seen her have any visitors other than a few people who come by in the fall to pick the strawberries and apples. The neighborhood whitetail deer work over her gardens nightly.

We've waved to her when she drives by, and on the few occasions when we'll get her mail delivered at our house, one of us will walk over to her with her mail because of all the dope fiends that know how to acid wash checks.

There was one time that we actually had a conversation with her, brief as it was. It was during the remodel of Billy's house before the trash people moved in. The remodel people were scumbags just like the new owners. They used a very tired and barely running old flat bed haul-truck to remove the debris. They would not tie or strap down any of the construction trash, wood and drywall along with plumbing and electric fixtures. When the workers left for the day we could see debris falling off the truck into the street as they chugged away. They never stopped to clean it up, they just kept driving. One summer day we noticed and heard a bunch of stuff hit the street as they drove away, so we went over to clean it up. Now we don't use that part of the street so it's not our deal, we just thought we'd be good guys and clean up the mess. There were dozens and dozens of nails and screws laying on the street just waiting for a car tire to come by to build a personal relationship. We only brought two brooms and a dust pan. I had to go back to the house and bring a 55 gallon yard bucket for all of the debris. Connie came out of her house and helped us and that's how we first met. We only had a brief conversation, she seems nice but she's not very social, at least not with us but then again, I'm guessing the word got out that we are the two people living in sin and we smoke cigarettes.

CHAPTER 6
My Head Hurts

OK, let's do that slanted roof beige house directly in front of you on the corner of the dirt street. The people that lived there when I first moved here, were a really nice young couple that had two little girls. His name was Nate, I don't remember his wife's name. We kind of got to watch his girls grow up over a six year period. They were just absolutely sweet little girls that played together like best friends. No whining, no fighting, just giggles and laughter. Mommy was a school teacher and Nate was a inhalation therapist. We didn't see mom outside very often. Nate worked six, ten hour days every week. When he came home from work it was as if daddy had been away for an entire month. His girls raced out of the house to meet daddy. Those little darlings mauled him like he was Santa Claus and the Easter Bunny all rolled up into one. The poor guy never made it into the house. The girls took him over as if he was a new puppy. He didn't even get to change out of his hospital scrubs before the girls had him rolling in the grass, playing tag, pushing them on the swings of the well appointed play set. It was, "Let's teeter-totter, push me higher, catch me on the slide daddy, let's catch some grasshoppers." It was him and his girls loving life and each other. The wife was very rarely ever seen outside, unless she was driving her car. Daddy was always out in the yard with the girls. In the Winter months it was all about snow angels, snowmen, sledding and toboggans. Daddy made cool little toboggan runs and he pulled them around on their sleds. He was really a good guy and a good neighbor. He never asked us for anything and never had a bad word to say about anyone. We would chat briefly with him on the days that we were both out mowing or doing yard work.

Their home was once a rather sizable chicken coop in the 1950's and the entire hillside was a large feedlot for dairy cows. Obviously the house was built in sections over the years. The house was small and only had two bedrooms. Nate bought a sizable rural lot with plenty of room for a large house along with a greenhouse and a work/craft shop. Nate and his dad drew up all of the floorplans. Nate sold the house and moved into his parents home while their house was being built. Nate told me that he wished he could do some of the building himself but he knew he would lose far too much time with his girls. I have never witnessed that type of such a deep family bond. They made me smile, they warmed my heart.

The current resident has been there for I'm thinking maybe two years. She is more than just a bit interesting. Heather calls her stump. She's maybe in her late thirties, short and squatty, all ass and no body. She has long, straight (below waist) super thick, flaming red hair. I don't know anything about that hair extension stuff but her hair doesn't look quite natural. We only get brief glimpses of her as she does not use her front door. Her driveway and garage are off of the avenue. We never saw a moving truck come to deliver anything when she moved in. She gets food delivery daily and sometimes, twice a-day from one of those restaurant services. She has a lawn maintenance company to take care of her lawn and a snow removal company to take care of her driveway.

Jesus Christ you guys, I sound like one of the lady huddle gossips! If I'm not at my computer writing with all glass in front of me, I'm outside at the deck table using my laptop, doing research or editing corrections. Yes, I see everything during my split-shift of seven hours of writing during the daytime and four hours of late night into the morning hours, six days a week. Our oldest lil fur baby needs to potty more often then the other two, due to her age. I'm on night watch from 10pm to 1am so Heather can sleep.

Now, getting back to 'Stump'. You all know that Heather and I like to make up silly little stories about people. So Heather figures that she's a witness protection program kind of gal and she must avoid people, either that or she is just a recluse. I don't give a shit either way.

So now look at the ditch in front of you. That is our property right up to the edge of the dirt road. That ditch pisses me off. Hell, that dirt road pisses me off, all by itself. There are very few dirt roads in the city. There are no curbs. Now remember that the entire hillside was a dairy farm up until the 50's. The corner house of Stump's and the one next to it were both farm, out-buildings. They both have stone basement foundations that, of course, leak. In case you're wondering, our house was built in 1967, we have a concrete basement. Both of those houses across the street were built below grade as it was a hillside and not a street. The ditch was put in to protect those two houses from flooding from heavy rains and snow melt.

Which now brings us to the second house and the potheads who live there.

I am not a fan of either of them, Heather on the other hand, straight up hates them! They are both retired and in their mid-sixties. He is a short, sizzle chest fool that struts around like a Bantam Rooster. Whether it is summer or winter, hot or cold, windy or calm, day or night, he is constantly bitching about the weather. He is a habitual bitch.

Their names are not important, I just call them Dumb and Dumber. He is just flat out dumb. She is even dumber for staying with him.

They seemed like nice enough people when I first met them. We had a few conversations in the first month that I moved in. One rather hot day (mid-week) I was mowing the lawn, Heather was at work. The wife (Dumber) came over with a young girl, (I thought too young to be hanging out with her) and suggested I remove my shirt because it was such a hot day and she didn't want me to get overheated and all sweaty. I just straight-up told her (without a smile) that my shirt stays on and I already have a woman. After that conversation she spent plenty of time in their tiny little front yard posing for me with a whole bunch of butt cheeks being flexed and open blouses being displayed.

Their house is narrow and appears to have had at least one addition built on and looks like fourth graders did the roofing and siding. It looks like rough cut yellow pine was used in the attempt to make it look like cedar siding, which was a huge failure.

They have a large, 'Angel of Mercy' metal work attached to the front of their house which I heard her husband had cancer at one time. Another neighbor told me that she was a retired neonatal nurse and the metal work was to honor the babies that she cared for that died. Her entire 10x12 foot front yard is laden with multi-colored Mardi Gras type beads. There are also several assorted cartoon Pez dispensers and one area has all the same theme SpongeBob SquarePants Pez dispensers. This chick (or should I say 'Dumber') lays in her front yard every day and talks to the trinkets like they are little children, she does this from early Spring until late Fall. I don't know if she's into some kind of witchcraft stuff or if she's doing some heavy drugs. As a side note, I was sponsoring a guy in his quest for sobriety. He pretty much told me his life story and none of it was pretty, which is quite common amongst young people in these times. He drank heavily and did so many drugs that he couldn't work so he sold drugs to live off of. After a meeting one night, I walked him to his car and I could smell fresh marijuana coming from it. He knew I smelled it but I wasn't going to confront him. He would just deny it and start building a lie to cover a lie to cover the next lie. Instead I said, "So you claim to have been sober for four months now, but we both know that your path has not been true or totally straight. What gives with what's stinking in your car?" He denied smoking dope or drinking but admitted to still selling high test grass, "Because I need the money and my customers won't leave me alone because I have the highest quality magic mushrooms and kick ass grass in the entire area." I smiled as I told him to spread his feet as wide apart as he possibly can. He had a look of, "Fuck, he's still a cop" as he did what I told him. I enjoyed watching him starting to freak. I stood within a foot of him as I said, "Sport you fuckin listen and you best listen hard. Sobriety is not just about not drinking or drugging, it's also about changing our ways and living right. Now, look down at your feet. Do you believe that you could stand in a lake with your feet spread as they are now and think that one foot will be in cold water and the other in warm water? My point is this, you can't have it both ways. You, as all other dopers that sling dope to get by are lazy, you don't want to work. Get a job to pay your way before some judge makes arrangements for you to work in chains. You are on probation now with a deferred sentence on drug charges, let's face it, the only reason that you are sober is that you have been court ordered not to drink or drug and you have to do weekly random drug screens. If you get caught with that dope, your fucked and you'll pull six to eight years, all because you're to fuckin lazy to get a job and make an honest living.

See that dumpster over there, get that shit out of your car and lay it on the ground on the side of the dumpster. I have some friends who will come and pick it up for disposal, I will stand right here alongside you as we wait for them. If you don't trust them and think they will sell or use it themselves, they will be happy to show you their badges. Now stand up straight like a man!"

I dialed a number and the voice said, "It's been a while, we'll be there in fifteen minutes." Two men pulled up next to us in a new white Jeep. They got out with smiles as they greeted me by name and with handshakes. They looked at the kid and said, 'Well Brown, I guess that this is another one of your ruptured ducks?" The three of us had a laugh, the kid was a bit green around the gills. "How's about you boys doing me a solid by showing my charge here some silver badges and hauling that sack of shit away next to the dumpster and use it for some controlled sales and catching some bad guys. This young man is buying us all coffee and apple pie."

I had the kid ride with me to the restaurant. One of the Jeep officers called and said they just got a call from dispatch that a warrant they had been waiting for was just signed and they had to roll on it. When I told the kid that the cops had to take a call and would not be able to coffee with us, I think that at that very moment, he may have had a spiritual experience.

Over pie and coffee the kid got real serious and asked if I would keep a secret that he needs to tell me. I laughed with, "Muther Fucker! You seriously have to ask me that? You little prick, I might just put you on the floor and cuff you and use you for a fuckin footrest until a squad is available to haul your ass off to jail!" He blankly stared at me and was obviously in mental vapor lock. I smiled and said, "Catch your breath, dick head and say what you need to say."

You guys will find this rich. The kid told me that he had to deliver that marijuana and a small sack of, "Magic Mushrooms" that the cops took to who else but, (drum roll please) Mr. and Mrs. Dumb as fuck!

Well now the little shit is in the county jail for one year for stealing a few packs of cigarettes out of a gas station.

My first fallout with the 'Dummies' came on one Winter day. She walked up to our house and rang the doorbell. It had just freshly snowed and there was probably four to six inches on the ground. She asked if I would snow blow their parking spots because her husband was feeling a bit under the weather. My only comment was, "Gosh, I'm feeling a bit under the weather as well. I hope your basement doesn't flood. Sorry, but I can't help you."

What prompted my response was that last summer they used the city public works department to fuck us. Both of the 'Dummies' were always bitching about us not cleaning out our ditch. Heather and I had both cleaned that ditch several times that summer as we get tall cattails and high grass that grows in the ditch from all the runoff water. One mid-summer day, Heather was using the weed wacker in the ditch, when that asshole came out of his house, walked to the center of the street and hollered at her not to leave the trimmings in the ditch. I was on the deck writing and was not sure of what he actually said but I sure as hell didn't like his tone of voice. I came down the stairs fast enough towards him, that that phony little bitch scampered back into his house and watched out his door window. I waved for him to come out but the little sizzle chest, bitch boy just stood there and smiled. I walked up to Heather and asked what he said. All she said was, "If that little bastard would have stepped a few feet closer, I would have taken both of his ears and his fucking nose off with this bad boy" as she revved the motor of the weed wacker. I didn't have the chance to confront him that day.

However, I vowed to all things holy, that him and I would dance and when that time came he sure as fuck wouldn't like the tune.

Two weeks later a city work crew showed up with a track hoe and two dump trucks. The work crew dug six feet beyond the ditch deeper into our lawn. The city has the right to do that but it was clearly based on Dumb's complaint of water overflowing the road and flooding his basement, which of course has never happened.

On several occasions prior to the city crew ruining our lawn, I saw that there were slots cut into our lawn obviously by 'Dumb' in the dark of night to assist rain water to run into the ditch and not flood the road and his property. I knew that if I got a hold of him that I would end up in jail. He is the type of asshole that would call the cops without even a word being exchanged between us and claim that I roughed him up or threatened to kill him, eat his liver, rape his wife and burn his house while they slept.

I needed a master plan that would end this bullshit and shut him down. Surprisingly it came to me rather quickly, I think fast when I am pissed off. I giggled with my insta-plan, I was quite proud of myself. If there was a trophy for, "Mind Fuck of The Week" it would be sitting on my fireplace mantel.

I was about to put that phoney little fuck-stick into the fear of his lifetime, that would hopefully last him for his entire lifetime. It will take me a few days to put the ball into play but we will definitely be playing ball and he aint gonna like it. Not one fuckin bit!

CHAPTER 7
The Set Up

The last time I caught him digging trenches into our lawn I shouted, "Hey, ass breath, this is our property, do you want to go to jail? You can't be doing this shit. You bought a converted cow birthing barn that was built below street level. I don't give a fuck about your house, you're the dumb-ass that bought it, deal with it. It's your problem! Those weeds are gonna stay there for fucking ever, if I can find a place that sells noxious weeds, I will plant that whole fucking ditch with them, then you will have a flooding problem!"

It took me four days to develop and refine my award winning masterpiece. One of the most common denominators amongst dopers is that they are creatures of habit and they almost never shy away from their routine. Dumb drives off every morning at 8:40 am. Not 8:30, not 8:45 but 8:40. After a period of time I came to understand that he was driving up to the convenience store gas station six blocks away to get a pack of cigarettes. I thought, "That's where it's gonna happen."

My plan was to contact my buddy, the county jail Commander and ask him for a day pass for my little friend that's doing a year for stealing cigarettes, so I could take him to an AA meeting. Here is where this gets good. Part of the plan is to have my uniform friends in marked patrol units block him in at the convenience store and do a felony stop on him. Pull him out of his car at gunpoint in the parking lot while he shits himself. Put him in the cage in the back of a patrol car and drive into the isolated alley behind the C-store. Then have the white jeep undercover narcs, pull up with me pulling up behind them with his drug dealer in my truck. The uniformed cops get out of the squad and I slide in behind the wheel with the greeting, "Hello asshole, where's your ditch cutting shovel?" Then have his drug dealer stand in front of the cop car and hand the narcs a manila file folder as he points towards 'Dumb' and nods his head several times as the narcs talk with him as he points towards 'Dumb' a few more times. "You see that dick breath, in that folder are all the delivery dates and times and amounts. Obviously you and your wife like to repackage and resell narcotics. Those narcs know who you have been selling to. They will bust them and your customers will sing like birds and burn your ass, for a lesser sentence and you and your lil Mrs. will go down for drug trafficking."

I would then say, "Hey asshole, you see this shotgun, you see this AR15, they're both fully loaded and resting in these locked racks. Look what happens when I push these two buttons. That's right darling, they are now free and ready to rock. But I don't need these big long guns. My everyday carry, Smith and Wesson performance center 45 caliber with a four and three quarter inch barrel would nicely do the job. If you prefer to continue to be an asshole I'd be more than happy to drop a round into your ugly fucking skull or if you prefer an open casket, I'll just pump a few rounds into your guts and be done with you. Here's the deal asshole, it's time for you and your sweetheart to move. I suggest you go home and start packing. If you're still in that house in seven days from now you will face your maker. You fucked with the wrong cat and this cat is about to fuck your life hard, long and continuous! Capace?"

Sadly, none of that happened. I was sitting on the deck at around 9:00 am drinking coffee, smoking cigarettes and doing some edits. Sirens were sounding nearby and a fire truck and ambulance pulled up in front of the Dummy's house. I got kinda giddy with thinking that she got tired of his shit and finally shot him or maybe they were overdosing.

The next day, one of the 'Huddle' ladies was making the rounds and came to the door to tell me that Mr. Dumb fell down the stairs in his house and broke his hip and pelvis. My only response was, "At least he won't be digging in my lawn for a while" as I closed the door.

So on to the next house, an elderly lady lived there, who rented several rooms like military barracks. She is known as "The Church Lady" in the neighborhood. Word has it that she finds single men at church and rents rooms to them cheap. Most of these fellows looked to be downtrodden and without family. Anyone ever heard of the many homicide cases throughout the country where people will use a church or a soup kitchen to recruit homeless fellows without families who are down on their luck, buy life insurance for them and list themselves as the beneficiary and the gentlemen soon die unexpectedly? So this old broad lives alone with all these renters, she probably plucks them from the church, invites them home to live with her in the barracks and unbeknown to them, signs them up for some kind of a welfare assistance and the payments go into her bank account. She collects a shit load of money for room and board.

I had a run in with one of her renters who was a drugged out psycho from hell. He walked up to me one day when I was mowing my lawn and said, "I understand you used to be a cop." Which put my hackles to full attention. He went on with, "They told me at the house that you may still be a cop." I said, "Why is that a topic of conversation at the house?" He said, "Well I guess I just don't like cops. I've had some bad experiences with them." I said, "Yeah you know what, assholes have bad experiences with cops and I think you're one of them, get the fuck away from me and don't come back on my property."

The next day he came over and stood in the street in front of my driveway and shouted, I'd like to talk to you, I'd like to make amends, I didn't mean to offend you in that way. I want to be a good neighbor. I want to get to know everybody in the neighborhood and make friends."

I stood in my lawn and told him to stay in the street and we will have a chat. He goes on to say, "I hear you're an author and you write books about alcoholism and PTSD. I got both of those and I struggle every day with my alcoholism." I said, "You ever try a meeting, you ever try to stop drinking? You do know that the struggles are over once you put the plug in the jug?" So he knew enough about it that he asked me to be his sponsor and I said, "No I don't have time, I'm a writer these days, I'm no longer a sponsor. You know where the meetings are. Go find one, I go up to my normal Monday night Piedmont Heights meeting and those folks got it right." He again said, "I want to be friends with you" as he put out his extended hand to shake hands. I said. "Wait, stop, we're not gonna be pals, I don't ever want you to come near me or talk to me. You're welcome in this meeting as everyone else is, just don't try to talk with me."

One fine evening, a few weeks later, here comes a fire truck and an ambulance and a couple of police cars, they obviously loaded up the old doll that owned the house. One of the neighbors said that she fell and severely injured her spine and hips and would be in the hospital for an extended period of time. Well the son who lives out of state came to town (who I had yet to meet) who came to my door, introduced himself and made mention of the condition of his mother and they might sell the house, they weren't quite sure yet but they're going to leave one renter to stay there to care for the house. Well this one renter was the clown that wanted to be my friend and hated cops.   He came by and told me that the family had a suspicion of him pushing the mother down onto the floor but he wanted to argue his case before there was even an accusation or investigation, which tells us all a whole bunch of truths. According to the home owners son, this little psycho bastard bothered him every week with phone calls of, "I want this fixed and I want that fixed and I don't like these neighbors, these people should be made to move out and on and on. The old doll had a car in really good shape. He somehow finagled a way to buy the car on a monthly payment plan with the old doll's son. He was driving the injured mother's car around until a month later when a cop came and had it towed because the car was parked at a strange angle and blocking the middle of the street. Suddenly the prickhead was gone. The son came over and wanted us to know that his daughter will be living there and she is also an engineer in the family business and they have plans on developing the rest of the block from this house next to us, all the way down for eight city lots to put in an exclusive condo building.

My answer to him was brief, "So that'd be fucking charming, I can't wait for two years of continuous construction noise and the putred smell of diesel exhaust every fuckin day."

I only spoke to the girl once and that was because the night before there were three bears, (not the three bears in the book you assholes, quit grinning) in the street in the late afternoon. She runs and bikes after dark. The daughter was obviously an exercise freak, I would be surprised if she weighed a hundred pounds. I warned her of the bears and the only thing she said (she didn't even introduce herself as she was running in place) was, "I'll be fine, bears don't scare me" as she went on her way.

OK the next house down, and this is my favorite house because of the asshole that lives there. This clown was married to the number one neighborhood gossip until she died and that was before I moved in. I guess she was a real piece of work, she was in everyone's business and broadcast it like she owned a fucking radio station. I understand that the husband is no different. Whenever anyone on the street is gathered for any kind of conversation he has to be right in the middle of it. I understand that he's a retired electrical contractor that owned a sizable successful business with more than twenty employees. He has a very nice home, he's done a ton of upgrades and just recently had a gorgeous concrete four car driveway installed as well as added onto his garage to be a six bay garage, attached to the house. He's always got some kind of a contractor project going on. Every year he buys a new car and a new pickup truck. That's a pretty nice gig when you're retired don't you think? Well he strolls down the street three or four times a day. I guess he's just cruising for gossip. Last week I was in the garage with the doors open cleaning guns. He stopped and asked what I was doing, when I answered, "cleaning guns" I saw him shudder which told me all I needed to know about this guy. He went on to say that, "Somebody told me that you're an author, I love to read!" Of course he, like every other asshole I've ever run into who loves to read, gives me his list of his favorite authors and his favorite books. It's always the same, no matter who I'm talking to because that's what makes you cool, I guess. So he asked me about my writing and I told him that I had published seven novels and one of those was a joint venture with a dear friend of mine who has recently struck out to be an author on her own. So this asshat says, "I'd like to borrow one of your books to read." I smiled and I said, "I don't have a lending library, I have books for sale on my website and I ship them out of my home but I don't loan books. He acted a bit miffed and responded with, "Well I just want to borrow one, I'll be real careful and I won't get it dirty and then I'll give it back to you when I'm done with it and you can still sell it." I had to struggle not to tell him to go fuck a tree. I knew a little bit of this guy's background, he was some kind of a religious fanatic well entrenched into his church. So I said, "Well there's a lot of bad words in my books, I use bad words as sentence enhancers, I use the word fuck a great deal. He shook his head and said, "I don't like that word." I said, Then you're not going to like my fucking books, I fucking assure you!" Without another word he left my driveway and we haven't spoken since. What a fucking asshole this prick is. He has the latest model snowblower attachment on his riding lawn mower with a cabin mounted and a heater and this asshole wants to borrow one of my books? Go fuck your entire self!

Next to him is the guy, who I wrote about two books ago that favors himself as an author but has only written five pages in the last three years. Once I showed him my six published books and told him about the publishing business. I think I crushed his fantasy and he stopped waving and talking to me.

Lastly there's a house at the end of the dirt road and those people too are a couple of real beauties. I think she is self-appointed as the official keeper of all the rumors of the neighborhood and I'm sure she catalogs them like a librarian. I think a couple of times each day she makes her rounds and chats with neighbors for hours on end.

Well, they too are below the road grade and somehow they've got some kind of a hook into the city street maintenance department. There's maintenance trucks going down that road all the time on our tax dollars. The city workers refer to her as, "The cookie lady" because she bakes cookies for all the city workers so they'll come when she calls. I don't know what the fuck they do down there but they're down there on a very regular basis. Her husband is a flaming prick and he favors himself as a traffic bully. He loves to drive down the street in the center of the road causing you to have to veer almost to the edge of the roadway, again there's no curbs but I hold my ground every time I see him. I even turn a little bit into his traffic lane just to let him know I don't back down. The story I got on him was from some of my friends that came over to visit that remembered him from being their high school PE coach. The story goes that he slipped and fell at the swimming pool and developed some kind of brain injury that required surgery. When he returned to work he was just a mean nasty son of a bitch and was throwing kids around all the time. I guess that at some point the kids had enough and they had a blanket party for him which brought him into early retirement, the poor son of a bitch! It's a beautiful thing to hear stories of bullies getting bullied.

So that's it my darlings for the neighborhood tour, I hope you enjoyed the visit. I'm done for now, I need a nap. You guys do whatever the fuck you're gonna do, I'm gonna do me.

I woke from my nap hearing Heather saying, "Our friend Sean Carrigan flew out from Colorado that night when I told him of David's lighting, side-strike, followed by his cardiac arrest and he went into a deep coma. Sean came to the house (he knows where the spare key is kept) and the next morning he had a landscape company stripping the grass where David's body was outlined in the burnt grass. He had a large area replaced so I couldn't see the exact location where David was lying dying."

I jumped off the bed with a rage like I've rarely experienced. "Holy shit, they are making Heather relive the nightmare that even we, rarely speak of. I gotta shut that shit down, now!"

Something stopped me in mid-stride. The thought came to me that maybe Heather initiated that conversation.

Maybe she needs to vent her anxiety. Maybe she can't talk to me about it yet, for her fear of upsetting me?

Hell I have some secrets that I can't talk about for fear of upsetting her, she has been through enough. I guess we both have.

CHAPTER 8
The Honest Lie

The following morning somebody had the hotel restaurant deliver an elaborate breakfast which was quite nice. I didn't really feel much like talking today but I thought we'd finish up, shake hands, have some hugs and I'll take my life back.

Everyone said that they thoroughly enjoyed the virtual and physical tour of the neighborhood yesterday and how they greatly enjoyed the way I talk about people.

Ann: David, you have this incredible ability to say it like it is, you don't hold anything back, you're absolutely fearless and you don't care who judges you. I wish I had the courage and skill of saying, "I don't give a fuck." I'm sure there's a lot of freedom in that.

Heather came out onto the deck and said, "Kids, after breakfast we're going to cut this deal short. I need my husband, my mother is quite ill and is in the process of dying. As a matter of fact she's been non communicative and pretty much gone for the last several days. I have family matters that I need to attend to and I need some of David's attention, so let's have the handshakes, the hugs and the kisses and I have to ask you all to be on your way."

Well I had to agree with Heather. We needed our time and I've been holding back on my secret, even from Heather as well as our close friends. There are just some things that I don't feel I need to burden other people with. As a matter of fact I haven't bothered to burden Heather with it because of her looking at her mother's potential passing, perhaps in the next day or two. Her stepdad is right behind her mother, he may go before her, so yeah she's got her plate full and she's going off to work every day. It's no secret to Heather that I'm neither a fan or a friend to either her mother or her stepdad. Those two did all they could to separate us because they wanted Heather back for their own personal playmate and they wanted to live vicariously through her, as their lives were so pathetically mundane. They were the ones that said to Heather, "You choose, it's either David, or it's us, it can't be both."

Since then she's had very little contact with her mother or her stepdad in the last eight years. Tragic, but it's all about control and power with them, I detest narcissists, people can be such fuck heads.

I felt I had to stay quiet and support Heather. She knows my feelings for her family but now's not my time, it's her time and I have to support that. I have to be her best friend and be considerate and patient with her. My time will come later, hopefully a lot later but I've got suspicions that shits about to hit the fan with my health and it ain't gonna be pretty.

I have been trying for the last two years to get in to see a doctor but because of this covid bullshit and all the restrictions, you couldn't get near a medical facility unless you had the jab along with all the many boosters, well Heather and I refuse to be anybody's fucking lab rat just because the government says we need to be, so they can control people and so people will mail in their ballots and avoid the polling booths. Well that certainly did work, you see the asshat that we have for president now, along with his cabinet of total thieves and losers.

I received a reminder in the mail from my doctor's office that I was due to have my annual physical. I showed it to Heather and she said, "You are past due, call tomorrow for an appointment."

I have an appointment to see a doctor tomorrow and it's gonna be a party. I'm not looking forward to it but I know I have to face it. I went to my reckoning day (Monday Aug. 1st) and I had several notes that I wanted to discuss with the doctor. Heather helped me with the notes because she has noticed some symptoms that I haven't. I know she had some fear but I also don't think she fully understood what was going on with me. I did a pretty good job of hiding it. Again, I had to make these last few months to be about her and her family and not about me.

As soon as I was registered they took me in. The PA did her thing quickly and the doctor came in. My original doctor left the clinic due to their covid policy and the way they threw away loyal staff who served the clinics and hospital for several years who refused the jab. This doctor seemed like a nice guy. He was the replacement physician from my last doctor who left because he refused the jab and the hospital all but fired him. He now has a private practice somewhere in southern Wisconsin. I liked him, I wish him and his family all the best.

I sat with the doctor and read from my list. Twice he asked me if there was anything else that I would like to add after I thought I was done. He acted like I was the only patient in the entire building. He was very calm and his voice was reassuring. When I was done he smiled and said, "Part of what you're talking about I can see as I sit here with you. I'd like to run a few simple tests as we sit here and then we will move on to the lab stuff. Before you leave here today, I will schedule a series of medical test procedures that will take place at the hospital but nothing invasive. I want to check your cognitive capabilities at this time."

He said, "I will present five, one sentence statements to you. As I read each line, I want you to concentrate to remember them as I read them off. We will discuss those sentences a few minutes later, so please try to remember them." I didn't remember them nor do I now, but I failed his test. I was only able to remember one partial sentence of the five. He then laid a piece of paper flat on his desk with pictures of different denominations of coins. There were five lines of coins numbered I-5. He told me to add each line in my head and write the totals at the end of each line. He then told me to add in my head and write the totals from top to bottom and place each total on the bottom of each line. For the next test he handed me a standard size sheet of paper with a printed circle the size of a small shirt button printed in the center. He said, "Now look at this paper as a clock. I want you to write where the numbers go on the face of the clock." So I did that. I thought this was quite silly but I went along with it. He then said, "I want you to show me on this clock, with this pen, what eleven minutes after eleven o'clock looks like. I drew two lines for the big and little hands to the eleven. The doctor pointed out that the big hand should be on the twelve. That's when I knew that I was more fucked even then I thought I was. He smiled and said, "David I think you have a problem and I think you're right about how you described your problem, but I want more testing. When you had your blood pressure taken a few minutes ago, it was a little high so I'm going to take it again." He had me sit board straight with my feet flat on the floor. My blood pressure was normal. He leaned back in his chair as he said, "David, you are going to be a real challenge for me. You are a perfect patient with good manors and with a willingness to cooperate that I personally find refreshing. You don't play any games, you know what you're here for. The challenge I foresee is that you know too much about medicine. With your family history of early age deaths from Leukemia, I understand your concerns. Your chart shows that you were a fourteen year rescue paramedic and later you were a twelve year police officer. You have witnessed most all of life's many ill's, tramas and tragedies. Have you ever been debriefed?"

"Well doctor, If you can count consuming extreme amounts of booze and babes on a daily basis then I guess the answer is yes, I've been debriefed. Doctor, I'm an alcoholic, with thirty-one years of continuous sobriety. I am a seven time published novelist. I have a high school diploma and nothing more. My book sales suck because I can't afford an agent, but the few that do read my books, claim it has added value to their lives. I write about many of life's ill effects to reach other people like me. I write about myself, I write about my failures, my sorrows, my shattered dreams and how I found the courage to have hope and climb out of my hole."

I reached into my briefcase and pulled out a copy of, "Daddy Had To Say Goodbye" and asked him who he would like me to sign it to." The doctor grinned as he said, "Mr. Brown, I think that you are smarter than even you think you are. Yes, my friend, I believe I will enjoy this challenge."

I signed his book, we shook hands and I was off down the hall to the lab for my blood draw. The Phlebotomist acted a bit surprised as she said, "You're getting the E-ticket of all blood work. I may have to draw from two sites, I'll try to be quick so you won't bruise too badly." She had to struggle to get seven vials for the CBC work-up. She was fast and smooth. I went home for a nap.

You would think that most people would be freaking out upon realizing that their brain was no longer their friend, as a matter of fact, my brain was attacking me. Strange to some perhaps but I felt relatively calm. I had to wait for the blood work results before I could have a more clear picture along with the brain scan results. My nap was relaxing.

Heather came home from work and she wanted to play twenty questions about my doctor's visit. I didn't want to frighten her with my only getting a score of 10 in the cognitive tests which shows severe cognitive impairment. I knew that she wouldn't allow me to brush anything off, so I just told her that I am scheduled for a battery of tests in the next week, before we will know anything.

I received the blood test results online through my 'Patient Portal' the next day, shortly after midnight. I had a couple of flags in my blood work. The first flag was that my Chloride level was above normal which signifies that I have too much acid in my blood, which explains my constant fatigue. The next flag was a high Glucose level, which simply means my intake of red meat and carbohydrates is beyond normal. That ain't going to change, I eat meat. Lastly, I have a high LDL along with the rest of the world, who don't exercise. Well no shit. I don't have the interest or time for that crap. I sit for twelve hours or more each day writing. It's what I do, I write. My and my doctors true concern was whether or not my red and white cell counts were in the normal ranges to cancel out Leukemia. The cell counts came back normal. I'm clear with my blood work, on to the next.

My brain scan was scheduled for that Friday, August 5th. I went to have my brain scan and of course I got lost in the hospital. It's a huge layout and it's like seven poorly attached but different buildings with connector walkways. I had to ask for an escort to show me where I needed to go because I couldn't understand all of the directional signs with all of the arrows. Well, I've had brain scans in the past but this machine was something right out of Star Wars. The scanner was pretty wild, it made a lot of strange sounds but I stayed calm and went through the exam. At exactly 12:35 am the next day I received the report from the radiologist of his findings on my patient portal. The findings told me that I was fucked. I have a number of dead blood vessels on the right side of my brain and my brain is shrinking. Which of course validates my suspicions that either I have a blockage in my brain or I've had a number of Mini-strokes. My doctor is out of town until Tuesday so I won't be able to get up with him until then. I, of course, tried to soft-pedal the scan results. Heather wasn't buying it, any of it. She wanted answers, the best answer I could come up with was, "Baby, I'm seventeen years your senior, I'm seventy-four years old, all of this stuff points to what we already know. I am aging, the only question in all of this is at what rate and of course, what's next in the natural progression? We still have more tests to go. We should have a better idea in the next week or two."

So now here it is, Thursday night, Heather's mother passed away earlier in the day. Heather didn't get a chance to say goodbye to her mom, (her mom had been non-communicative for the last week and lasted longer than her doctors thought she would). Heather was at work, she had planned to leave there at 1:00 o'clock to visit her mother but of course in her job, there's always emergencies that she had to tend to, she didn't get to the nursing home until 3:00 pm. Her mother passed at 2:45 pm. I'm sure that Heather will suffer some fallout for most of her life from that decision, but as most of us know, we all have to live with our shit and regrets, sadly regrets are something we can never change .... ever!

My next exam was a chest-lung screening the next day, Tuesday August 16th. Heather wanted to come with me but she needed to care for her mothers funeral arrangements. The chest-lung scan took less time than it did for me to enter the building and register! I got that report early the next morning. My chest/lung scan was clear.

My next and final exam in this round of tests was scheduled for Thursday, August 30th .

I was a bit pissed that I had to wait for two weeks. If I had a blockage or bleed there is a pretty good chance that I could have a stroke or just bleed out. This test was an Ultrasound to check for suspected arterial bleeding and arterial blockage.

The day before this final exam, I checked my online patient portal for any restrictions of liquids or food intake. What I found was that my appointment was changed to Friday, September 23rd!

No email, no phone call, the schedule clerk just decided to change my exam appointment. My ass was on fire, I called my doctor's office, he wasn't available at the time. I told his receptionist of the situation and asked that the doctor call me back because I needed some muscle to straighten this out. I waited until noon and thought, "Fuck this, Mr. nice guy just left the building." I called the hospital and asked the operator to put me through to the hospital's administrators office. I was connected to some kind of Patient Advocacy Office. I explained the situation and got the feeling that this lady was probably filing her nails as she listened. I knew that If I couldn't snap her awake, that nothing would happen. I started with, "Ma'am, I need you to understand that I am not looking for a tanning booth session, I am fighting for my life. Please help me understand how a schedule clerk can override a physician's written orders. Beyond that, how can that same person change my appointment with no communication with me. I guess she views your patients as toys to move around like Chess pieces. Yes, I get it, we're talking about the number one function of the Ultrasound department is to take cutesy pictures of developing fetuses for show-n-tell with family and friends. Let's face it, young people get an enhanced treatment service because those customers have young families and are guaranteed return customers with top level employer health insurance whereas, I'm on my way out and I only have medicare. My next phone calls will be to the State of Minnesota and Federal Government offices where I will file a claim of Elder Abuse and Age Discrimination. I don't know or care what you have to do, but you best damn well do it now! You have one hour to call me back before I go public. I do know how to get loud, damn loud!"

I got a call back from the lady that I was speaking to earlier. She said, "Sir, I would like to bring the schedule clerk online with us and see if we can move your appointment up. The clerk came on line and asked what she could do for me. I responded with, "What you can do for your employer is keep them out of court and cost them huge attorney's fees and countless days of answering to several government agencies. What you can do for me, is explain why you undervalue senior citizens and our rights to timely health care."

Her response was, "I am sorry but I have no openings at this time. If we get a cancellation, I will call you for that appointment." I chuckled and responded with, "The only time you get a cancellation is when a patient dies waiting for their appointment!

Ladies, this is not over. The storm clouds are building and it's going to be one hell of a storm. If you will excuse me, I have some phone calls to make to the storm center, Good day"

I received a phone call from my doctor (obviously the wheels were turning) who talked as though he had been briefed on the situation and was told to call me to settle me down. Of course he was trying to play it off as his concern for my message that I had left with his assistant. He asked me what the problem was with my ultrasound schedule. I almost started to laugh. I gave him the overview with the ending, "Your hospital executives better get their lawyers lined up and call their wives, mistresses and bankers and tell them that there would not be a quarterly bonus this time around." Of course in my brief statement to him, I made it clear that I planned to sue for denial of medical care for the elderly based on their discriminatory practice in this matter. I almost heard him gulp as he was back peddling with, "Mr. Brown, we do our utmost best to ensure that all of our patient's rights are protected. Once I order a test for my patients it is out of my hands and becomes hospital procedures and policies. Let me make some phone calls and I will call you back shortly.

It was no more than forty minutes when the schedule clerk called and said she just spoke to my doctor and she was able to open a slot on the following Monday.

I will call that a win and I most certainly will change hospitals and doctors. But then again, I would have to think about that for while. I'm thinking that by now, my file has a red star or skull and crossbones on it. The smart money would tell most people that, 'This is nobody to screw with, we better treat him right'. Yup, I'll have to think it over.

I went for the ultrasound exam and the technician was almost too caring and jovial. Her concern for my comfort during the exam was a bit over the top. There is no question about her being briefed as to who and what a pain in the ass I was.

The test results came back negative. It did not show any signs of arterial blockage or a dissecting aorta. That evening I received my doctor's final report which pretty much said, "You have dementia, there is no treatment for it, it's all part of aging, deal with it." He closed the report with, "No further testing needed until the patient's next annual physical."

CHAPTER 9
Getting Dirty

I wasn't about to tell Heather, (who was absolutely exhausted due to her mothers death followed by her step dad's death four days later) that I was in some rather serious medical trouble. The next day was Saturday, we had a number of errands to run, her brother was working on their mother's obituary. They had to empty out the condo of which her mother and step dad lived, so she had that on her plate as well. So I knew that I just had to keep my mouth shut until all the dust had finally settled. There were a couple of small pieces of furniture that Heather wanted to have from her mother's memory so we were waiting for the sister's husband to break free from what he was doing to let us into the apartment to retrieve these two pieces of furniture. It sounded like it would be a couple of hours yet. Well I knew I had to take the time now. I didn't feel like it but I knew I had to just look at her and say, "Baby, I need you to set aside all the stuff that is swirling around us and for the next few minutes, let's sit together on the couch, I have something to tell you."

I had the printout of the doctor's report and his initial and final findings with the explanation of what the report means. We sat together, and I handed her the report. She asked a few questions but she knew what it all meant. I said baby, "I'm sorry but I've just now become a liability to you. I'm sure that's all you need, stacked on top of what's currently going on." I told her that if she needs time to process all this shit, that I would go stay somewhere else for a few days and if it gets to be too much for her with my condition, I'll just move away and allow her to live her life.

Many people do medical searches the minute they have a symptom out of their norm. WebMD and Mayo Clinic seem to be the most popular sites. I'm sure that doctors must lose their minds when their patients self-diagnose off the web. In my case, I did the same. My greatest fear initially, was of course Leukemia. I am the oldest living male on my dad's side of the family for the last three generations. Leukemia was the main cause of death in his family. Twenty-six people succumbed from Leukemia, all before the age of forty. Yes, I have reasons to be concerned. Once my blood work came back negative, I knew what my problem was. My brain is eating itself.

I don't and never did have a great fear of dying, just in the way I was going to go. For me, I would much rather die quickly in an accident and I don't much care how gruesome it is.

As a Paramedic, I witnessed great suffering from both the patients and their family's at the time of death. The worst way to die, at least in my experience, is waiting to die. With as much violent death involving people of all ages that I've witnessed, my worst flashbacks come from the soulful heartache of resignation in a patient's eyes when we had to transport them to a nursing home. Their eyes said it all. Many times, I could see their spirit leaving them through their eyes. Their homes, their pets, their furnishings, the things that defined them, the things that they sacrificed and worked hard for all of their lives, were now, all gone. The only thing of value in their life now, are their memories and their dignity.

Sadly they will lose all of those things in the very near future and they know it. There was a time when they looked forward to holidays and family gatherings. Soon they won't remember when the holidays are. Oftentimes they won't remember who their family members are. Worse yet, those family members won't come by to visit them anymore.

Suddenly, those poor souls will no longer receive the neurotransmitters that they have taken for granted all of their lives, to tell them that they have to relieve themselves. Now they are diapered and can't even wipe their own ass. They are now completely dependent on being bathed and fed by a total stranger. I have witnessed the surrender of once vibrant, and meaningful people with being completely mortified. They can only sit, day after day and watch their wick burning lower and lower as they pray that their candle will soon burn out.

Heather took my hand as she said, "Lets go lay down, I want to hold you." We laid on our backs, held hands and let our tears flow. We talked of our fears, both present and future. It was the deepest level conversation of gut stuff that we have ever had. Heather assured me that she would always be next to me in every step I took. We did have a bit of a struggle when I took the conversation to my end of life wishes. I made it clear that, "I will not die at home because I don't want you to have those memories. I will die in a Hospice, I can't live with the thought of you avoiding an area in our home because that is where I died. I always want you to feel comfortable and safe in our home and for you to never dread going to bed at night. But that ain't now. I won't surrender to death, it will have to come to get me and I will fight it till I can fight no more. In the meantime, we need to concentrate on living and I

CHAPTER 10
I Thought I Knew You

Well that sure didn't take long. I was shocked but sadly, not surprised. There are times, many times that I wished I didn't know what I know about human nature. I have watched families self-destruct during times of sickness and death within the family. Whether it be about division of money, real property or personal property. There are times where families get into disputes over the planning of a funeral service that will not just divide loyalties but also cause siblings and extended family members to never speak to each other again.

It was no different with Heather's family. She has a brother and a sister who are both retired. Her brother Sam and the two of us were the best of buddies. He lives a few states away and we only see him every few years. Sam and I talk a few times a week, every week, sometimes he calls me his big brother, other times he calls me dad. Sam's relationship with his dad is nonexistent. They are both stubborn to a fault but neither are ever at fault. They don't try that crap with me, they know it won't fly. Those two have been at it for years, neither is willing to give in and repeatedly make reference to the other as 'Narcissistic'. The dad asks me to appeal to his son to be kind to him because of his age. I've listened to that BS for too damn many years! The son gets pissed and blocks his dad on their phone systems and the internet. They at some point will temporarily agree to a truce but each time it is short lived. As soon as they part company they both try to convince me that they were wronged by the other and are looking for me to take their side of whatever the argument was about. My answer to each of them is the same each time, "I don't have a dog in this fight, It's not my deal, either work it out or don't."

But these last three weeks have become personal and now I do have a dog in this fight! It started with Sam. Sam elected to write their mother's obituary a week before their mother died. Sam is more than just a bit anal in just about everything he does. This self-elected project was no different. He claimed that he has written and rewritten his 'masterpiece' several times. He sent me an email copy of his work. I found three typos and he totally missed the name and spelling of his mother's employer that she had worked for, for more than twenty years. He got pissed and defensive and challenged me. I laughed it off as I said, "You pride yourself as the great research analyst, check it out."

He also sent a copy to Heather and she caught the errors as well. When she told Sam the same thing I did, he snapped back at her with, "I haven't slept for several days on this project that you girls consigned me for!" He sent an amended copy a few hours later. For the next three days he called me a couple times each day with nothing but him bitching about the other sister as she has the power of attorney. He called the house for Heather every evening with his rants of dissatisfaction in the way things were being planned. He used vicious and vulgar language and went on for an hour or more with threats to sue everyone involved. I stayed out of it for the first two days even though I could see the hurt in Heather's eyes but on the third day I had enough. Now understand that he had not bothered to visit his mother for six years as he would always say to me, "My entire Minnesota family is so damn toxic that I don't ever want to be around any of them, I don't want my two adult children around any of them and I forbid my kids to ever bring my grandchildren around any of them, excluding you and Heather of course."

Me: Sam, If you want to direct the show then haul your ass up here. Further and more importantly let me remind you that your sister, who you have been ranting to, also is losing her mother. This is no way to behave because you don't know how to process loss and can't deal with your not coming to visit your mother all of the times that Heather called you over the last year to report that your mother was failing. Yes I understand that you're pissed off because the girls didn't submit your version of your mothers obituary. Sam, everyone knows of your huge interest in genealogy and how you pride yourself as being the puzzle maker and solver. It may be important to you but listing your grand children's full names and ages is unnecessary. Your grandchildren are your mothers great grandchildren (who she never met) is a bit over the top. In your case, none of your mothers passing is about her, you have made it all about you and your family lineage. You had already stated last month that you are not attending the funerals because you have plans with friends for the next two months, so who is bullshiting who?

Sam sent a last and final (according to him) email to Heather that was nothing more than cruel and poisonous hate. That is how he justified his not attending his mothers funeral. He is out of our lives, I wish it weren't that way but I will not tolerate or forgive him for the way he treated Heather.

If all of that silliness wasn't enough to set Heather back on her ass and tear her heart apart, along came her asshole dad and his wife.

CHAPTER 11
The Clown's Of Family

It has been said by most all people at some point in our lives, "You can't choose your family...... That is certainly a true statement but I have learned through my own negative family experiences that I don't have to approve of or accept any of their bullshit. I have learned to dismiss them from my mind and heart. Would you feed a dog that bites you every time you feed them? Heather's dad is that biting dog. He finds some kind of sick joy in causing discomfort in his children. It's how he can feel superior and empowered to belittle his adult children. I think he is greatly bothered that both Heather and Sam out earn him, it's part of his weak ego. He has always been an absent and selfish father. He, very much like his son (Sam) is a dedicated narcissist. He downplays everyone's accomplishments because he has no accomplishments. He is more than just a fibber, he is an outright lier. The only reason that I ever had anything to do with him was for Heather's comfort. I had lunch or breakfast with him every week, for the last seven years. His mind has been slipping for some time now, but he continues to show his rude and condescending arrogance.

I haven't taken a meal with him for about the last four months, ever since he made a snide dig at me with, "You needed that girl to help you write your last book."

He was referring to Christine Bomey who was my co-author in the novel, "#BELIKEED." The silly bastard obviously doesn't understand anything about literature. That day in the restaurant, I fantasized about reaching across the table, grabbing him by the back of his head and holding his face in his soup bowl until he was dead. I gave him my best smile as I told him that I needed to visit the men's room before our meals arrived. I walked to the cashier, paid for my meal and walked out the door.

The joint funeral services for both Heather's mother and step dad were still four days away. Heather (bless her heart) returned to her mother's and step dad's apartment to help clear it out so as to avoid paying another month's lease. Heather gathered up several boxes of mementos for her brother Sam's two adult children. Her mother and stepdad were very active with their grandchildren even though they lived several states away. They visited the grandchildren every year when the children were young and gifted them for their birthdays and all the holidays. They spoke to them on the phone on a regular weekly basis. Heather being the considerate and kind-hearted auntie contacted Sam to tell him that she had gathered some things that belonged to both Grandma and Grandpa that she is going to forward to them. Sam lost his piss-ant mind, he all but screamed in his emails, "Do not send anything to my children, we want nothing of anything of you people from the north. We are done with all of you!" Of course none of the adult children attended their grandparent's funeral. That's how much control this guy has over his family, which I find disheartening at best. The day of the funeral I almost wanted to drive my fist into the back of Heather's dad's skull. That jerk and his wife attended his ex-wife's and her husband's funeral, with him wearing a faded and thread bare knit short sleeve shirt and shorts. His wife was wearing some kind of denim pump pants or whatever the hell they're called and a badly worn sweatshirt as they explained, "We're going to the cabin as soon as the service is over."

They clearly never came to the funeral to support Heather, they never came there to celebrate a life or to mourn the loss of a life. No, they simply went there to be seen, oh and they also carted along their daughter, her husband and their new baby. So this whole deal was nothing more than a, 'Show & Tell' with a, "Look at us, we are here and you should probably celebrate us!" I just wanted to puke.

Heather's dad, at no point tried to console his daughter for the loss of her mother, it was all about him, his wife, his daughter, daughter's husband and of course the newborn child.

Three days after that service, a dear friend of mine passed away. Jerry was a quality guy, I very much enjoyed him and his friendship. I knew him for fifteen years. He was in his early 80's when he passed and had been in a nursing home for ten months, Jerry suffered quite a bit of discomfort. It's one of those times when you pray for their passing, for their sake. Jerry was a lot of things to a lot of people but one of the things he was best known for is that he was an alcoholic in long-term recovery. Jerry's favorite word in his extensive vocabulary was the simple word, 'Willingness'. He used that word in every AA meeting as well as everyday conversations. He would always say, "You don't need a car, insurance, or even bus fare to get to an AA meeting, I will get you there one way or another. There are no dues or fees to attend an AA meeting. Just bring your willingness and the rest of the good things in life will follow, in time." Jerry had been sober for more than forty years and carried a lot of young people along the path of sobriety. He was like the car dealerships that advertised, "We take all trade-ins, push, pull or drag in your trade."

Jerry was also very much involved in his church and with his family. Jerry was a man to admire if not to emulate!

Jerry's vision had been failing him for the last several years to the point where eye glasses no longer worked for him. He had not been able to drive for the last two years before he went off to the nursing home. One of the things that Jerry did for me and for countless of many thousands of others, came over us having coffee after an AA meeting more than ten years ago. We were sitting in a late-night Diner. At the time, my first novel had been in print for only two months. Of course I was proud of my work and I wanted to gift Jerry a copy to show my respect and to show him how much I valued our friendship. I brought the book to the meeting in a bubble mailer. I opened the bubble mailer in the booth of the diner. I signed and personalized it in front of Jerry and handed it to him. Jerry's facial expression at that moment is something I still visit with in my mind on a regular basis. His smile of approval was also memorable as he said, "I have heard that you were a writer but I had no idea that you actually wrote and published an actual book! Holy Christ man, what an incredible accomplishment for just another, old falling down drunk. I'm proud of you, old-bold son! But I have a confession to make. I've all but lost my ability to read, as a matter of fact, when I read, "How it Works" during a meeting it's all from memory. I can't even read the fourteen point print. It won't be long until I can no longer see well enough to drive a car. You know buddy, if that's the worst that's going to happen in my life next to dying, I'm okay with that. I have lived the life of many Kings through the grace of God and the principles of Alcoholics Anonymous. I want for nothing, I long for nothing, my life is complete. Now let me tell you about something. Have you ever heard of the NLS which is a National Library Service for the blind and print disabled, that is sponsored by the United States Library of Congress? Well my friend, it's a pretty cool thing. It's part of the BARD program which stands for, "Braille And Audio Reading Download." All anyone needs to do is be registered with The State Department of Disabilities or The Minnesota Braille and Talking Book Library. The talking book library collection is available to all disabled people. All they have to do is access the Minnesota Department of Health to find The Braille And Talking Book Library, you only need to register and it costs nothing. The state sends you a free Talking Book Player. You can either choose a book from their library to listen to or you can submit a book to have it read by volunteers, all free of charge, even the postage is free! You can order up to three books at any one time and when you're done listening to them, you just need to return them in a post-paid envelope. It's really a wonderful program and it's my only outlet to the world at this point in my life. With your permission, I would like to submit this book to have it recorded and read and I'll give it back to you when it's complete."

All I could do was smile and say, "Jerry you SOB, so you've been faking all of the AA literature readings during the meetings. You actually have them all memorized, word for word! I listen when you read and it's always word for word. How in the holy hell did you learn to do that?" Jerry said, "I have a god of my understanding. He is my guiding light, he is my eyes and my ears, he is also my heart."

From that moment I made it a point to gift my friend Jerry a copy of each of my books as they were released. What's interesting is that an author cannot send their book to have it voice recorded, it has to be sponsored by a registered member of the Minnesota State Dept of The Visually and Physically Impaired. I guess that's to keep the riff-raff authors out from trying to get their books in front of people. Yeah, sadly there are people like that.

One night after a meeting Jerry pulled me aside and said, "Come over here, I have something for you." He had a plastic shopping bag that he opened for me to look into. It was almost as though we were doing a drug deal with the way he was looking around to see who might be watching. He said, "I'm not supposed to do this but, here is your book on this cassette. I will loan you my player but you can't let anything happen to it and you can't tell anyone that I have loaned this to you, I'll need it back in the next few days. I want you to hear your book on tape, I hope you like it."

It seemed that I drove home a little faster than normal. That book was three hundred and thirty-six pages long. The face of the cassette showed, 'twelve hours of listening.' I sat up throughout the night and well into the mid morning, listening to my twelve hour book on tape. I was startled, surprised and humbled and any other words you can come up with to identify my gratitude to both Jerry and the good people who volunteered to read the book and of course my God, the God of my understanding.

When I finished listening I just sat in absolute disbelief of how the gift of writing was brought to me. I felt the true joy of the gift of sobriety deep within me. I sat with a wide smile and tears running down my cheeks.

As I now write this, I get the giggles thinking about Jerry slipping me his player and a cassette like we're in the middle of a huge drug deal as he says

"Keep this between ourselves, no one else can know, I'm not supposed to be doing this!"

What is not to love about Jerry? Jerry was one of those guys that had to make sure that everyone else was okay. He sponsored a great number of young people and not just young people but people of any age who needed help. It seemed like he was ageless in his efforts and he was never spending too much time helping someone else.

Well, here is where things got stupid. Jerry worked with Heather's dad several years ago. Jerry knew that I was living with Heather, he met her and knew who her dad was. On one occasion, a few years back, Jerry asked me how I got along with Heather's dad. My only comment was, "I tolerate him for Heather's sake." I received an email from an AA friend of Jerry's passing before the first death notice came out. I forward it to Heather's dad. Although I was done with the prick, I still felt an obligation to let him know that his long-term work associate had died. Well Heather's father of course (being the asshole he is) sent me a lengthy email telling me all about his relationship with Jerry to let me know that they were the best of friends with a bunch of drivel, alluding to the fact that him and Jerry, were much better friends then Jerry and I were. Once again, he had to show me of his great value to all of mankind. I didn't pay any attention to his silly bullshit.

The morning of Jerry's funeral service, I arrived forty minutes early. I stood in the foyer of the church, against the far wall across from the podium to sign the memory guest books. I stood there for more than a full hour during the visitation, greeting friends of mine and Jerry's of which there were many. Jerry had a large family, the church was as full as any church could be I guess. When the actual service started I left. I'm just not a church guy but I wanted to be there with Jerry's family and friends. Well I got an email from Heather's dad saying, "I was there and I didn't see you." I told him that I was there and where I was standing and thought I'd have a bit of fun with him. "Geeze Sport, I didn't realize that you were taking attendance." I knew that I was lighting the fuse for a gala display of fireworks. He came back with something like, "Why didn't you offer to pick me up and bring me to the church, my wife had to work that day and I had to employ my other daughter to give me a ride to the funeral service of my dear friend, when you could have given me a ride but you never offered!"

I didn't even respond, it's just more of his bullshit, more of his manipulation, more of his being a victim and being mistreated by his family. I finally had a gut full and I answered him back as I took him right between the eyes with his truths of his arrogance, self-pity and what a narcissistic prick he actually was.

He writes back, "I don't know why my son and you have to be so mean to me. I'm 88 years old and I don't deserve to be mistreated the way you two treat me. I'm done with you both, do not contact me ever again. I just smiled and responded with, "My pleasure!" I'm pretty sure he broadcasted to the rest of the family that I once again was being mean to him and I misunderstood his good and kind intentions. I am so totally done with that piece of human waste.

CHAPTER 12
The Haunting

I believe it was mid-summer of this year (2022) and once again Heather is locked into watching Hannity every night. That particular night, Hannity had Nancy Grace on his show as a guest. I can only take very small bites of Nancy Grace, as she is so pathetically overly dramatic. It's almost to the point where she wants to be the story rather than report the story. This particular evening she was talking about the JonBenet Ramsey murder case in Boulder, Colorado that took place on December 25th (Christmas Day) 1996. My belly dropped into my toes.

I have a rather intimate story of the JonBenet Ramsey murder case, which I've never told to anyone, not one soul, it has been and still is deep in my heart for the last twenty-six years. Something told me that it was time to tell of what I knew.

Well at the end of the interview, both Hannity and Nancy Grace gave their contact information and asked viewers to please contact them if the viewers had any information on the case. I attempted to contact their show producers the following day. I couldn't get through to anybody on any platform with all the websites they gave out. I once again knew that I had to accept the ugly reality that it's not about the story or the people, it's only about them telling the story. Nancy Grace and Hannity spend a great deal of time selling themselves because viewership ratings are what creates more fame and money for them. So they have huge staffs to sniff out or dig up stories, to find the glamor or heartache of whatever kind of story that is going to get the most people to listen to them. I'm damn certain that they would be climbing the side of my house with briefcases full of cash to get my story ahead of their competion and increase their ratings. It has been three months now and no one has bothered to contact me. I could however not just let this go, it is now my mission to come forward to whoever will listen but at the same time, not jeopardize the case.

    This case was so poorly handled that the investigators should have all been criminally charged and fired. The murder took place, or at least the recovery of the child's body took place on December 26th 1996. JonBenet Ramsey was only six years old. Her parents propped her up as a beauty queen and had her professionally trained almost like you would have a bear performing in a circus. The child competed in several beauty pageants all around the country. As far as I'm concerned, it was all about the mother living vicariously through her daughter, as the mother was once a beauty queen of some sort. The family was extremely wealthy and it showed with the child's costumes, media coverage and extensive travel.

So, the story goes that the child was missing from the home, both parents were at home at the time along with a number of family and friends celebrating Christmas. The family found or supposedly found a ransom note and notified the police. I don't care to go into any more of those details, it smells really bad right from the beginning.

So here is a snapshot. It is Christmas Day in Boulder, Colorado. As with most any national holiday and especially within the public service community, seniority rules.

Most every Police Department moves the third level officers and rookies up to the top level, so all of the veterans can have some time off with their families or whatever the hell they do.

Tragically the Boulder Police Department had the "C" team on duty over the Christmas holiday. As is most often times the case, the "C" team gets all giddy with the thought of, "This is my time to shine. I'm not going to ask anyone for any help, no matter what's going on. I'm gonna strut my stuff and show them that I am more than capable and it's time they bring me up to the next level!"

I have watched that kind of silliness unfold for several years during my career in law enforcement. I've always enjoyed watching the 'Temporary fill-ins' wag their tails and look for a pat on their head as if to ask, "Did I do a good job, well did I, did I?" It was like watching an episode of, "The Andy Griffith Show" when Andy has to leave town or takes Opie fishin and leaves Barney in charge. Much like the character Barney Fife, when the returning 'A' team leader doesn't give the proper accolades with plaques and ribbons and uniform stripes, the 'C' team player pouts and bitches to their fellow officers. I have seen cops quit their jobs because in their mind, they were being ignored by ranking officers.

The JonBenet Ramsey case was jam-packed with weak egos and lack of knowledge and experience in professional police work. That level of incompetence is what has kept this case alive after twenty-six years, without an arrest. That and of course the many lies and cover-ups by police, prosecutors and medical experts.

I personally don't care to go any further into any details of the case. You can google your life away in this case. The facts, strangely enough, will not speak for themselves. Evidence was so poorly gathered and protected that there will only be a conviction in this murder of this lovely child with a confession.

This case is more about principal players protecting their jobs, their retirements and their bullshit images.

If I sound cynical and pissed off, it is because I am. The State of Colorado, Boulder County, the City of Boulder have all intentionally failed the people, the law, the victim and her family. The coverups have led to deep corruption and criminal activities amongst the "Trusted Servants" of the people. Currently the denial and 'Blame Game' is operating at its maximum output.

CHAPTER 13
The Dirt

Well I knew I had to write something about this. I didn't know where I was going to go with it, but I wasn't going to waste my time or my readers time with reviewing the entire JonBenet Ramsey case. I did a post on Facebook asking if anyone had a connection with the Ramsey case because I had pertinent information that I felt needed to be known. I received an answer from a gal that I'll call Connie. Connie sent me a very nice email. She's a Facebook friend of mine who I've never met, we rarely if ever had any contact but nonetheless she is still a Facebook friend. So I got an email from Connie, it read, "I saw your post yesterday for your deceased infant daughter's birthday. I can't begin to imagine the pain over the years and all the wondering about her and who she would have grown to become. Your whole life became something different the moment you lost her. I'm so sad for you and for your lifetime loss of your baby girl. Thankfully you came to a place not of acceptance but of self-preservation. You have managed to right your world onto a path where you are good to yourself and encourage others to walk through their own personal fires and come out of the other side. Sending you strength from the line for whatever comes ahead."

Well, that note set me back a bit and I spent a few days processing the kindness and understanding this was tended to me by my new friend Connie.

A few days later I did a Facebook post asking for information in finding the principles in the JonBenet Ramsey case. It just so happens that Connie is in fact a principal and she has researched this case for years. She is currently a retired police officer and of course knows the insides of most everything to do with police investigations. Her final assignment with a major metropolitan police department was investigations. So yeah, she has some extreme knowledge and further she has knowledge on the JonBenet Ramsey case. Connie directed me to a very active website that I didn't know existed. It's called, "JonBenet Ramsey SLEUTHS." There's a large active number of everyday people (non-police) involved in that group from all around the world. For the most part, these are people who would like to see this case solved and the perpetrator brought to justice. I made a post on that site that read, " I have first-hand knowledge of why the Boulder County prosecutor's office, the Boulder County medical examiner's office and Boulder Police Department are all withholding evidence."

And so it began with a flurry of members that wanted more, theymore like demanded that I tell them of what I know.

I was simply asking for direction as to whom to speak to. Well the floodgates definitely opened. I received several comments on that website, very few were warm or welcoming. It was like I just stepped into their private sandbox or peed in their wading pool. A lot of people were trying to work me over for my information to add to their, what I don't even know. Maybe they were all frustrated authors who hoped to write a best-seller book off the back of a dead child. Hell, I don't know, maybe they wanted to be cops or just famous. I was very cautious and spoke nothing of my knowledge of the case. I wanted to see the case solved, I don't need to be famous nor do I have that desire.

I was contacted by another Snoops member who is well-entrenched in the case. She directed me to the (I guess you would call the official amateur investigator and supposed authority on the case.) This woman advertised herself as the official representative to the actual main players of the case and to the Ramsey family.

I sent her an email asking her if she would be interested in hearing of my information or if not, who I could forward my information to. It didn't take her but a few moments to establish who she was and what she was all about. She wrote, "I'm in direct contact with the Ramseys as well as Lou Smit's daughter and her team. You can check me out in the Ramsey book and online, my email has been the same for 26 years." She went on to say, "I do not forward everything sent to me as let's face it, there are insane people out in our world, who might want to hurt the case or certain people, but I do work with media on documentres and I have worked with Sydney Mara to get DNA for testing. If you have information that exposes the killer, make your case to me, do it in email so you will have a record of our conversation. I would never want to take credit for solving this case if someone else does. If you can convince me this needs to be heard by John Ramsey and the others, I promise to forward it to them." She included her email address.

My thought was simply, "Are you fuckin kidding me? You are going to examine my information and make the sole decision on whether or not my information is credible or of value, who the fuck do you think you are?"

I get the part where yeah, there's always a nut job or two in any situation who has a need to clamor for attention. The part that she mentioned she does media work on documentaries and made mention that she is already in a book, was all the red flags I needed to see. Is she trying to steal my information and use it for her own financial gains or maybe just to look good, who knows? Then she goes on to say that I have to make my case to her, are you shitting me? She goes on with, "If you can convince me that this needs to be heard by John Ramsey and others I promise to forward it to them." It sounds like she is a frustrated wanna-be game show host. My thought was, "You know what young lady? I wish you all the best in life but you really need to just step around the corner and go fuck yourself!

Another one of the principal amateur investigators sent me an email saying that she would like to discuss what I know and she would be happy to talk with me. I gave her a date and time for a phone conversation. For some reason she writes back the following day, "Okay, I will pass along your phone number to our investigator, if that's okay with you. I'll let him know your time preference." No call came.

Two days later I wrote back to her that all of my information in 'Report Form' has been forwarded to detective Ron Gossage but thanks for your lack of Interest!" She came back with, "Okay, not sure why you feel you need to attack me like that but we were very interested and would still love to speak with you."

I haven't bothered to speak with her. I refuse to be treated that way, there's a lot of ego's in play with a lot of players, I don't need that silliness in my life.

This is where things finally started to take off. Connie introduced me to a friend of hers who is also a Facebook friend of mine, who again, I have never met or had a true conversation with. This friend I will call Sarah and Sarah is very much involved in the JonBenet Ramsey case. She too is a retired police investigator. What's ironic, is that both of these women came from the same metro police department and currently live in the same city, a city with the population of less than 20,000 people, now that's quite ironic

Sarah and I shared a few conversations in email form. I sent her what I wrote as a report and said she'd be happy to read it.

Following is the report I sent in reference to the JonBenet Ramsey case:

I was working part-time, (thirty plus hours a week) at Boulder Community Hospital, in Boulder Colorado at the time of the JonBenet Ramsey homicide. I worked in the security department. One of the many responsibilities of the job was to remove expired patients from the medical floors and transport them to the hospital morgue located in the basement of Boulder Community Hospital. It is also the official Boulder County Morgue. We also received bodies from the coroner's office for autopsy. Just down the hall from the morgue was the maintenance shop for the hospital. I took strong exception to the way that the morgue was operating and the poor care of dead human remains.

Infant children were stacked on the shelf like cordwood on an unfinished pine wood board. These precious, tiny babies were just wrapped in thin blankets with a patient sticker on them.

After autopsies the bodies were put back in the body cooler without body bags. Sometimes the bodies were covered with a sheet but most often times, the contents of the body cavity were just stacked on the chest and sometimes were covered with a thin Saran Wrap type material. Bodies were not isolated from one another. I would find arms and legs laying over on another body from the cart next to it. When I was assisting the body transport people to move the body onto their transport gurney, the deceased had black marks from the limbs of the body next to them. The body cooler had doors much like you see in a grocery store, meat department. They were just thin metal swinging double doors with windows in them. The morgue doors never closed properly and were always standing a bit askew and partially open. Inside the morgue body cooler, was a wall rack to place bodies of John or Jane Doe's for extended stays, until they were identified and the survivors were properly notified.

Part of the security assignment was to constantly check the temperature of the morgue body coolers. In the same area but not the cooler room were the autopsy drain tables. The body carts in the cooler and the autopsy tables were filthy and oftentimes had standing body fluids on them. The floor drains oftentimes had particles of human flesh or other body parts stuck in the grates of the drains. I was appalled by the condition of the morgue and the unceremonious way that the bodies were treated. I complained to my supervisor to no avail. I wrote letters to hospital administration, the board of directors as well as the County coroner's office with my disgust with the operation of the morgue. The only response I ever got was for my immediate supervisor who said, "You're just being overly sensitive because your baby died and you don't like the way it all works. There were two hardbound books in the morgue. One was for receiving a body and the other for releasing the body's. Of course bodies were released to mortuaries or transport Specialists to be delivered to area mortuaries. The sign-in books had a line for the patient's name, date of death and cause of death. On the day of JonBenet Ramsey's death, I was working the morning shift from 7am to 3:30 p.m. It should be noted that the morgue entry doors are secured and can only be opened by security personnel or hospital maintenance who had grandmaster passkeys. Of course the pathologists have their own set of keys. It wasn't uncommon for me to walk into the morgue to check temperatures and to find a Mortuary Transport person inside the morgue who wasn't let in by security. It was common that if a transport person was standing outside of the morgue waiting for security with their transport cart, and a maintenance worker was coming down the hall going to their shop, they would oftentimes let them into the morgue unescorted. Sometimes a body was missing and had not been signed out. At the beginning of each shift there was a briefing by the off-duty going officer. The first duty of the day was to always check the morgue temperatures and do a body count and compare the numbers to the sign-in and sign-out books. Of course I noticed JonBenet's body bag that was zipped and padlocked. Three hours later, I did another temperature check and when I opened the cooler door it was very obvious that there was a slice in the body bag of JonBenet. The cut was approximately ten inches long, approximately five inches from the body bag zipper center and near the head, the padlock was still in place. That slice was not there the first time I checked on her. There was one body that had been picked up but not signed out of the morgue. I was not present and I was the only security person on shift at that time. Somebody let somebody in there, I would have to guess it was one of the maintenance people helping a waiting transport person. The following day when I did my first rounds to check the morgue temperature, I checked the login and log out books. I noticed that the sign-in page for JonBenet was missing, it was there the day before and now it's missing. Where this brings me to, is that there was a body transport person who was arrested in the metro area for making paper and cardboard signs and hanging them around the necks of the deceased as if it was their last statement. The police found several pictures of dead bodies with signs around their necks, in his possession. I guess he'd been doing that in all of the morgues in the metro area for some time. He did a few pick-ups a week at Boulder Community Hospital. Did he slit Jonbenet's body bag open? Did he photograph her body in the body bag? I don't know. but I highly suspect that he stole the morgue sign in sheet as some kind of perverted trophy? I don't know, my point in all this is quite simple. Boulder Community Hospital lost the chain of evidence with Jonbenet's body. Is her body bag somewhere in evidence to be examined? I don't know that either, but if I were to speculate I would look much closer at the body removal person who obviously took a great deal of liberty's with human remains. I vaguely remember the articles in the Rocky Mountain news and the

Denver Post about his arrest but since that time I've lost track of the case. I don't remember his name. Shortly after Jonbenet's body was removed from the morgue, my supervisor and his supervisor, along with myself, were all-fired.

The reason the Hospital Human Resources gave me for my firing, is that I failed to list that I was a former police officer on my job application. Which equals "You know too much, you're a liability to us, and you're gone." Boulder Community Hospital stands to hopefully lose millions of dollars to victims whose loved ones were abused in the morgue.

Please note I have intentionally left off my home address as I have received numerous death threats over the years. I've had notes put on my windshield and house door saying, "We know where you live, keep your mouth shut" I also have received threatening phone calls, which were long before there was caller ID. Please respect my right to privacy and my family's safety. I hope this finds you all in good health and with peace in your hearts.

Most sincerely,

David J. Brown

Sarah read my report along with her friend Connie. They both decided that there's some credible information, so they forwarded it onto the true principles in the case. Sarah sent me an email that read; "I sent it to BPD detective Ron Gossage who is in charge of the case. Mr, John Ramsey, Cindy Mara and Lue Smit's daughter and Boulder County DA, Michael Dougherty."

    At this writing, it's been over three months since I sent that information. I've heard nothing back, nothing at all, not even a receipt or confirmation that they received it from any of those principles. I was told by a few Snoops members that none of the county and city people involved in the case respond to anything written and refuse phone calls since the very beginning of this case. Well, I'm only a party of one and strange as that may sound, I have a life to live too. I hope this case does get resolved. I have no idea who the true perpetrator is nor am I willing to guess. It's time I pick up my marbles and go somewhere else. I still have a book to complete.

CHAPTER 14
Gale Warning

The phone calls started three days ago and they have continued. I just thought I would let it simmer for a bit. I, of course, knew who it was and maybe what she was up to, but I was waiting for her to make the first move. I'm not going to rescue her, she has to come to me, it's the only way that I can reach her. Finally her call did come through, she sounded guarded as though she was afraid that she might be in trouble with me.

Norbs: Sir, you probably already know that I'm in town, right?

Me: Woman, if you call me sir again, I'm hanging up this phone. Well no shit, you're in town, I have people too, what's your game this time?

Norbs: David, I have been trying to find the pulse of your effects on other people. I've been in town for three days. I've been attending AA meetings, morning midday, afternoon, and evening and even late evening meetings, all throughout your city. You claim that you're not all that well known and yet everyone does know you. Many will say they've never met you but they've heard of you and what they've heard makes them like you! How do you have that effect on total strangers? They don't see you, they've not met you, they've never heard you speak and yet they adore you!

When I do question those people they say, "Oh I just heard that he was this or that that's more than acceptable to me."

Me: Well all that shits mighty cute, what the fuck are you doing here and when are you leaving. I need some rest, I need some goddamn rest!

Norbs: David, I just can't get it, I just can't get it and I have to be honest with you about it.

Me: So you've been lying to me and you left your family to fly more than halfway across the country to do what, confess your many sins? All of that's swell, so what is it you have to be honest about in living flesh, rather than with a simple phone call?

Norbs: David, I know that I'm an alcoholic but I just can't believe that AA will work for me, I can get this whole AA program thing. It makes sense but I don't trust it's going to work for me.

    Me: Of course you don't, because you think you have all the answers. How could it possibly work for you? So what is it that you are looking for, my permission to go back out and requalify? Do you need to convince yourself that you really are a drunk but you're not quite there yet? So what are you going to do, drink until you're hospitalized? Maybe find yourself in handcuffs in the back of a squad car, on your way to detox or maybe jail? What's it going to take baby, maybe your husband divorcing you and taking the kids? What's it going to take for you to believe that you're an alcoholic and secondly that there's hope for you, as there is for all of us? Don't even try to bullshit me with any answer because you don't have those answers either.

    Norbs: David, I have been such a liar! When you shanghaied me into that treatment center in Colorado all I was doing was mouthing all the right words. At no time did I feel any truth to whatever I was speaking. I'm a whole bunch of nuts but sometimes I'm convinced that I'm infallible. I'm not really me, I'm an actress in a book pretending to be me. My personal life is phony as hell. I had to take a, "Fourth-Step" in treatment before they would consider letting me leave. I lied about everything and I easily justified my lies because of my need to protect my public persona. I'm not comfortable with telling anyone anything about me personally because it will reflect back on my business. People don't want to see me as a human being, they want to see me as someone who's larger than life. People love people of fame because it gives them hope that they too may someday reach that level of success. At the same time, they resent the hell out of me because I have things, I've accomplished things that they can't ever possibly dream of. Yes, and before you ask, it was a clergyman that sat with me to hear my 4th step. I justified lying to him because of my suspicion of all people. What's to keep him from flapping his gums to some tabloid? We all strike out for a bit of fame, maybe that's going to be his way of being somebody?

    Me: Okay where the fuck are you right now?

    And that's when I heard the other voice and a bit of a stifled giggle. Well then I knew who she was with. I said to Norbs, "Shut up for a minute, baby, what's that east coaster broad doing in your office?

    Heather: Well I was going to tell you tonight, but I've only been working half days for the last three days. The rest of the day I've spent with Norbs. We have been racking our brains to figure out how you do what you do, because I don't know, I honestly don't know. I know who you are but I don't know how you got to be that, nobody knows how you got to that. I have never even thought to ask you how you get to be who you are. I have to tell you truthfully, sometimes I try to hide it as best I can, but there are times I look at you and I hear your voice and your words and I get starry-eyed like a fourteen-year-old at an Elvis Presley concert. Being with you gives me the shivers all down my spine and then I snap out of this trance that I fall into and realize that this is my man, sitting here with me, in our living room.

Me: So what you two are doing is you're ganging up on me? You think I'm like a motherfukin Mr. Potato Head and you get to rearrange me until I fit your ideals so I'm not such a puzzlement? You're trying to recreate me! Do you have a truckload of Legos being delivered this afternoon so you can build a safer and more comfortable image of me. Let's do this, how about if we just sit, the three of us? We can look at each other, we can listen to each other because that's what I do. That's who I am, I am who I appear to be. For you Norbs, I want you to lock this deep into your brain. Honey, you are who you are but you don't have to be who you've been. I'd like you to have that tattooed on the insides of both forearms because you're not getting it. Babe, you're still developing that public persona, stop that shit. You don't need to study anyone other than yourself. Ladies, I don't have the goods, all I have is a talent extended to me by the God of my understanding and that's it, there's nothing more. Why I have the voice I have, I don't know. I never went to school to develop it, I haven't taken voice or speaking or wherever the fuck kind of lessons you would have to have to have my level of voice. It's just the way I talk and that's it, there's no magic, I have no magic.

Norbs: Everything about you is so natural that people think you've spent years in training in everyday conversations. You are wrapped in a magnetic field that draws people to you. You can tell people to go to hell and they will happily start packing a bag.

I've been staying at the Corker Hotel. Heather said I can come and stay at your house but I have to get your permission first. I know that I'm making you nuts with all this, but I need to feel safe. I always feel safe with you.

Me: How could you think you're that powerful? You think that you can make me nuts? Honey you come pre-nutted but you don't make me nuts, you are nuts and you probably will stay that way until you find the level of humility necessary to break out of it. You're not broken, you're not shattered, you're just unwilling. Maybe we need to sit down and I'll tell you about my friend Jerry and his take on willingness. I will never lose sight of Jerry's teachings that you and I are an alcoholic and you and I deserve to live a better life. So if you plan on darkening my doorway this evening, leave the bullshit out on the front stoop. You're more than welcome to spend the night. Wait a minute, why do I have a feeling just in talking with you that it's going to be more than just a night? What's your plan? Don't tell me that a world renowned author, who is a multi-millionaire, can't afford a hotel room?

Norbs: David I'd like to spend a full week with you just you and I with mostly Big Book readings and discussions. I really do want to break free of my denial and develop the trust to be able to engage in a lifetime of sobriety. No, I haven't drank ever since I left the treatment center but I've been on a dry drunk. The most painful part of it all is when I look at the mountains of amends I need to make, David that scares the shit out of me. Yes I've made a few safe amends but not the real ones I need to.

I can't even dig deep enough in my own heart to admit my truths because of the shame I carry. Does everyone have this level of shame when they first sober up?

Me: Oh heavens no, just you because you're so fuckin unique! Shut up, hang up the phone and you two shake your asses up here. We're going to have a face to face sit down. I'll throw on a fresh pot of Folgers coffee and when you get here we'll order a

Sammy's Pizza and then we'll have a chat but I'm not going to let you control my time. Remember that I too, am an author and I have an audience who is anxious to read my next bit of work, Mrs. Big deal!

CHAPTER 15
Road Trip

I made two very important phone calls after I hung up from Norbs. One was to her husband, the other was to my friend Tom. They both agreed to my requests. I was looking forward to tomorrow morning.

The girls were overly giddy when they came into the house, I could smell their apprehension. Heather's eyes were pleading for forgiveness, for not telling me that she was meeting with Norbs for the last three days. Norbs' eyes spoke volumes of a combination of fear and guarded hope. I was proud of Heather for her tending to Norbs. She understood that I was still processing the loss of my friend Jerry. God, I love that woman!

Me: Have a seat you two sinners. I'll get you coffee, Norbs, where is that Patsy chick who is supposed to be such a bad-ass bodyguard that she thinks she can take me?

Norbs: She peeled off when we pulled into your garage. She knows that I'm safe with you. Her and Tim have been with us for the last three days. You do know that Patty would fight you to the death, if you tried to harm me, even though she knows that she would lose.

Me: Honey, that's why I love her. Dial her up and give me your phone. Patsy answered with a chopped, business type hello. I responded with, "Patsy girl, how fucking dare you come to my city without giving me some lovings the moment you arrived. Grab your bags and check out of that shack you're staying in, you're camping out with us. I could hear her smile as she said, "Don't tell me what to do, I don't fucking work for you, you jerk. I can't wait to see you!"

We all made an unspoken truce that afternoon. We kept our conversations lite and with humor. It was more like a family reunion with favorite cousins.

We all turned in early. I went out on the deck for my final smoke. I heard a very slight sound of a foot step on gravel from the alley, at first I was thinking it must be a deer. But nope, once my eyes adjusted to the dark, I saw two dark figures up on the patio of the airbnb like they were spanish pillars and I finally saw the figure that had made a misstep on the gravel, that was now sitting at the base of a tree. I glanced at the vehicle in the driveway. I was not at all surprised to see license plates that read, "In transit." The "Numbers" boys were on the job! I wanted to give them the finger and grab my nuts, but that would catch the attention of any potential evil doers.

I slept like a baby. Heather woke me to say goodbye as she was on her way to work. She said that everyone was up and showered as she left the bedroom.

It took me a minute or two for it to register that Heather said, "Everyone."

There's only two of them. Who is everyone?

I went into our bedroom master bath and created the greatest sin of all times! Although Heather and I are both smokers we have never smoked in our house but I knew that I just couldn't walk into those women without bracing myself. I opened the window and flipped on the ceiling fan as I lit a cigarette. I needed to gather my wits. So why are they really here? Did Heather call in the calvary for help? Am I showing greater signs of dementia that I'm not even aware of? Is this my Waterloo, of sorts? Has she spilled the beans or is she going to twist my arm and make me tell my friends the truth? I fuckin hate this old age bullshit. I don't give a fuck what anyone says, that's not me! I don't give a shit what definition you use, I'm not an old fuck, I'm not worthless and I'm not ready to be put out to pasture. Anyone who thinks that, can most certainly kiss my ass and they better be prepared for an ass whooping. I was getting an ass ring from sitting on the toilet for so long. I had smoked enough cigarettes while sitting there that I left the window open and the exhaust fan running as I closed the door. I guess I just have to haul my wrinkled ole ass out there and pour a cup of coffee and go outside. I found the two girls sitting at my computer on some kind of a live chat or conference call. I realized that it was Amanda they were talking with and maybe a second or even third person as well. I softly said good morning as I poured my cup of coffee and went out to the deck to escape and to enjoy my first legal cigarette of the day, rather than sneaking around in the back bathroom like a little bitch. Heather is probably going to know that I was smoking there and yep you know, that I'll hear about it.

My pal Patsy was the first one to come prancing out onto the deck. She had a shit eaten grin on her face when she said, "I want to see those 'trophies' you have! What the fuck? People actually give you cans of Dinty Moore Beef Stew and you keep them as trophies? There's got to be a story behind all that shit, tell me about that."

I got the giggles as I thought about it and all the people involved. I said, "Well babe, here's the deal, try to keep up. I've either sold or gifted my books to a number of people that would tell me they are some kind of super speed readers and how they can devour a three hundred page novel between after dinner and turning out their bed lamp. The more humble ones would say they plan on reading it in one day, over the weekend. I've always laughed as I say, "No, that ain't going to happen. I don't care what kind of speed reader you are, you're not going to push through that book in one sitting even if you start at sunup, unless of course you enjoy a very flat ass and reading deeply into the late night hours. No baby, this is not a breeze-through book, it'll give you reason to pause, you will have to close the book and look away, maybe look up and stare at the wall because you will suddenly find that you're reading about yourself. That nondescript character is who we all are, we just haven't come to terms or realized it yet."

I smiled with remembering a conversation that I had with a newspaper editor in Los Angeles. She told me that, "I was a bully, that I'm mean to big people because when they read my work they at some point, come to the understanding that they are reading about themselves and they cry!" I will call that I win!

Then we would have a little back and forth of "oh yeah, oh yeah, oh yeah" so I would tell them, "Here's the deal, I will bet you, one can of Dinty Moore Beef Stew, that you cannot finish that book in eight to ten hours."

What none of them could have possibly known is that I've listened to my book on tape through the Minnesota Department of Health Services for the Blind and Handicapped. There are no pauses in any part of that recording and it goes for a solid twelve hours. What, nobody goes potty in twelve hours? Nobody has to have a meal, tend to a child or dog, run an errand? That's nonsense, I love making that bet.

I'm most certain that I could never lose that bet. If by chance they did read it in under twelve hours, I would gift them a copy of my next book, free of charge. So Babe, go in the kitchen, open the bottom cupboard door next to the refrigerator and on the bottom shelf you will find fourteen neatly stacked cans of Dinty Moore Beef Stew and yes, those are my fuckin trophies! Honey, there's a lot of different ways to win in this world, that's just one of them. As a matter of fact my little love bunny, my first book is just bait for the trap, you see, I'm a Hunter and a Trapper. I collect and repair shattered dreams and lost souls.

Patsy: Brilliant marketing, you're so fucking insane that you're actually brilliant. What's next, you're going to cut off one of your goddamn ears, like that painter guy?

Me: Patsy, such language! You girls have breakfast? Did you feed the muscle up across the alley-way? Those boyz look like porch pillars in the dark of night. Norbs and I are going for a drive, and no, you are not invited. It's just going to be Norbs and me.

I picked up my cell phone and I called Tom. I said, "Tommy Boy, do you have everything all set?" Tom came back with, "Ready and waiting my friend, anytime you get here is a good time, the range is yours. I looked over to Patsy as I said, "Sweetheart, go grab your boss, I need a few minutes with her out here alone. Norbs came out and smiled as she asked, "Mind if I sit?" I said, "Norbs, we're going to polish up your shooting skills this morning."

Norbs smile told me that she had already been thinking about that.

Me: Sorry honey, we won't be going downstairs and shooting in our private range. We're going on a bit of a road trip. It's only a twenty-five minute drive. We're going to run up to our outdoor pistol and rifle range. It's gonna be just me and you babe, just me and you. So tell your little bodyguard pals that they better stand down. I won't tolerate any interference. I don't want to hear any feet scraping on gravel. I don't want to see any shadows, I don't want any of that bullshit, just me and you and no, I'm not going to whack you. This is not a replay of the movie, 'Good Fellows'. Do you have your shooter in your purse? Norb's nodded her head. I said good, we don't have to fuck around with any of the shit downstairs then. Let's roll.

    We went out to the driveway and got in the truck. Before I could back out onto the street, here came those special secret cars with black windows, along with a few of those vans that can change colors with a push of a button. I had to laugh as I was wondering what color they are going to be by the time we arrive at the range. I backed out of the driveway and those protective cars were right on my ass. I didn't get fifty feet down the street when two more identical cars pulled out in front of me. I quickly realized that I had no business doing this. I drove to the end of the block, turned left, drove to the end of that block, turned left again and pulled back into my driveway. I said, "Honey, I think we're going to ride with these ghost people, I don't quite have the juice to steer a vehicle this morning."

Yeah, I guess things have gotten worse for me, without me realizing it. Is this the why of we're having this visit with these nice people? I have to guess that Heather told them of my current condition. What are they here to do, see what part of me is still left? Shit, I don't know what part of me is still here or what has left.

I strolled to the first car and his blacked-out window came down. I said, "Sport, tell your pals here, that we're going on a bit of a road trip, go ahead and Google, 'United Northern Sportsmen's Club' on Island Lake. We're going to an outdoor shooting range, once we get there you are all going to get lost, get it? This is just for Norbs and I, it may not fit your protocol but I don't give a fuck, I don't work for you guys."

I had Norbs get into one car and I got in another and off we went. I'm sure there's a whole bunch of people including Norbs with the, "What the fuck" look on their faces. That pleased me greatly.

I had them stop at QuikTrip because every time we go up to the outdoor range we always stop there and get 'range' donuts and a package of chocolate chip cookies. Heather only likes plain donuts but these donuts come in a hard plastic twelve pack container. There are three rows of four each. There is one row of plain in the center row, with two different flavored powdered donuts on each side. Heather does not want powdered donut stuff on her plain donuts. She wipes them off like they must have boogers on them or something. She can't take any bit of that powdery stuff on her plain donuts. I enjoy watching her trying to blow the powder off of them. I remember the last time we went up and got our range donuts, we got everything set up at the range and I opened the plastic donut vault and by the way who the fuck designs these plastic boxes with those little snaps on each end? Son of a bitch, you'll wake up the whole goddamn household if you git the munchies in the middle of the night. Those goddamn things are so loud, that the minute I open one of them, son of a bitches, all the donuts go into baggies cuz I'm not going to fight that goddamn plastic! Who is the psychotic asshole that designed those fuckin containers?

Just before we arrived at the range, I told my driver to tell his Pals that there will be one person there standing at the pistol range waiting for us. He's solid, you're not going to shake him down, you're not going to pat him down, you're going to be perfect gentleman and you will treat him like he's my brother because in some respects he is.

When we pulled up, there stood my buddy Tom with a big grin and welcoming open arms. As I got out of the car I glanced back and saw that the entryway to the range was now blocked off. I don't know where the fuck those other cars and vans came from. I take it that the range is locked down tight, that's for damn sure.

I introduced Tom to Norbs and her security team. Norbs got a strange look on her face as she said, "Wait a minute, Tom, you are the range safety officer here right? You're that same Tom that David gifted you several cases of bullets because he received even better bullets and you asked him if you could sell off the bullets to buy fishing equipment for the kids "Learn to Fish Weekend" you're that Tom?"

Tom tipped his hat as he said, "Yes ma'am, the one and only I'm afraid. Excuse me Ma'am I need a moment with David."

We just stepped aside a few feet and he said, "Everything is ready, look down range it's all set up, look over towards the rifle range, there's a utility cart that is all set up for you. The range is closed, it's all yours my friend. I guess I'm going to sit with these big beefy guys with bulging sport coats?"

I opened one of those plastic containers of donuts and intentionally took a white powdered donut and smeared it all over my mouth, my nose and my chin. Norbs was in hysterics as I was eating that donut with a second that quickly followed.

I said "Norbs, look down range, this is of course, a pistol range, club rules say no handgun larger than 45acp. Fuck em! I shoot my 10mm's here all the time. We have a few newly appointed members on the board of directors that don't know shit about ballistics, they just need to feel their power. Fuck em twice!

Me: Norbs honey, what do you see in front of us?

Norbs: Well, there's twelve shooting lanes with twelve targets set up, all with green paper in front of them, there's something under the green paper, what's going on?

Me: Come on honey, we're going to walk down to these targets.

As we stopped in front of the first target, I put my arm around her waist as I said, "Baby check this out" as I peeled back the green paper on the target. There was a collage of her three children and her husband's faces, all with red bullseye rings on their faces. Norbs looked more than startled as she gasped, "What the hell is this?" I was glad that I had my arm around her waist as she started to crumble. I said "Oh no you don't, stay on your feet and come with me." We walked over to the next target. I pulled back the green paper and there were three different pictures of her three children and her husband, all with red bullseye rings. I took her all the way down the line. Every target station had collages of different photographs of her children and her husband. I never let go of her as she was so unsteady with her trembling. I glanced back at the bodyguards a few times and each time they were braced to pounce on me and rescue Norbs. Tom did a great job with holding them back.

I walked her back to the six foot, (with my arm still around her waist) painted firing line and turned her to face the targets as I whispered, "Now are you willing to draw your weapon and shoot any of these targets?" Norbs looked at me like she wanted to shoot me. She said, "Christ no, what the fuck is wrong with you?" I said, "No baby, the question is what the fuck is wrong with you? Each of these twelve targets are actually your family and you can kill them with your next drink as easily as if that drink was a gun. So my dear, do you want to go ahead and shoot them now and blast their hearts and eyeballs out of their bodies. Either that or you better get damn fucking serious about living sober! Capiche?

Norbs was so shaken that I nodded to a few of her people to help me walk her back to the shooting table where she could sit down. For the first time I saw Heather standing with Patsy. I motioned the girls to come forward, Heather mouthed the words, "I love you," as she draped a blanket over Norbs. The girls sat on each side of her as I motioned everyone to move back as I myself did.

It was her time now, time that she confronts her own truths. It was time that she sees what she has and what she may potentially lose. One of her people came from the car with a box of Kleenex. I waved him off and whispered, "Let her wipe her nose on her sleeves, don't bother her, this is her time. I poured another cup of coffee from my thermos and just stood there. It was like watching a baby fawn being born. I could feel her letting go and I was standing a good ten feet away. I don't know what the time span was from the time we sat her down on the shooting bench to when she was able to bring her head back up and look at me as she turned and said, "You are the sneakiest and craftiest bastard I have ever met in my entire life, but I'll tell you this, you are also the most effective, loving human being I've ever known. David I had no idea. It just never came to me that I was in such deep trouble and just an arm's length away from my next drink and from losing everything and everyone that I've ever loved."

Me: Yeah baby, egos a bitch isn't it, denial is a bitch too! Now are you ready to start working the 12

Steps of AA , no more fucking around, no more pampering just gut honesty?"

She nodded her head and I said, "No good babe, the word is yes. Say the word yes, head nods are for pussies. Say it loud and say it proud!"

One of Norbs people came to the far edge of the table and slid down a box of Kleenex. Sweet fella I guess, he had his priorities too. It's obvious that they're more than just bodyguards to protect her physical being. Yes compassion lends to comfort as well.

Norbs threw back the blanket and reached over and grabbed the container of donuts. She took a powdered donut in each hand and smeared them all over her face, while laughing her ass off. She had chunks of donut in her hands and just slammed them into her mouth and chewed like a horse. Even a couple of her stoic protector guys couldn't help but to chuckle.

Yep, I think this old broad might have a chance after all. I extended my open hand to her as I said, "If you're ready young lady, gather yourself up and walk this way.

I walked her over to the rifle range and to the utility cart and told her to get in, as I slid behind the wheel. I drove the cart to the back side of the three hundred yard target butt.

In the back were two very large and thick red 'Hudson Bay' blankets, a 6 pack of water, a thermos of coffee and two cups and of course another box of tissue and lastly, a copy of the 'Big Book of Alcoholics Anonymous.' Norbs looked at me and asked, Tom too? I smiled and nodded as I said, "Why not Tom too? Grab your blanket sweetie, it's time for your come to Jesus meeting. You might want to roll up in that blanket, there is about to become a chill in the air.

Me: Baby there's some things that you may not quite understand or if you do understand them, you simply don't like them. Today is not about liking, today is about doing. It's time you do you. Still love me babe?

Do you really think that your confession of your not getting it and you're fibbing a priest a little bit in your fourth-step gets you a pass? You have no business in the fourth step. You haven't even been able to grasp the first step and part of that I understand. I've never had that type of trouble, but you are different then most, actually you are quite different than most. You can't admit that you're powerless over alcohol and that your life has become unmanageable, which of course is the first step. The reason being of course is because you have had people to manage your life. You had your people, you had meal chefs, housekeepers, servants, you had childcare people all living in your house. You have personal shoppers who deliver to your house. You never had to balance your checkbook, you had accountants to pay your bills and you had plenty of money. You have private secretaries that make all your travel arrangements and lodging. I won't even ask when the last time was that you strolled the isles of a grocery store. You really never came to your bottom, whereas most of us garden variety alcoholics think we've dug our way to our absolute bottom when some son of a bitch throws in a bigger shovel. But that's not you, you are different in that respect. I want you to think back to those targets you just saw. I want you to think about the eyes of your children looking back at you. Now you can admit that you are powerless over alcohol and that your life had become unmanageable because you were ready to lose it all, just like the rest of us. Listening to you, I have to say that you're not the least bit as common as most any common alcoholic. I have met a lot of people that can't even admit to being alcoholics but they still go to meetings. Some will say that their therapist told them to go to AA because they used up their insurance allotment for mental health care. Some may say, "I have a small drinking problem." Sometimes they introduced themselves as Chemically Dependent because well, alcoholic just sounds so crass and unrefined, then of course then you have the self-identifiers and all of the pronoun people. Hey listen, I don't give a fuck who you fuck, and I don't give any part of a shit if you or your friends do nasty things with kitchen utensils on your countertops, that's your business. But don't ever try to bastardize the one thing that has saved hundreds of thousands if not millions upon millions of lives throughout the world. There are a lot of people that say AA is too rigid, or, "I don't dig all of this God bullshit in the Big Book. I'm going to write my own Big Book. Well, I've yet to see a customized AA program work for anyone. It's simple, follow the rules. The very first line in how it works reads, "Rarely have we seen a person fail who has thoroughly followed our path." Look at all the celebrity deaths of older and young people who have taken their own lives, perhaps unintentionally but they're still just as fucking dead. You jumped ahead in your step work because you want to think that you're special and can pick and choose your sobriety due to you're being a celebrity. You believe that you qualify for the accelerated program of AA so you can take a bow for not drinking. Humility is not your strong suit. Your jumping the steps to making amends is a thousand miles down the road. Slow your roll, learn to breathe and then learn to absorb. You've been a 'Gasper' from the moment I met you. You need to learn to breathe, inhale…exhale repeat. Stop it, you're gasping, it's very unattractive if not deadly. Yeah babe, I get that whole drive to make amends because you want to cleanse yourself and you want to move past that to the next best good thing in life. It doesn't work like that. If you want to remain sober follow the rules, they're there for a reason, the steps are in numerical order for a reason. Your legs aren't long enough to hop from the first step to the sixth, you will go right on your ass. We take it one step at a time. It's no different than the wise old cowboy that tells a green horn youngster, "We're going to eat this here Buffalo one bite at a time." One bite at a time, one step at a time is how you do it, it's not baby steps and it's not lunges. What it is, is walking with purpose. Identify your purpose and your steps will come. Now I'm sure you've been wondering what's in this small briefcase, am I right?

    Norbs: Jesus Christ David, when are you not right? You say the simplest shit with the strongest voice affirmation that I've ever heard. Okay, I'll bite so what's in the case?

    Me: Baby we're just going to sit or lay here, wrapped up like a couple of tortillas in these massive blankets and we're going to listen to music. If you start tapping your foot I'm going to hit you with a stick. I want you to listen and more importantly, I want you to feel the lyrics. Listen to the lyrics, it's the lyrics that tell the story. The Rhythm and the background is just to draw your attention to the lyrics. Sadly not enough people understand that. We're going to listen to lyrics that happen to be in the form of music, the music draws your attention and the lyrics tell a story.

The first songs we listened to were the first three songs of, Tears for Fears, "Everybody Wants to Rule The World" "Head over heels" and "Shout." I'm going to pass on "Woman in Chains.' You can listen to that on your own time. Don't forget to open your box of Kleenex.

I could see the message was well-received just by listening to Norbs breathing patterns. I looked over at her and said, "Babes, you want to hear those songs again?" She smiled and said, "Yes, yes I very much would like to hear them all again" as she was wiping her tears. The next song of Solomon Burke's, "Cry To Me" brought on the water works. Norb's looked over at me and said, "I could listen to that all day and all night long, that is my song, all these songs describe me, the inside me! The me that I never show to anyone. I try so hard to deny and not show my depression because I'm afraid that my children and husband will think that it's their fault. That would just kill me!"

I patted her hand and said, "Honey there's more, there's much, much, more. Next came Elvis Presley's, "You're the Devil in Disguise," followed by, "Suspicious Minds" than on to, "If I Can Dream," and

"In the Ghetto" followed but what I think was his finest gospel song that was still a smash hit, "Kentucky Rain" but It didn't get a lot of airtime.

Before I could go any further, Norbs reached over and asked me to hold her hand. I smiled as I said, "Yes, but no funny business young lady." As the tears were now streaming down her twenty year younger looking face.

I felt a great internal sigh of relief, she's getting it, she's finally getting it! I can almost hear her surrender through her sobs. Yep, this is a day well spent. Once she gathered herself I told her about how I wasn't a big fan of country western music most all of my life, until I actually started listening to the lyrics and not to the beat. I think Brooks & Dunn brought it all to me. I think when Ronnie Dunn would take a break while playing in a Honkey Tonk he would go into the back room during a break in his early years and would sit and study me and write lyrics, either that or he sat outside my bedroom window listening to me talking in my sleep. Their song, "Neon Moon" was my life anthem. Listening to Neon Moon was hearing my story, it let my heart bleed and I found a cleansing. I listen to all this music almost every day along with a whole bunch of others. On those days that I can't find my center, I have to rely on other people to help me pick myself up. You're no different. What the Big Book of Alcoholics Anonymous does for us, is it allows us the strength that we can rely on to help other people pick themselves up. We don't lift them, we let them pick themselves up. So let's get to this, are you sponsoring anybody? All I got was a shake of a head. "Oh what, you're not far enough along in your sobriety, you don't have this thing all mastered, to where you can be of vital importance to another human being's life? Oh baby you got a long ways to go. Listen to a newcomer who walks in the door, you've got three months of sobriety and in their mind you are a rockstar with three months. It's rare that a newcomer will ask an old-timer for guidance, they want someone fresh from the fight like they are. Someone that they can relate to, somebody early on in sobriety. You own your gifts, you already have them but you're so busy seeking for yourself you're missing your true purpose in life. You are the example of the power and freedom gained from continuous sobriety. Put your humility hat on and help them walk their path to happy destiny.

Got it babe? OK, this lecture series is now complete. Let's get the fuck out of here, what do you say we all go down to Coney Island and wolf down a couple of those nasty chili cheese dogs?

Norbs was laughing as we started to drive away while she was still drying her tears. As we neared the one hundred yard target butt, Norbs started to giggle, she grabbed my arm as she said, "Stop! I want to run back the rest of the way. I just feel so damn good, I feel like I'm floating." I reached down and grabbed her leg just above her knee as I said, "The fuck you will! If you jump out of this cart and start running towards your gun happy goons, I will gain several pounds of molten lead in the thought that I hurt you. Keep your happy ass in this seat." We had quite a welcoming crowd as we returned. Norbs did a beeline to Tom. She threw her arms around him and held him tight. She whispered several words to him. As we started to the cars, Norbs turned back and waved to Tom saying, "Thank you Tom, I will never forget you and what you taught me today. I love you Tom."

CHAPTER 16
Damn Right She Knows

There are times that I wish the world would just stop and let me off.

There are also times that I would give a major organ just to be left alone for a few hours or even a few days. I would like to blame it on people and their constant interruptions. Maybe blame the TV and radio, blame facebook and social media, blame Heather and our fur babies, blame street noise, squirrels and birds, the wind, the clouds, the sun and the list goes on. In truth, I cannot shut down my brain. It's like one of those perpetual motion toys! I can't nap any longer, I can't sleep undisturbed, I wake myself up with my own thoughts and thrashing. Every morning I awaken with the same fatigue that I took to bed with me. I can't get away from it, what sucks is that I know exactly what the problem is.

I am full of fear. The very same fear that I shout to the rooftops that fear doesn't exist. I have sold the concept that fear is not a word at all, but an acronym that stands for: False... Evidence... Appearing... Real... I have peddled that concept for many years in my books and public speaking engagements throughout the country. Yet here I am controlled by my fear while waiting for the horrid and painful end. It has nothing to do with my personal discomfort of dying. It's about the people I will leave behind.

Mostly, I worry about Heather and it consumes me every moment of every day.

I fight with myself constantly, in asking if I'm too protective of her? I have been withholding certain information from her, thinking that I'm doing the honorable thing in protecting her. But am I?

I don't like what I've been doing lately. Part of me says that this is what love is truly all about, the other part tells me that I am a coward. I have been quietly throwing away my favorite comfy shirts that makes Heather cringe when I wear them. The collars and cuffs are badly frayed, might be missing a button (or two) and have a few small holes in the elbows. I have boxes and totes of 'someday clothes' that I've outgrown due to weight gain that I've hauled off to the Goodwill. But that's been the easy part. My truest life's passion has always been camping, hunting, fishing and of course the shooting sports. I can't do any of those things any longer due to my health challenges. I have been secretly giving those things away as well. I want to believe that I'm again doing the honorable thing....but am I? Am I just being self indulgent in my sorrows? Then comes that damn list. Not a bucket list as much as a list of the things I'd like to see before I die. I would like to see our country recover from the socialist, communist democratic party's fuckery. If there is a civil war, I hope to be able to answer the call. Not a lot or people know of my condition and that's the way I want it. The few that do know, don't know the depth of it because I don't want their sympathy, I want their friendship, the way it has always been.

    I may have been a bit overzealous in giving away most of my camping, hunting and fishing stuff. A few guys have stated that they would be honored to have a few of my guns and ammunition with saying, "I'd be willing to pay you a fair price for anything that you want to get rid of." After they saw my half-smile glance, they have not repeated that statement.

    I do have two guns that I want to go to my two dearest friends. They have admired those custom guns from the first day I let them shoot them. Those guns are in their factory cases with their names on them along with a brief personal note to each. All of my other guns go to Heather to do with what she wishes. Knowing her as I do, I know she will never part with them, any of them. She will add them to her collection and keep them until she dies.

I have to laugh at myself sometimes. Oh Hell, I actually have to laugh at myself most all of the time! I want to believe that I am somehow protecting Heather by under-reporting my test results and daily challenges. Heather is nobody's fool, damn far from it. As much as I try to hide the progression of my illness, she clearly sees through it. It's her way to leave me with my dignity intact. Yes, there are a lot of ways to say, "I love you" without muttering a word.

I think Norbs was still smarting a bit from our morning trip. I could just barely see her sitting on the back side of the big cottonwood tree off the deck. She must have had one of her muscle men haul that iron chair off the deck. Obviously she was hiding out from me and I found that fucking delightful. We keep a large tin of boiled unsalted shelled peanuts on the deck for the squirrels. We don't put them out until the fall because we didn't want more than we can afford to feed. Squirrels are opportunists and they will tell everybody about their new found wealth of peanuts. I could only see a part of Norbs right shoulder and leg, so I started lobbing a few peanuts at her. One peanut hit her on the foot. She came up out of that chair like it was a jet fighter ejection seat. I smiled and waved while asking, "Are you mad at me or just pouting?

Perhaps what you are doing is acting like a cell phone that doesn't have any bars?"

Norbs: Up yours dick head! I am journaling, it's one of those newer age things that people do when they don't have a mind like yours where you write a complete book in your head before a single word ever hits paper. Some of us mere mortals have to write everything down before we can develop our thoughts around it, whereas you just shoot from the hips! Yeah, you're rare all right, be sure to let me know if you have trouble spelling you bastard, son of a bitch and motherfuker. I'll be happy to help you with those big words!"

We both started laughing as I said, "I'm ready for another cup of coffee, care to enter into the enemy camp, my lady? Norbs came up the stars like a little kid that knows she's in trouble.

Norbs: I need to ask you a few questions.

Me: Go ahead angry girl, what are your questions? Remember that you said, "Few."

Norbs: Well I saw on Facebook that you did a post about you being ready to sign a contract with a voice actor, is that true?

Me: Of course it's true, I'd never fib on facebook.

Norbs: And he's going to record which book, hopefully he'll record all of them?

Me: My problem is that I don't have the budget to support my end game. All I've ever had in my life is a dream. I continue to stack that dream on top of the last one and the many others that came before that dream. Nothing has ever come to fruition, whether it be romance, finance or something as simple as peace of mind. I've yet to recognize any financial success. Babe, don't get me wrong, many people have reached out to me in the last seven years to tell me that I have made a difference in their life. Yes that of course is definitely success, yes that's personal success but I'm talking about a different level of personal success.

Now back to the facebook post. I wanted to see if people would be interested in listening to my books on Audiobooks and iHEART. I have been in contact with a few voice actors with phone calls and emails. I've also gone to the actors' websites to listen to their work. I've listened to several voice actors' promos on ACX, which is a Amazon's site.

I have found the voice actor that I think would be a perfect fit to do my first book, "Daddy Had to Say Goodbye" and all seven of my other novels including this one. The only problem is that our finances are all tied up and we're not liquid, not to mention that Joe

Biden's spending bullshit has killed our savings that I put into a private 401K. This voice actor is charging a very reasonable fee, but it's a big risk at the same time. I have to sell 208 audiobooks before I can realize even one cent of profit and there's absolutely no guarantee of sales. He is a very accomplished actor but I don't have any experience in marketing my books other than my website and Amazon, who only pays me $1.82 per book for a $17.95 retail price. How's that for a fucking, and it took me three years to write my first book!

If I have learned anything in these last seven years, it is that just because people say they can't wait to read my books, doesn't mean they will buy them! It's all about marketing and once again, I don't have the money for marketing and no, I'm not going to take a dime from anyone.

Norbs: But David, don't you have a friend that wanted to do that for you?

Me: Yeah honey, I did have a friend, 'did have' are the operative words in this conversation. This cat was all geared up, he came from a family of radio personalities in large markets, he even had his own radio show as a young person so yeah he's got the voice without question. He does a podcast where his voice carries very well. There was a big secret amongst him and some of my other friends, was that they were going to set up a professional recording studio in his home just to record my books. A number of people donated materials and large sums of cash to build this top of the line soundproof recording studio. The studio was built and everything was set to record. He sent me a video presentation of the set up. He was very proud that he had read my first book into his system and was close to doing the final edits. This was back in early December of last year, he told me and the listeners of the live podcast that he would have two of my books complete and in the market by the end of March. Well, we're now in mid November and I have no audiobook. What had transpired was he had met a woman. Suddenly he couldn't get anywhere close to record my books. He kept talking on-air about how busy he was with re-roofing his house and outbuildings. He was saying that winter was near (in June) and how far he was behind in his preparations.

  I get it in part, I get the whole lonely-heart deal for a man, who lives in an isolated rural area with some personal challenges in front of him. Yes I get that, I get every bit of that. But don't fucking lie to me and treat me like a child and think I'm too stupid to see what's actually going on. He is no longer the man he once was, there's no question about it. He used to tout that honor, integrity and loyalty was everything and the only true measure of a man. He sadly does not measure up to any of his own ideals.

I'm not going to cast any aspirations on this woman because it's all on him. No man or woman can be manipulated unless they want to be. Maybe he wanted to be, he may have set the whole thing up, was she his out when he realized that he didn't have the skills he bragged so proudly about having with reading and recording? Hell I don't know. I am not a relationship expert but what he did to me is unforgivable. Yeah I'm hurt, I thought we were friends, I thought we were close friends. It was disheartening at best to realize that you can be replaced, regardless of the history between people all in the name of romance.

Who I feel sorry for are the other wonderful people involved who believed in him and wanted to do good, the people who donated money and materials because they believed in me and my writings. Yeah, I won't realize my dream but they are not going to realize there's either. So that 'old friend' has become a past friend. He gave up both his honor and his dignity to be with a woman. Again, I can cast no aspersions upon her as life is all about choices, we all get to make them. He made his....so fuck him!

CHAPTER 17
Confusing Fear With Shame

Me: Baby, you needn't seek the truth, you already know the truth. It's the acceptance part that you're drowning in and believe me, you will drown!

Norbs: Damn your hide! Those words leave your lips so smoothly, yet when I hear them, they are crushing blows! Will we ever just have a respectful, level playing field, friendship?

Me: Probably not, at least for now. Please forgive me for my unwillingness to watch you die.

Norbs: Damn you again David, I have never hated and loved the same person at the same time, I love the fact that you care so deeply for me, I hate the fact that you care so deeply about me! I can't get out from under you. Will it ever end?

Me: Only if you want it to. For me, I aint changing shit! More coffee?

It was the day after we came back from the shooting range and Norbs was still feeling tender. Yes, I roughed her up quite a bit to get her attention. If she is willing to listen and learn from others, I think she can earn the life she has always longed for.

Me: You being a famous aristocrat and sitting on millions of dollars, I have to ask you babe, can you cook?

Norbs: So your highness, I'm guessing that you want me to make you breakfast?

Me: Not on your life, sweetmeat. The way you despise me, no fuckin way. We'll order delivery. Just so you know, I have absolutely no interest in being your AA sponsor. I'm old school, men sponsor men and women sponsor women. Capisce?

I am your loving friend who cares so deeply for you that I smile every time I get to drive my boot up your ass. And that's all I am!

Norbs: If Amanda hadn't warned me about you and your crude ways I would have shot you some time back. Amanda is coming in tomorrow and we will collectively beat your snarky ass, if you keep hacking on me. I will call for breakfast.

Suddenly I needed to pee and went to my bedroom to sit on the bed. I knew what that meant with Amanda coming, I am worse off than I thought I was. In a few minutes I found a reason to smile. If nothing else, I got to reach one more soul. Norbs is well on her way to her and her family's best life, if she stays the course.

Our breakfast arrived. Norbs called the muscle from the airbnb from across the alley to join us. Six rather sizable men and a female walked out of the place and were walking toward us. Lucky that Norbs had an accurate headcount.

I didn't know who this new woman was. I never saw or met her and for whatever reason I was not introduced to her. I guess that she is just another ghost, standing in the dark of night, doing the good deeds that the fearful will never understand.

My cell phone rang before my breakfast sandwich was half over. It was Amanda, her playful little brat voice came across with, "Have you showered lately?" I didn't answer. She asked, "Are you still there?" I said, "Yes I'm here, I'm waiting for you to come here and to put me in the shower!"

Amanda: I'll take care of that, I'll be there in less than an hour. I had a schedule conflict so I had to push our date up to today. I hope that's not a problem?

Me: Babe that's not a problem, I'll brush my teeth but I'll be damned if I'll shower, that's on you!

We both giggled and exchanged I love you's and hung up. Norbs people looked at me like they so much wanted to burst out in laughter and shake their heads, but they knew that they were on the job, so it was stoic faces but the twinkling eyes that gave them away.

Well I had to shower of course. Norbs insisted that she come along to the airport as she hadn't seen Amanda in sometime. I was not comfortable with that but said okay. When we got to the FBO side of the airport Amanda's advance team had already arrived and was standing next to the portable staircase waiting for her bird to land.

I have known all of these guys for a couple years now. We pranked each other when nobody's looking, we've shared jokes, meals and spent some quality time sending molten hot lead down range and spinning brass in the air and on the ground. Of course they'd already taken up their positions. When I walked up to them, all I said was, "Hey fuckers!" They all broke rank and started laughing and extended their hands with several hugs. With that, something told me that they already knew. These guys are the top security professionals in the world. They were not overly affectionate but their hugs and handshakes were more sincere than at any other time. I asked, "Which of you gun slingin, muscle heads are in charge of this detail?"

There was a quick and subtle hand flick that most people would never catch, even by their competitors. "Do you have communication with the aircraft?" "Yes sir, right now they are four minutes out, on final approach." "Great, let them know that once they touch down and taxi that I'm going to come aboard. I want a few private minutes with Amanda. Can we do that, fellows?" There was no hesitation, just a head nod and a crisp, "Yes sir." It told me that I'd finally been accepted into the "Inner Circle" and I don't mind admitting that it felt damn good. As the aircraft door opened and the portable stairs were rolled into place, Amanda came to stand in the open doorway staring down at me.

Me: What are you doing?

Amanda: I'm just checking to see if you have any bald spots, besides I love looking down on you, I feel so superior to you!

Me: Knock that shit off, you wear those power strutting, six inch hooker heels so of course you tower over me. Just another indication that you hate men because you can't be one!

I knew that I took it a bit too far when the FBO ramp workers who were plugging in the power unit and opening the cargo doors were trying to stifle their giggles.

Amanda: I understand that your Royal Highness is demanding a private confab? Right this way good sir.

Of course she had some security people on board with her. As I entered the cabin, the flight crew were lined up like little ducklings to welcome me. I was handed not one but two cups of coffee. I smiled and I said, "If this isn't Folgers, someone is out of work."

Amanda had her hand on my forearm. She nodded her head towards the office door in the tail section of the aircraft. I said, "I need some private moments with you baby." The flight attendant led us back to Amanda's office cabin. Amanda extended her courtesies to invite me to step across the threshold first, saying, "Have a seat my love." as she stepped in and quickly walked around her desk and took a seat. The door was still standing open.

Me: Push that little button at your right knee. I need to hear a whooshing sound from the airlock and the heavy metallic click from the door lock, so nothing outside of this cabin can be heard or recorded.

Amanda: So you're running the show? Need I remind you that I own this show?

Me: So baby, you don't trust the current reports and you came to do a personal damage assessment on me? Do you have a shrink back here somewhere hidden in the luggage compartment perhaps? Baby, I want you to understand, and I'm going to be the one that tells you how I am. Honey, I can't be fixed, there is nothing to fix, there's less of me than what it was before, and there's nothing to replace it. I guess in street terms that condition is known as, "Fucked Forever." My brain is shrinking, my thoughts are often scrambled, and at times I can't finish a sentence. My motor skills, or lack of, frighten me. Oh and just so you know, you forgot to hug me just now. You can't break me either, I'm not frail, I'm just different, more different than I've ever been before, but I've made my peace with it. It's just part of the deal of aging and yes, it totally sucks.

I have to tell you, that I look at the obituaries in the newspaper every morning and it screams, 'you may be next.' So many of these people that died are dying younger than I am. It's gotten pretty weird all right. Just a few days ago I was driving around town just out of boredom and I realized that I may be looking at these things for the very last time! Who's to know but at least I have a warning, there's a lot of people who left home this morning with every intention of coming home tonight for dinner with their family, who will never make it there. I can't allow myself to continue to think like this, my only concern can be about the people I'm leaving behind. My greatest concern of course is that I'll become a babbling idiot and poor Heather will have to care for me. I may call you someday and ask you to smuggle a gun into whatever kind of facility they got me locked in. Now girly, that I've laid it all out, what's up with you?

Amanda stood and came around her desk, stooped down and kissed me full on the lips and sat down next to me. She had tears in her eyes as she looked at me for a long time without saying a word.

Amanda: Tell me tough guy, you ever cry?

Me: I stopped with that nonsense by the time I reached 20 years old. My parents taught me that if I cried as a child, I would feel even more pain from my next beating. I don't know if I cried because it hurt physically or because it hurt my heart that my parents who were supposed to care for me and love me but didn't. They taught me plenty about non-love, those were the people that I needed the most, but what they taught me is that I didn't need anybody. So yeah, I grew up hard and stayed that way. Even when it came to loving a mate, I couldn't connect with them because I didn't know what love was. To me, sex was love and love was sex. Heather and I have been together for ten years now. She is the first woman that I have trusted to not betray me.

Back to your question, Heather and I cried together six weeks ago after I got the brain scan report. I didn't cry for myself, I cried for her fears, loneliness and future suffering while taking care of me as I continue to degrade.

Amanda: You're still a big strong fellow. I want you to get on your feet and let me hold you.

We both had a few tears. The embrace was genuine with a 50-50 body melt. It felt good to feel her true love.

Me: It's time that I ask you how you are. Before you answer, I already know about Robert and how he fancies wearing womens dresses and under garments. Baby I'm sitting right here, if you need to talk about it I would like to hear it, if not we'll just go to the house and I'll slap your ass every chance I get.

Amanda: You do make me smile, you crass bastard. This is a genuine smile, I always knew there was something a little off about Robert. We as a family told him about, "The Company " the morning of our evening engagement announcement. Before that, he seemed a bit uncomfortable with our security people and all the precautions and protocols. He hated to have to be driven everywhere he went. Want to know what's funny? He was afraid of guns and people with guns. Even our own security people! Do you know who the one person is who scares him the most? I'm looking at him! You scared the holy hell out of him. He would have nightmares about you sneaking up on him or seeing you in a crowd or him thinking that you're looking at him through a scoped rifle from a distance. I never got that, but he was a little strange that way even at work. There were times where he would just jump and look around, I would ask him what he was looking for and he said, "I thought I smelled David!" I thought I would have some fun with him one day and I said, "You don't need to worry about David, if he wants to kill you he will make it very personal, you'll never know what happened. He carries a common small pocket knife, he would just slam it into the small of your back and separate your spine!" That poor bastard didn't sleep for almost an entire week, he was so terrified. You pretty much had the read on him all along. The way I found out who he actually was, was when I came home early from an evening meeting. He had the music playing awful loud. I found him in the living room dancing to the song, "It's Raining Men" by 'The Weather Girls' from the 1970's disco era. He was wearing a woman's blond wig and one of my party gowns. He finally turned around, and passed out when he saw me standing there. He crumpled to the floor in a thud. So here I was on my knees leaning over my husband, trying to bring him to while he is laying there with a Shirley Temple blond wig and my gown up over his waist with my nylons and panties on. I guess I must have screamed because our home security team came in, in a rush.

Before that I just didn't know what it was with him, but I thought it was something I could accept and at some point he will confide in me.

Me: Honey, this is a smile of compassion, I'm not laughing at you. That would have been really nice if that would have taken place before you two got married.

Amanda: Well yeah, that would have been nice wouldn't it. Well I don't know how much you know, so I'll just lay it all out, it's not a long story. I came to find out afterwards that Robert has been gay or bisexual or whatever the hell he wants to identify as, most of his life. What is amazing is that my dad and my brother both did independent background checks on him and nothing came out. So the way the story starts and ends is that Robert wanted to move his man lover in with us. Robert was escorted from our home, he was fired from his job at our office and I'm not sure just what transpired but somehow it was made crystal clear to him that he had to disappear. The only money he got out of me was just his last paycheck. My prenups were bulletproof. He took nothing, he got nothing and I'm done, at least I'm done with him. But you still look mighty tasty! What are you doing this afternoon, sweetheart? We both laughed and she called up front for a fresh coffee.

Me: So sweet cheeks, why are you here if not for damage assessment, what are you here for?

Amanda: I don't know baby, I just, I just needed to see you. My dad and my brother are the only men I've ever been able to trust and love, more importantly I had to come here and personally offer you anything you could possibly need. I didn't know if there's a word for it in your illness. I've talked to our doctors about your condition. I've talked to your doctor about your condition and how I got to that is none of your fuckin business. Oh yeah, I just want you to know that we will do everything possible to make you comfortable and more importantly I believe you would like to know that Heather will always be comfortable and want for nothing. David you have the Roberts family pledge of our lifetime of care for Heather. I guess that's just pretty much it, other than that, I just came to be with you. and yes I've gotten reports that told me that I should spend some time with the most lovable asshole on the planet. Mostly, I want to learn from you. I heard what you did out on the shooting range yesterday or was that the day before? I don't even know what day it is at the moment. Sweetheart, your level of brilliance far exceeds beyond any scriptwriter's abilities. You do know that you saved that woman's life don't you? You do know that Norbs is going to pick up your banner and she will run with it until she can run no more. You got to her when no one else could, she will always be grateful and she will always pass it on.

  I've talked to Heather a few times on the phone but I couldn't get a good fix on her and how she is holding up. That poor girl has been up against the wall with all this family death and her asshole brother's bullshit. Mother said that she would take him out for you guys, just say the word.

Me: I'm actually grateful that Heather hasn't had time to fully realize what the future holds in the middle of this family shit show. Heather is slow to trust but I'm far more concerned about Heather's well-being rather than my own. Maybe I'm being a little egotistical and I know that you would find that amazing. This it's just another painful disappointment in her life. She is damn tough, I think she's going to come out of this whole deal okay. I can see her getting a few more dogs in the near future because dogs are the best friends anyone can ever hope to have. Human beings suck, dogs don't lie to us, dogs don't betray us, all they want us to do is have us love on them.

Are you spending the night, how long are you here for? Please tell me that you didn't bring your jammies.

Amanda smiled as she squeezed my hand and said, "Yes, you're that same old nasty pig and if things were different I would not sleep with jammies. I would trust you to keep me warm, that is if things were different. To answer your question, I think I'll hang here for a week if it's okay with you guys. I don't have to stay at your house, I can hang out at the hotel, maybe we should all get rooms at the hotel, wouldn't that be fun? We could have one big sleepover with room service and a swimming pool, you up for that big boy?

You know I just have to be honest, yes I'm scared, yes I'm not ready to lose you, any part of you. The girls told me about their last sit down with you on your deck, when you took them on, 'The Neighbourhood Tour'. They are still in awe of your abilities to identify and say things as they are. That's something I've never known how to do. I must always weigh and measure every word before I speak. I will never forget how you spanked the High and Mighty's of The Greater Chicago Area. You shamed them to their core and in less than twenty minutes you took them from wanting to toss you into the Chicago river…..to they wanted to commission a statue of you. You emptied more billfolds and purses that day, than any team of armed robbers could ever hope to!

Now sweetheart, I have an announcement to make and you are the first one to hear it. David, I'm backing out of both, "The company" and the family business. I don't know what I want to be when I grow up. I'm embarrassed to admit that I've always had everything put in front of me, handed to me, and sometimes even gift-wrapped. You may think this is silly but I have developed a romantic interest in your writing. I mean come on, if Norbs says that you're a better writer than her, that means that you have arrived! I want to witness that, I want to feel that, I want that to be part of my DNA. Aren't you the one that said the greatest flattery is when somebody tries to copy you?"

Me: So what is this? Are you planning to dissect me? I'm not going to let you interview me, please don't give me anything you've writtin for my approval, nor will I do any proofreading, I won't fucking do it! I've been down that road before and it's not very pleasant. The view sucks and the roads are rough. I'm not going to do it babe! Hell, I don't know how to identify what I do, or how I do it. I just do it, it's just something I can't explain. I'm not going to try to explain it, it's a gift. If you were given a new laptop would you tear the back off of it and look at how everything is laid out? No, of course you would not. So why would I try to disassemble my gift, just to see where it came from and how it works. Now if you want to spend some quality time rubbing tummies together and maybe you could get some of this…oh hell, nevermind.

Amanda squeezed my hand and said, "Sweetheart I hope you never change. What I enjoy the most about you is that I feel so safe and peaceful around you. It's cold out today and yet when I look at your eyes, it's like I'm on the warmest beach with the lightest of breezes and I have a cocktail in my hand, watching the waves gently coming ashore. You've done that to me every time I've seen you regardless of where we have been or the circumstance. You give me a sense of peace and safety that I have never experienced with any other human being or any other location. That's your gift, that's what I'm here for. I want to witness your gift, I want to feel your gift, I want you to teach me how to extend your gift to others, I want to learn to be a mini you. One more thing my good man, I'm here to collect my inheritance ahead of time.

    Me: Why do I not I know that already? Well I've given my best two guns away to my swell local pals, that is after I die of course. They are still in my safe and I will still shoot them until I no longer can. These are not the guns that your family gifted me. These are the guns that I bought from my meager profits from my book sales, stimulus money for the covid deal and a few bucks from savings and my social security.

    The guns that your family gifted me are the sole property of Heather, she can do with those what she pleases. Remember now, before Heather and I got together she had never fired a handgun in her entire life. I'd like to say and and I do pride myself in the fact that I taught her everything she knows about firearms. Especially about the 1911 style handguns. She has become her own master with knowledge and abilities with every modern day manufacturer of firearms. I taught her the proper shooting techniques and more importantly, I taught her how to respect firearms and how to admire the craftsmanship. I have spent countless hours teaching her how to clean every gun in our inventory. I have hammered into her head that if you clean a gun in less than an hour, that you've committed a crime against nature and the gun God's!

Guns are to be respected, nurtured and massaged. Due to the high humidity with living in the front yard of Lake Superior we spend some quality man/women time wiping down our collection, I personally find it soothing. It's part of my zen time. Heather likes to say that she is headed to the vault to pet her babies. So yeah, I don't see her parting with anything to do with firearms. She deeply respects the gifts your family gave us. Firearms to her, are like the doll collection she never had when she was a little girl. Now that she's a big girl and she's got some big beautiful toys that she greatly admires and covets.

God help the poor bastards who tries to hustle her after I'm gone for our guns, in thinking that she is just another dumb broad that doesn't know what she has and tries to screw her over. Those fucks are in for a very rude awakening. But again I just don't see her selling anything, the house is paid for, our home appliances were all replaced two years ago, and we have very little credit card debt. She does need a new vehicle and she can easily swing that with her current income and our relatively safe investments. We see that owning guns and a strong inventory of ammunition is not just a hedge against inflation but as a real life bartering tool when paper money loses its value.

Gold, Silver, and Platinum along with jewels will all be worthless. All that bullshit is only of value to the people that already have big money. But who are they going to sell it to when peoples only concern is to find and hopefully stockpile food and medicines? When the shit hits and I believe it will, Heather will have the best buying power of most anyone I know. We've even talked about and have developed a solid plan as to how she would sell guns if she needed to and where the safe platforms are to sell. She is smart enough to never make mention of the number, types or calibers or where our firearms are stored, nor would she ever invite anyone to our home to inspect them. Our friend Craig, who owns, "Hammer Down Firearms" (the catsup sandwich chef who will be catering my funeral) will be her sales agent. Neither of us mind paying him a reasonable fee if we needed to offload some of our weapons in our collection. As a matter of fact, a few times Craig has been on the ropes financially and somewhat overextended with his gun suppliers from people ordering high dollar specialty guns that they can't wait to pick them up and suddenly they have a money emergency and Craig is stuck with them and he has to eat it because the guns are so specialized and damn expensive and most people can't afford them or the people that can afford them don't understand what they are looking at. On more than one occasion he has called me for help to buy some guns from him so he can put gas in his truck to get to the next gun show. Now that the panic buying from the mostly former anti-gun assholes who overpaid because they realized that their disbanding the police movements only created more crime. Now those same idiots have settled down and don't even know which end of the gun the bullets go in and the run on guns is pretty much over and the crowds at gun shows have shrunk by a strong 40%. The latest trend at gun shows now, are the sissies who had to have a gun and now no longer want a gun and try to sell their unfired new guns back to the dealers at the price they bought them at. You can tell by the long faces as to who fucked themselves with their panic buying. So now, Craig has to compete with those dummies at the gun shows that he has to pay a healthy floor space and table fee for. Six months ago people gladly paid the over inflated asking price for a gun but now everyone asks, "What's your best price?"

Craig also has a great deal of ammunition for sale but he doesn't bring them to gun shows because it is once again a buyers market and the problem he now faces is when people say, "Well I'll buy the gun at this price if you throw in a box or two of ammunition."

That box or two of ammo is his only proffit. People don't respect anyone's property any more. The dickheads at gun shows will drool over a gun pick it up and get their slimy mitts all over the finish, rack the slide on a semi-auto and release the slide lock to hear the upper receiver slam home on an empty gun which will fuck up the rails and internals in just a very few times. Then you have the same pricks that will pick up a revolver, open the cylinder and flip their wrists to snap it shut like in the 'B' rated westerns they watched as a kid. Then they just toss it back down on the table like it's a used Kleenex and walk away. Yeah, maybe I'll go to a gun show and stand around at Craig's tables and knock the holy fuck out of a few of those type of people, right before I die. On a much lighter note, I'm dead serious about wanting my funeral service to be fun. How can they call a funeral service a celebration of life when people are sitting with a box of Kleenex in their laps? That's not how I want my life celebrated! I want laughter, I want smiles and I really do want to have strippers or at least 'go-go' dancers from the 60's that came out of West Hollywood's Sunset Strip. I want them dancing in a cage doing the Watusi, the Jerk, the Fruge, the Shimmy, the Boogaloo and stuff like that. That and whatever the hell Heather wants, and yes, I want her to do a 'split the pot' deal for the cover charge at the entrance to the mortuary. Notice that I said Mortuary rather than Church? Babe, even God has his limits as to how he deals with heathens. Of course I am really serious, as a matter of fact. I'm deadly serious (pun intended) that I do want my pal Craig to be there to serve up his world-famous ketchup sandwiches. The story behind that came from when I would try to make a deal with Craig on a gun. He would whine that I hurt him so badly and that he loses money on every deal we make that it's to the point where now he has to steal those little ketchup packets from fast food restaurants and gas stations just to bring home to feed his family dinner!

Baby, I'm tired, if we're done here, what do you say we head to the house?

Without another word we both stood up, full well knowing this would be our last private embrace and this time we melted into each other's arms as one.

This time I actually followed through with my threat of the last two years, I cupped her buns in both of my hands and firmly squeezed. We both laughed and then we cried. As we broke apart Amanda giggled and said, "You might have wrinkled my dress with the way that you were groping my ass, but I was so much hoping that you would do that!"

Me: I got a swell idea, how bout we do the nasty right here and see if we can git this gazillion dollar, super jet a rockin like we did in the olden days in our parents car at the drive-in?

Amanda: Cute idea except for the trained killers who would come bursting in with guns drawn all aimed at your head. I love you David, I have loved you from the first time we met. Thank you for your friendship and your passion for life and the people in it.

I will miss you and always remember you and think often of the lover I never had. If I ever get married again and have a boy child, I will name him, David J. Brown, the same as it reads on your book covers.

Please sit down for just another minute, I have a huge favor to ask you. I've been fibbin you a little bit as to why I'm here, but only in part. I asked Heather last week if you were healthy enough to do this, she said she wasn't really sure but if you're willing, that she would go along with it. With your approval of course, what I would like to do is a reenactment of sorts. I want to do a professional movie studio type video of you doing one final book signing, as you did at the Corker Hotel almost three years ago. I want my children to someday sit with me and watch their Uncle David in his glory days. I believe it will be the performance of a lifetime. So they can better know his namesake. Kick it around see what you think, the invitations have already been sent out and the film crew is on its way. This coming Saturday, (six days from now) we will, er…ah…you will be live!

All I could do is smile and say, "Yep I know there's also something going on with you, there's always something with you. I think it will be a blast, yeah I'm all in with that but don't think for a moment that you can play that at my funeral service and not have the strippers there. I guess you'll have to pay for some additional time in the funeral parlor."

CHAPTER 18
The Round Table

I thought especially now, with fall coming on perhaps we should move our activities into the Corker Hotel for the next week. There's a lot of great staff there that I have very much enjoyed over the last two years. Who knows, I may even want to go up to the penthouse to look things over, to see what changes were made. I'm glad Heather handed those keys over to Tim but I miss that place. Who knows, someday I may even want to buy it back if I live long enough. So it was a brief stop at the house. I gathered up the dogs and their toys, my and Heathers shower kits, and a couple changes of clothes for the both of us. The only place to all sit together is in a conference room or the garden. I asked for the garden because the conference room is just too stark without all those grease boards hanging in there. Times sure have been changing, almost too fast, but isn't that the thought of every dying man. We want to hold onto every last minute while the universe rushes by at warp speed. It wants to remind us that we are no longer the future, we are the past.

We had to have Building Maintenance come in and move a number of the big potted trees so we could sit at a convention size round table that would seat twelve .

Me: Okay, you guys called the ball and that's just fine as long as you understand that I carry that ball. capiche? Who wants to start where?

Norbs: Well I picked up on something just the other day, that you are somehow involved in the JonBenet Ramsey case, the beautiful little girl that was murdered in Boulder Colorado, twenty-six years ago.

Me: Let's step away from that bullshit that you picked something up! That's total bullshit. Yes, your people 'encrypted' and blocked out others from hacking into my systems but you all left a little back door open, just for yourselves. I don't need to see your heads nod, I know what you fuck you have all been doing and you've never stopped. So I have to guess that in part, is why you're all out here. Listen, I've actually written about this in my book that I'm currently working on. Of course you probably already know that the reason I got involved with the Ramsey case was that I was there. Not at the crime scene but I was there where her body was kept in the hospital morgue and I witnessed why they couldn't possibly prosecute the case from any evidence obtained from her body in the morgue. The chain of custody was not just broken, it was severed! That's the whole reason that I got involved and sent a three-page letter to all the principles involved. I was trying to give Colorado Governor Polis and the rest of them a boot in the ass and put pressure on the governor to order the DA's office to release the DNA data gathered at the victims home and from her body in the home. DNA processing has moved leaps and bounds from twenty-six years ago, to today.

When I was briefly involved with that on-line organization of Snopes last month, I think it was called the 'JonBenet Ramsey Snopes', a lot of people in that group wanted to tear up the family's lives and hearts. The finger-pointing and the blame game was just everywhere and multi-directional. I think that some of those long-time members of Snopes now want to point a finger at me. People are begging for closure but they don't want to go through the process. They just want to build a gallows on Broadway Avenue and hang somebody, anybody so they can jump on to the next fresh unsolved mystery and return to their sorted and pathetic little lives. I wanted to give the father, Mr. John Ramsay and his investigators , some level of valid evidence. I'm willing to testify to the condition of that morgue at the time I worked there. Yes, I also wanted to deeply shame Boulder Community Hospital for their unintentional complicity.

We can only hope that they have changed since then. At the time, those people should have been crucified for the disrespect they showed for the dead and the way they treated dead human bodies like it was nothing more than a kill floor at a meat market. It sickened me then and it sickens me now and in all honesty, I hope that every criminal case or every civil liability case that was prosecuted from any results obtained from Boulder Community Hospital Morgue be thrown out and anyone involved gets another trial but mostly, I want to make damn sure that that shit doesn't ever happen again anywhere in our country. Maybe I'm a little sensitive because I know someday that they're going to open me up like a dead deer as they will the rest of you when our times come. So that's pretty much that, I haven't had any threats come across that I'm aware of for speaking out about this terrible miscarriage of decency and justice, all because the hospital wanted to protect their bottom line. I need a nap.

I wasn't looking forward to this Q & A stuff to do what, document my final days and last nights of my life. I feel fine, just a bit tired is all. Hell, don't we all?

Besides, I have a little secret of my own and it's a beauty. My secret is that I've had this thing in the back of my mind for some time and now that a few of the principles are showing up uninvited, I think that maybe this plan just might work. I think at this point they're willing to do anything and everything for me.

I know it's a hell of a stretch but it sure as hell won't be the first time with these guys. Who knows, it may not even be the last time!

We were all in the hotel restaurant drinking coffee when the head maintenance man came into the restaurant to tell us that the table set-up in the garden was ready. And so was I.

CHAPTER 19
The Arm Twist

Well kids it's a little before noon, after we have this brief chat I expect we will all be meeting in the ballroom. Here's the deal, you all came here to support me true enough, but you all came here to get something from me, well there's something I want from you guys in return. I want you all to think back to the early times we first met. Did I ask any of you for anything for myself, anything at all? That answer for the most part is no. Yes I did ask you for your cooperation, yes I spent a shit-ton of your money and what you got was a very handsome return as well as being instrumental in changing a number of people's lives, your own included along with the other principals lives. We will never know the overall effect on the people that attended our first gathering. Well I believe at this time I will call in my marker. Do any of you truly think that I just did everything I did out of the kindness of my heart because I'm a man of the people or some other assorted bullshit like that? I had a master plan from the very beginning. That time is now, and it's going to be a doozy. It's no secret that

I'm operating under a limited capacity, that's a given. We all know that that's why you're here. Here's what I want you cats to do, you will contact all and I mean everyone of our principles that went through this whole thing at the beginning, along with the whole book signing thing and the lecture thing attendees yada, yada, yada. I want the other principals to meet us in the next 4 hours in the ballroom. I don't know what it's going to take for you to get your movie producing people and those other folks here but you better tell them to step it up. I'm not going to wait for anyone. Time is not my friend nor should it be yours. We're going to fast track the fuck out of this thing and I'm not going to tell you what this thing is until we get all of our principles together, so I suggest you all pull out your contact lists and decide who's going to call who. We best be having a rather large gathering at 4:00 this afternoon, tell them to bring their laptops, pens and tablets. We're going to get busy, damn busy!.......Tick-tock sweethearts, Tick-Tock!

I went to my room for a nap. Before I knew it there was a tap on the door. It was Heather with a guarded quizzical smile as she said, "I don't even dare ask you what the hell you just stepped in the middle of, but you got people bustling and busting butt. It's 3:30 and I understand that you have a 4 o'clock appointment? You might want to freshen up.

We strolled into the ballroom, I looked at close to twenty faces all with the same question and a healthy dollop of apprehension, maybe even a bit of excitement on their faces. I didn't greet anyone, I just said, "Let's get started, we don't have a lot of time. Excuse me, let me rephrase that, "You don't have a lot of time", so here it is, once again in a very large fucking nutshell.

Okay, most of you are from this area, most of you know the situation in the West End area of Duluth with it being a grocery and small business desert. Yes there is a movement afoot by a true visionary who is doing his damnedest to revitalize the West End, of course all the business sweethearts have renamed this part of the city as 'Lincoln Park' to break the negative image of the West End. As far as I'm concerned this is total bullshit, it's where I grew up. As a matter of fact, the entire revitalization is in the hands of just two or three people who are only interested in huge financial gains.

They have realized a relatively positive success with their investments. The problem is that these businesses are mostly restaurants, bars and Microbreweries. The area is teaming with pedestrians towards the evening hours. Most of those folks are locals from other parts of the city and tourists. It's a poor and rundown area with mostly junkies and gang bangers. We still have all the crackheads and other assorted junkies who are like sitting in the bleachers all around these new developments like cats watching a fishbowl. There are constant conflicts with aggressive panhandlers and strong armed robberies. Assaults are commonplace. At some point, there will be some serious if not deadly repercussions. Junkies and street people don't like successful people. They resent people that have money or a job. Hell they don't even like people who are like themselves and they don't like many of their own families. Our mayor forbids the police dept. to do press releases on the many assaults including stabbings and shootings. Why, because it's bad for business, we are dependent on tourist tax dollars. When there is a shooting or stabbing the standard press release with the suspect still at large will most often times read, "The parties are known to each other, it is believed that the public is not in danger." That's why we have so many beatings, shootings and stabbings. That and we are down 28 police officers because of our mayors mistreatment of the police, good cops either retire early, go to another police department and some just say, "fuck it" and turn in their badge. My point is that at some point a citizen legally carrying a firearm will legally defend themselves. A whole bunch of innocent people may get hurt or worse.

Amanda, you owe me, you all owe me. Does everyone remember how I never asked you for anything and you all prospered from what I delivered. I'm officially calling the outstanding debt due. This is how you will all repay me.

There's another part of the West End that used to be a vibrant part of our community. This is where I grew up. There were two small Mom & Pop grocery stores, three corner stores, a bakery, a full service pharmacy, two gift stores, a shoe repair shop, a dentist's office and a handful of other small shops and stores. They're all gone, now everything is empty. I want to see that change. The West End is currently a grocery store desert, there's nothing here anymore! I get it, I understand why, because all the drunks and junkies have taken over this area and nobody could stay in business. Retail theft is at an all-time high. This shit has been going on here for the last twenty years. People don't want to come into this area after dark, nor should they.

Well you people are going to change all that! Every bit of it. What I'm talking about Amanda, is the success of your grocery store program in the greater Chicago area which has been mimicked and brought to several other major cities all across this entire country. Well babe, I want one of those right here, right here in this area but I want to do it with a couple of different twists. In your Chicago stores we used young children as guides and shoppers assistance. This is going to be a little bit different. I want Junior High and Senior High students only, this time. I want, "at risk" kids. The kids that are at risk of dropping out of school and life itself. Either because they just quit on themselves or because of a broken home, family addictions or they've been incarcerated and believe they have no future. We're going to give them a future, these kids at this grocery store will stock shelves, they won't just be shoppers guides they're going to be employees and they're going to get paid a living wage. We will still have a classroom, we're going to have tutors as well, we're going to keep these kids in school. We're going to show them that they do have a future, we're going to empower them to become who they want to be. We're going to help them develop their dreams and more than just develop their dreams, we're going to teach them how to realize and live their dreams. So y'all wanted to know about my end game, well there it is. Pretty simple wouldn't you say? With one hell of a lot of work of course. There is an existing former grocery store which has been closed for several years on 27th Avenue West and 3rd Street. Well we're going to bring this store back to life and the other four buildings next to it. I understand that nobody here has time for this colossal undertaking. Stay with me on this. We're fortunate enough to have a small chain of grocery stores in this area and up on the Iron Range, I think they may have a few in Wisconsin too. This is a locally family-owned company and believe me when I tell you that the owners of this company are of this community, their hearts are of this community. They do a ton of charity work, not only public but with several very quiet private and personal donations for people in need. This family has also suffered personal tragedies with the loss of young family members. They personally understand the sorrow of a young person giving up on life.

    I'm going to romance them as best I can, to open that store under their own banner, all with their own management people. I just want a grocery store to serve the community where shoppers will feel safe. I hope to have two uniformed police officers to be there as the store is opened and to stay until the last employee leaves the parking lot each night. It's time these thugs move along and we are going to move them. I want young people to receive the validation necessary to believe that they too can thrive. Am I asking too much? Of course I am, remember you owe me, each and every one of you owe me, so you will want to break out your list of all your contacts you have from the book signing deal. And here is something else, we will again be doing book signings, as a draw but it won't be our sole purpose, the "Meet The Author's" and book signings events will be the breadsticks and salads before the main course meal, if you will. The main course will consist of bringing in some guests to give testimonials as to what brought their lives together and how that got them to where they are today. Amanda, I'm of course talking about the Chicago kids who worked in your Chicago area grocery stores. It's going to be an annual deal. It will be a two to three hour event. I will speak of my vision for no more than twenty minutes. Again I can't be involved in this to the depth I once was. I don't have the juice for it, but I do have the vision and if nothing else, my vision is crystal clear. I want to serve my community and the people that live here. I want to see them (the local children) prosper, with no other investment other than their own time and good behavior. I want those book signing people to be invited all over again. We have four universities within a twelve mile area. What's going to be different in this presentation to the public is the first several rows will be filled with local and national celebrities of all walks of life. TV and big screen folks, professional sports people and the like. Here me clear on this, no fucking politicians! You can and will set their little fannys on fire.

Amanda, you wanted to become a mini me? I don't believe you're in a position to do that. I think there's somebody here amongst you that is in the position to do that on this local level. Amanda I want you to go national, we need a local face for this event.

I'm leaving it up to you to choose who it'll be. I'm simply just the idea man, I'm not the doer man. Now if you don't mind it's time for our fur babies to have dinner and then I'm going to feed my wife. I expect to see the lights on in this room well after midnight, there's so much to do and so little time to do it. Oh, and I guess that you want to ask me when this all needs to happen, well this coming Friday morning. You have just five short days, I suggest you get to it!

    Tick Tock…Tick Tock

CHAPTER 20
I Won't Do It!

Amanda: David, I can't do that, it's not what I'm here for. You have some extremely capable people and you have to put them into play. I'm simply here to be with you. I will throw all of my political weight and finances towards this project but I can't be a part of it. I am just here to be a part of you and what is going on in your life. I hope you understand that? I need you to understand that. Let me tell you about some of my concerns, they're not just mine, they're also my family's concerns.

Do you think that maybe you're going a bit too far and that's on two fronts? The first question. Is your writing affecting your health? Secondly is your writing affecting your safety? You have gone after some big people and as you know, they could be quite dangerous.

Me: Yeah hun, I've got a pretty good idea of what I'm up against. My only concern is for Heather's safety. I know there's a lot of whack jobs out there.

Amanda: David I'm also concerned about your financial future as well. You have kicked off the lid to Pandora's box, once again! But this time, you've named names! You have taken on the mayor of your city, the mayor of Minneapolis, the Attorney General of Minnesota and the Governor of Minnesota. Honey, those people carry big sticks. Are you not concerned about financial loss with lawsuits for defamation or worse yet?

Me: I have trained all my life to deal with conflict and in some cases in combat. I'm as prepared as any man can be, I'm not fearful of retribution, at times I welcome it! As far as the financial consequences, I've mentioned before that I would love to have one of these dick heads come after me. I want them to file lawsuits as a matter of fact. I crafted a great deal of this last book, to do just that with, "The System Is Guilty-The Raping Of Lady Justice."

You shouldn't know any of that shit, you shouldn't have access to my stuff, but of course your backdoor builders and hackers did a hell of a job on my computer's and our phones and you probably have my house bugged as well, for all I know. Again, I fully understand that if these assholes come after me to shut me down, they're going to have to make mention of what has them all hot and bothered. They will have to expose themselves, then do it in a public forum complaint, and what does that do for me? It does two critical things, first it can be used to open an investigation. I don't think they want that. I think that's the last thing they would want, they just want to bully me and knock me down and tell me to stay down and walk away and go about their little sordid lives. Well you know damn well that's not going to happen. The other part is, they will claim that I damaged their character which opens another huge brass double door Investigation, that I hope to kick the fuckin hinges off those doors as well.

The real kick in the ass is that they have to try to expose me, they have to try to demean me, they will have to show that I'm just another whack job. How do they do that? By mentioning me by name and by mentioning the fact that I'm a published author and further having to make mention of my eight book titles that hurt their tender, tiny little feelers. That my child is publicity that nobody can afford, regardless of who you are! Yeah, I want to use those shit heads to sell my books. It's not about money or profit from my books, it's about getting my books distributed to the people that would have never known they existed or they probably wouldn't buy them. Once again, I write my books to reach people that have lived a life like mine and that's it. If I have to use these bottom feeders to do it, all the better. You see, it's like two-fers at a restaurant where you buy one, get one free! My books will have a much broader distribution. You know that my end game is about people finding freedom within their own lives. It's about people who are on the edge of that cliff with her toes dangling over the side. I'm trying to convince people to step back from the cliff and begin engaging in the life that they've always dreamed of, but didn't know that they actually could. It's pretty simple sweetie, there's nothing magical about me. We'll just call it a story of how a broken man was driven to deliver a better life to people like myself. So tell me, what's dancing in that pretty little skull of yours?

Amanda: I don't know David, I too am looking for some level of normalcy in my life. Yes, I know that people look at me as someone who has it all and in fact or at least in part, I did grow up and was raised in extreme wealth. I've lived my entire life of not wanting for anything and yet I feel this tremendous internal void. I have to tell you that I made some tremendous mistakes with Robert. I thought that he would fill the void within me. You're the one that kept telling me that it is an inside job. You knew what I was doing all along, hell you always know what everyone is doing and why they're doing it. How can you read people so clearly?

Me: It's not that I read them well, the real question that begs to be asked is to what avail? How do I reach these people that I read so well? You know as well as I, that people are reluctant to change and how they'll fight with you to not change, as miserable as they might be. Simply put, resistance is the only level of control that they believe they possess, it's the only thing that nobody can take from them. I see it all the time as well as you do in AA meetings. People want to make changes in their lives, they all want a better life but they have to let go of something to get something and what's the guarantee that what they let go of will be any better than what they get out of it? Is it really going to be any better, any different? You have to know that some of my very best sales pitches have to do with convincing an alcoholic that there is actually a better life ahead of them. As you and I both know, that better life doesn't just appear and it sure as shit doesn't come overnight. We have become a society of immediate rewards. "I want it, I want it now, because I deserve it!" Those may not be the very words they speak but that's what speaks to them from within. I don't have answers for any of that silliness. Let's get back to my AA friend Jerry and his constant reminder to all that listen, "Willingness is the key to sobriety!"

Baby, willingness is the one thing that I don't know how to deliver. I guess it comes down to the old adage, "When you get sick and tired, of being sick and tired, you'll make the changes necessary or you will perish." Well some people don't last long enough, some people go back out to their misery because they see no hope for a positive future. They will do all they can to avoid the disappointment of their failures from their own lack of trying. I guess I'd have to say many will embrace further disappointment in life, rather than take the challenge and risk of change. Don't get me wrong, you and I have both known people with long-term sobriety but neither of us could spend a day in their lives and stay sober. You notice how there's no rank in AA, no shoulder patches, and no lapel pins to self honor time served? Yeah, we have Medallions to celebrate years of sobriety but we don't march around to show our rank, we don't have hash marks on our sleeves and that's for a reason. And that reason makes perfect sense. If you set me up to be a leader, the first thing that happens is, I have to maintain my leadership to support my image and behaviors, which of course isolates me. It locks me down and now I'm playing look good games for other people and in the meantime, I'm not dealing with my own stuff. You and I have both seen over the years people with long-term sobriety that go back to the bottle. Why? I don't know those reasons, I don't think anyone knows those reasons other than they simply lost hope as they lost contact with themselves by trying to be all things for all people. It's all about maintaining an image even when your belly is on fire, it's a lonely and frightening place to be, when you believe that you have to deny your own humanism for someone else's wellness.

Youre falling into a very dangerous trap, life changing and perhaps even, life ending!

Amanda: Here's what's important for me. I want to learn from you, you get phone calls and emails daily and more than just one, when people will say, "Although we've never met, you've made a difference in my life." You respond to each and every one of those emails, I don't know how you keep up with it all and you're writing at the same time! Then I see you posting silly, nonsense on Facebook that gets a lot of laughs and even a lot of shares, all in the same day. How do you find the time for all of that? I will not mention that you've got a home, three animals and a woman to take care of. Don't you ever sleep?

Me: Honey it's all about respect. I will never meet 90% of my Facebook friends but yet they share their lives with me. I get some emails as you well know of course, from people who are in tremendous emotional pain. Who and what kind of person would ignore an email that says, "I'm hurting, I don't know which way to turn, I have lost the desire to live." I feel an obligation as a human being to respond to these people, other people like to tell me of their blessings and accomplishments in sobriety and then there are people who are not alcoholic, who will tell me how reading my books has made a difference in their lives. Of course I have to support that and of course to support that you continue to give them validation. As you well know, validation is that one gift that costs nothing to extend and it could mean the world to a broken heart with a lost soul. It's not that hard to understand. So now you want to ask me of course, why doesn't everyone do that for everyone else? Fuck, I don't know, we're all just people, we all have our own thing whatever that thing is. My thing is in part of my making living amends. Let's remember I have screwed up a lot of people's lives. I have broken promises, I've broken wedding vows, I am not what you'd call a, "Clean one owner" on a used car lot. *Capiche?*

So sweetheart what are the greatest emotional defense mechanisms put in play to avoid becoming vulnerable? I've witnessed and I often times use it myself, to turn the attention away from me. So now is the time that I ask you, what are you running from? You have an awful lot of questions and that's how you stay safe. You want to be standing with your toe on the sidelines, ready to jump into the game but you're sure you'll stumble and fall and embarrass yourself in front of the whole stadium of football fans! What is it that either you can't find about yourself or that you have found out and don't like about yourself? It seems to me that you have a bit of a struggle with balance.

Amanda: How is it that sometimes I feel so loved and protected by you and the very next moment you attack and pounce on me like a bloodthirsty mountain lion? How and why do you switch on me so quickly?

Me: Easy enough, it's what you need. That's the way I love you. I listened and I watch and identify what you need. You know me well enough to know that I'm going to give it to you, whether you want it or not. Our lives and needs are worlds apart, so I'm more than a bit lacking in social skills. Jesus Christ woman, in a large group you are the 'Belle of the Ball', everyone envies and watches you and they watch as you watch them. They watch how you move through a crowd, how you interact with people, they study your mannerisms, they watch your smile and your head nods. You are a very gracious woman but you hide behind every bit of that, but that's all your fluff. I won't call you a phony because you're not, I don't know if there's a name for what you do, so I'm asking you. What does Amanda's life and insides look like to you?

Amanda: David I'm trying to get all I can while I can still get it from you. I know that sounds selfish perhaps, I know it's almost cruel but I have to have some things to keep in my mind and heart, for when I can no longer have you. Please understand that?

Me: Oh so you are trying to fill your basket with goodies while at the very same time you're reaching for a bigger basket for even more goodies? You can't live in my home, you can live in my head and you can live in my heart but you can't live in my home. I'm not your answer man, I'm just a man. If you would have truly listened to me and you do want to carry any of my messages forward, do this. Amanda honey, do you, be you, that's your gift. That's what you can bring forward. Bring hope and live with hope. You can't carry me and no, Heather is not going to give you my ashes or have a limb removed so that you can encase it in a glass trophy case, like an autographed baseball bat! Sweetheart, you've already got the goods!

Okay, the deal with you and Robert was a piss poor decision. You went with your heart and your gut, somewhere you left your head out of the deal. Pick up your head and let it be a part of your process and control your emotions. Now tell me, what have you done as of late for the betterment of the fellowship of Alcoholics Anonymous and more directly, why are you sponsoring Norbs?

Amanda: David, she clings to me and it's exhausting. I have not been asked by her to be her sponsor nor have I volunteered! It's like she's a stray cat. I felt sorry for her and mistakenly put out a bowl of milk for her and now all she does is follow me everywhere I go. She gets really defensive, she gets really worried about nothing and she goes off to places in our conversations to where I can't even follow her and I sure as hell don't want to. In all honesty I've been avoiding her, I cut her short in conversations because she's such high maintenance. It's kind of like she's trying to capture me.

Me: Oh, like you're just doing right fucking now, with trying to capture me? You get that look off your face. Baby what you're speaking about is fear. You're afraid that if you let Norbs down that she may throw it all away and go back into the bottle and then you'll be the responsible party and it'll be all your fault because you wouldn't give her the time she needed, when she needed it? Do you really think that you're that fuckin powerful? Life's about choices, baby and we all get to make them. Give Norbs a reasonable amount of time but don't let her consume you and tell her that straight up! Your relationship with her has become a bit askew. Set boundaries and make it clear that you are the leader and she is to follow. Whatever you've been doing is not working for either of you. Get honest, fear robs us of our ability to properly deliver love. I know of some people who supposedly care about others but in truth they use honesty as a weapon to harm other people. You're not that kind of chick, so I'm comfortable with telling you to get honest with her and be direct. Her very life may depend on it.

Now on to you youngster. Yes I am diying, for the fucks sake woman, were all diying! I don't want anyone to witness me becoming a blithering idiot. Don't come to visit me when I cross over that threshold, I won't know who you are and all you will do is upset yourself. Remember me as the man who stole your heart and cupped your buns with both hands!

All this time Heather was sitting with us and did not say a word. She knew that Amanda needed this time. Heather stood and wrapped her arms around Amanda as she said, "It's time for us girls to have a hug and a good cry. Unlike my roommate here, I promise that I won't cup your buns!"

The three of us walked down to the shoreline of Lake Superior holding hands. We stopped at a candy store on the way back to the hotel. Heather said that she had to attend to the dogs and we only had forty minutes until the next presentation.

I wanted to continue with my and Amanda's conversation but it would have to wait. The afternoon presentation and book signing went well. As in the morning book signing, people bought several copies of each of the author's books as gifts for friends and family to support the scholarship fund.

When I finished signing, Amanda and I returned to the garden to finish our previous conversation.

Amanda: David, can we kind of take a break from all this heavy stuff? I want to ask you about Granny. The whole world is in love with Granny and you are as well. Tell me about your relationship with Granny. I've got the basics of how you met Granny but what's your deal with Granny.

Me: Better yet sweetheart, what's Granny's deal with me? Granny is an adorable old doll who is one of those women that you just know is to be respected and admired. Like everyone else in this area west of Lake Avenue, which is the dividing line of our city between east and west. It's also the dividing line between the working class and the privileged professionals. The shakers and movers are on the east, the blue collars are on the west. There is not and never was any industry on the east end. The two classes don't mix with the other side of the city. They have a different culture and a different work ethic. Sweet ole Granny being in the western part of the city grew up hard. She knows what it's like not to have even the very necessities in life. She's learned what it's like to do with what you have and if you don't have it, you humbly ask for it to feed your family and you pay it back. If you do have it, you graciously offer and share it. That's a whole story of true character, just right there.

Granny is my friend's Matt's grandmother. I had to get permission by the way, to call her Granny.

Maybe you shouldn't be calling her Granny, you're assuming an awful lot with your acting like you're allowed, like you have permission to call her Granny. Maybe you need to ask Granny for permission, as a matter of fact, I'm going to call Granny and you and I are going to go for a little road trip. It's only a couple miles from here, I want you to meet Granny, I sense your curiosity is more than just, "Who is Granny?" She's somehow hooked your interest.

Amanda: I hope to hell you're not talking about right now, Christ Almighty give me a few minutes to breathe. The way you jump around hurts my head, it hurts my neck too. I'm always willing to look at whatever the hell you're pointing at and talking about but damn you, you exhaust me!

Me: Baby girl, you love it. You love being a part of something bigger than yourself. I just find it humorous that an old broke down joker like me can hold your interest or anyone's interest for that matter. I'll just give you the end of the last time I spoke with Granny. I had contact with her (of sorts) a week ago, via her grandson Matt. Matt came over to help me remove some landscape blocks that he said he could use them at his house, I told him to have at it. We have rhubarb that is stupidly out of control and mowing the lawn around it is a bitch in that area. In the winter time, we snowblow our backyard in our dog run which is quite sizable, so the dogs who are just little teeny short guys, don't have to hop through the built up snow. After we got the back of Matt's truck loaded and as a way to show my appreciation to him, we had coffee and a few cookies. I also gave him the latest copy of my book, signed it and asked him to give it to Granny. Matt's not what you'd call a reader unless it's a beer label to see which custom brewery made it and the alcohol content. Don't get me wrong, I'm not hacking on him, I see Matt as a close and trusted friend. So a few days later, Matt came by and said that he gave my book to Granny and Granny has something she wants me to have. So Matt brings on his most delightful shit eating grin followed with a delighted chortil as he hands me this business card if you will, with the title that reads;

"10 reasons for swearing."

Number one: It pleases mother's so much.

Number two: It's a fine mark of manliness.

Number three: It proves that I have self control.

Number four: It indicates how clearly my mind operates.

Number five: It makes my conversation so pleasing to everybody.

Number six: It leaves no doubt in anyone's mind as to my good breeding.

Number seven: It impresses people that I have more than an ordinary education. Number eight: It's an unmistakable sign of culture and refinement.

Number nine: It makes me desirable especially among women and children.

Number ten: It's my way of honoring God who said, "Thou shalt not take the name of the Lord thy God in vain."

    Yep, that's Granny's way of saying to me, "I wish you would grow up!"

She loves my writing, she just hates the language I use. Seriously, would you like to meet Granny?

    Amanda: Somehow I get the feeling that Granny very much adores you, I don't think I want to mess with Granny. I think she'd come at me like a honey badger if she thought for a moment that I was disrespecting you.

    Me: Good read babe, yeah I think she would, she just wishes I would clean up my language a little bit but yeah, she's a very nice woman and she gets it because she too, has been there.

    Well now what do we do ? We can't go see Granny now that you fucked that up for me. What's next, do you want to get out of here? You have to admit that this is a pretty neighborhood as we're sitting on this perch overlooking the Bay of Lake Superior. Admittedly, I too get bored with it at times. Let's do something to change both of our moods. What do you say we just roll down to Lake Avenue where all the tourists are packed shoulder to shoulder and bounce in and out of all the trendy shops? Mostly I want to make your security people go crazy. There's a hell of a cool candy store down there that imports stuff from all around the world and they make all kinds of stuff in chocolate. There's a couple of bakeries, lots of clothing stores along with lots of touristy souvenir shops. We could just go sit somewhere at an open air coffee shop, drink coffee and people watch.

Amanda: I know I'm being selfish but I don't want to share you. I just want to observe you.

Me: What better place to observe me but in public around other people who are observing you, that's some funny shit don't you think? How long do you plan on gracing me with your presence? Did you say a week? Jesus Christ that will be the longest week of my entire life! Let's do this, there's a special antique glass dome train that was pulled by steam engines back in the day. I remember watching the old steam engines operating daily when I was a little boy. Now it's a big deal for the tourists to get on these trains that take them twenty-six miles up to Two Harbors. The tracks run right along the shoreline of

Lake Superior and you can see a lot of the old rustic commercial fishing net boats and camps, there's also several old logging camps all along the way that are now popular tourist traps with overflowing parking lots every summer and fall day. Minnesota has more than just one deciduous tree, there are at least fifty species of leaf trees, and at least another fourteen types of pine needle trees. I can't name them all but the different colorations are mesmerizing as you drive in the country. It's not like Colorado where you get two shades of green and one shade of rock. Unless of course that rock is called gold or silver. It would be kind of fun to find some of that shit. You want to play tourist?

I could stand to catch my breath away from all these swell folks. How about it babe? You better be sure to hit the ATM before we leave the city. Everything you are going to look at will cost big money. You have to remember that our tourist season is only five months long. These Mom & Pop shops got to get it while they can. Then I guess we have to make a stop at Betty's Pies. I don't know how the hell we're going to get off the train to make a stop or two, so we can go get some pies. But then again, you got some muscle with you, that can get pretty much anything you want. Let's do this, let's take the train up along the shore and have one of your pals drive my truck up to Two Harbors and you and I will drive back alone. Just me and you in my truck and the muscle men can lead or follow in those color changing muscle cars they tool around in. They can do whatever they want to do, but I'll call the ball as to where we stop. We will definitely go to Betty's Pies. There are also a lot of smoked fish and cheese shops up there as well as smoked, fresh caught Lake Superior trout and salmon.

As a kid I remember having smoked Cisco's wrapped in newspaper and soda crackers. Dress warm, I don't think that those rail cars are well heated.

CHAPTER 21
The Pitch

Ladies and gentlemen, good morning. I'm happy to report that today's three author sessions and the next two days, three hour sessions are all sold out. The four local authors will speak on their crafts and will be selling their books and signing their works at each show. Your four local authors, including myself, are donating the entire list price of our books to a very special college fund that you are about to learn of.

Folks, I'm here to tell you a story. I'm here to tell you about a man who thought he had no place in life, both as a child and later in life as a man. A man who thought he needed to leave this world to find peace. That child and now man, belongs to the voice that is speaking to you now. I'm here to tell you about a dream, but before my dreams there were many years of constant nightmares and those nightmares define impart, the man who I am today.

My adult dreams started as an uninvited haunting demand. Many of you have heard or read the story in my books.

But now, I want to tell you my story, in the first person. This is my story, in part.

In 2009 my mother passed away. I drove the 1,180 miles from Longmont, Colorado to Duluth, Minnesota for my mother's funeral. I had only planned on spending three days in Duluth and then returning to my home in Colorado. The things that transpired during those first three days turned into a ten day stay and the start of my true life's mission.

Today, I stand before you as a seven time published author and I am soon to complete my eighth and final novel. Prior to my mothers death, I have never, at any point in my life, had a desire to write a book let alone to become a published author! I struggled to complete a grocery list, prior to my Minneasota trip. Yes I'll be signing my books today and if you would like, you can pre-order my eighth book. That book title which I'm here to speak to you of this morning as well as during my other sessions. My in-progress novel is titled, "Betrayed … My Body is Killing Me."

Let's get back to my main story. A number of things took place when I was in Minnesota for my mothers funeral. I noticed that my stepdad (who I've known for over forty years and was actually a good friend of my father's before he passed) was failing. It was obvious to me that he had stepped over the threshold and well into the arena of dementia. Perhaps deeper than even I realized and that's what told me I needed to be here longer. I was honored to do my mother's eulogy at her funeral and as we all do, we may exaggerate a bit in our remembrances. In my case I went a bit over-the-top. Perhaps that is how I wanted my mother to be remembered just in my own mind and heart.

Something magical took place during my mother's funeral visitation. I was blessed with the presence of my secret, lifelong love. We hadn't seen each other at that time, for more than six years but there she stood at my mother's funeral service. It was no secret that she was there solely to support me and I fully knew it. When I approached her to say hello, I reached out to her, she came into my arms, but she didn't hug me, she held me. And for the first time in my entire life, I felt whole and I felt safe. I guess the word for that is I felt loved and I knew that my life was about to change. But that's not the only unexpected change, there was more, there was a lot more.

On my return trip back to Colorado, I had to stop for gas in Sheridan, Wyoming. As I was filling my gas tank I looked at a mountain face with a sheer cliff several hundred feet high. It seemed nearby but of course we need to understand that at that altitude everything looks much closer than it actually is due to the thin air. One of the things about Colorado and Wyoming is that neither hosts pollution for very long. The air is clean and clear.

Well, as I looked at that mountain face, something told me that I had to go to it. I had to stand in front of it, I had to touch it. Now please understand that I have always been respectful of people's property, even when no one was looking. I was an avid bowhunter and hunted all the big game species in the Colorado Rockies for forty years. I deeply loved my mountains, and I trust that I've stepped where no man have ever stepped before. The more rugged the better, the more pristine the better, it was my Zen time if you will.

That Wyoming mountain face didn't just beckon to me, it didn't just call to me, it demanded that I respond. I found a frontage road, it took me to a dirt forest access road and eventually brought me to what's called a, 'cattle guard'. A cattle guard is like a small bridge across a private road leading to a public road and visa-versa. Cattle guards are usually made of old heavy solid steel or old railroad tracks spaced about four inches apart. Cattle won't step or walk on steel. The guards are to keep the cattle from crossing over and yet making the roadway passable for vehicles at the same time. As I got to the first cattle guard there were several signs posted that read, "Private Property." With further warnings of what may happen if you came on the private property. Such as, "Trespassers will be shot, survivors will be shot a second time." Well that was always my turnaround point even without the threat of personal body harm. No matter where I was, whether anyone was around or not, it was just something I never did or have done. But on this day, the beckoning was stronger than my moral code. I've never violated anyone's personal property until that day and moment. I drove across that cattle guard and followed the road for perhaps another thousand yards. It took me quite close to that mountain face. I had to step out of my vehicle and walk less than 100 feet before I was standing in front of that sheer cliff. What it reminded me of was when I was a little kid attending parochial school. They had huge statues of the Apostles all over the school, when I would try to look up at the faces of the statues I would almost fall over backwards. This mountain face was no different, it was like looking at those statues all over again.

To this very day, I still can't tell you what took place. Whatever did happen, is not in my memory.

Please note that I'm not a religious man. I live a spiritually based life and sometimes a rather loosely spiritually based life. But that's as far as I go with that whole God and religion thing. My God is personal and private. However, I share him with anyone that has an interest in entertaining a God of their own understanding.

I don't know how long I was in front of that sheer wall but when I came out of whatever trance I was in, I found myself on my knees with my hands pressed in prayer. That is not how I pray. I don't know if I actually prayed or received a blessing. I got to my feet and took one last long look at that mountain face. As I looked down at the dirt I saw my knee prints in the blow sand. I turned and walked back to my car through the Yucca and Sage brush. Just as I opened my car door and was ready to step in, I glanced back at the wall and I heard the voice. I don't know was it my mother's voice who just passed away giving me permission to tell the truth, or was it even God perhaps? The voice clearly said, "David, you must write the book."

Well none of that made any sense to me because I'm not a writer. I'm not intelligent enough to be a writer, I don't have the education or skills to be a writer. What book am I to write? I still had 140 miles left to get to home and that stayed in my head the entire drive. When I arrived in my city of Longmont, late that afternoon, I drove past my home and went directly to an office supply store. I bought a large package of yellow legal pads, along with a five pack of gel ink pens. I went home knowing that I have to write a book.

But I don't know how to write a book. All I knew is that it would be a monumental undertaking. I knew it wouldn't ever come to fruition because that's not me, I'm not a writer. I struggle with just writing a grocery list and now I'm going to write a book? I have no knowledge, and again no skills. I felt that God was bullying me.

I started to wonder if maybe I had, "White line fever" like over-the-road truckers talk about. After all, I did drive the 1,280 miles straight through, without as much as a nap! Maybe that entire mountain face thing was just a colossal hallucination!

I don't take much pushback, as a matter of fact, I never in my adult life have ever stepped back. I step forward and sometimes I push harder than I probably needed to but nobody pushes me.

So I sat at the dining room table with my gel pen twirling in my fingers looking at a blank yellow legal pad, waiting for inspiration.

In truth, I already had the inspiration, I just didn't have the courage, I didn't believe in myself. All

I've ever had in life was a powerful body and a commanding voice. As a police officer, only a very few dared to challenge me, the ones that did, regretted it. I was still that same man without a badge. However when it came to an internal emotional challenge, I was all show and no go. I acted as though I was in control and could handle anything but the man inside of me was just a bunch of fluff. I was just as scared as an adult as I was as a child after my beatings. I never knew what comfort was, I never knew what trust was. The worst truth that I hid within myself was that I never knew what love was. Even though I was married five times to five wonderful women who all thought that they could somehow fix me. It took me several years to accept the fact that the fix comes from the inside, not the outside. I knew that I would have to take myself to task if I wanted to experience any true freedom from self doubt.

It took me three days before I was able to put ink to paper but I did sit for countless hours trying to figure out how am I going to do this and then the big question of, "Why am I doing this?" That was the real question. What, because I was told to by a voice I didn't recognize by someone who may be more of a dream than a reality? Maybe I've really lost it this time, maybe the crazy came to visit and decided to stay?

It took me three years to write my first book. I would dabble with it and become frustrated, set everything aside for a few days or even a few weeks. I never Googled anything about how to write a book and the idea of publishing a book was nowhere near any form of reality. I would periodically revisit my notepads, I would jot a few things down that actually made no sense to me at the time. My handwriting was so poor that I couldn't even read what I had just written, so that in itself was a hell of a challenge. Being a remedial student all my life, I didn't have a lot of tools to work with and even fewer skills but with the loving grace of God, at the end of three years, I quietly completed my first book, "Daddy Had to Say Goodbye." I didn't know anything about publishing and nothing about distribution. I just thought it would lay in a 3-ring binder and at some point, it would find its way to the trash. Towards the end of completing my book, I knew that if I wanted to make any of this legitimate, it had to at least be printed rather than the sixty-eight legal pads lying curled up in a binder.

My two dearest friends and roommates in Fort Collins, Colorado (my wife tossed me out two days after I returned from my mothers funeral) both had some very attractive computer skills and knowledge. One day my roommate suggested that I buy a computer. Now understand that my fingers would turn into hooves whenever I would go near a keyboard. I didn't know how to type and I didn't know how to use a computer. I didn't know how to use any of the simplest of commands. I see people do all these trick things of having several screens open on the same screen and do back and forth stuff but I don't get any part of that. It wasn't my era, computers of any kind were still almost twenty years away when I was in school. As a matter of fact, if a boy in school took a typing class he was tagged as being a little limp in the wrist. In all truth, I would have taken a typing class if it was strictly for bullies, of which I was. I just knew that I wasn't smart enough to learn how to type because I didn't know how to read or spell. Some people use the term over-reaching, for me that would have been a monumental reach. Well, I found myself standing in the middle of Best Buy with my friends, looking at different laptops. I of course had no input. I had little money but was willing to spend my last dollar to at least make my last three years of struggling not be in vain. They found a pretty good deal on a laptop and then of course I had to get all these other programs and I'm looking at them going, why? I don't know how to use them, I don't have time to learn to use them, Christ I'm already 62 years old, what do you expect from me? It's too late for me to learn all this! They wouldn't hear that argument, not for a moment because they knew me and they loved me! They knew that what I've been doing was of value, a much greater value then I even realized. So I brought home a $800 laptop computer, it was nothing more than a doorstop in my mind. My pal God, takes a great deal of pleasure in pranking me. One fine day and if I didn't mention this before I will now, I'm an alcoholic, I'm an alcoholic in sobriety. I've been sober for more than thirty-one years with the grace of God and the principles of Alcoholics Anonymous. I attended five meetings a week, every week. Well I went to an AA meeting one night and a few people who knew that I was writing a book, introduced me to a fellow AA member from out of the local area. I had seen her a very few times in the last several years. She said, "I understand that you are a first time author?" I replied, "Author, what are you talkin about, author? Yeah, I wrote a book but I don't consider myself an author, all I have is a three ring binder with a bunch of legal pads." The woman said, "Perhaps you should."

She invited me to coffee early the next morning. I met her for coffee and she asked me if I knew what she did for a living? Of course I had to say no. She smiled as she said, "I am a literary agent, I want to talk to you about your book that you've written. Your roommates are quite impressed with your work! Tell me more of your writing.

Suddenly it's well past the noon hour in the same restaurant in the same booth. Over lunch she explained to me the entire publishing process. To me it was mind-boggling at best. I don't know how it all transpired but she said, "I want copies of your entire book and all of your rough notes. Hold your originals but I want a copy of every page that you've written." She then told me that our chance meeting last night was a set up. She had been a close friend to one of my roommates for several years. I think it took less than two weeks before she sent me an email that read, "This attachment is your book typed and formatted, your sister in sobriety, Lois."

I wasn't quite sure how to open an attachment, luckily one of my roommates was there as I asked, "How do I open this damn thing?" She just smiled and with a little chuckle, took my mouse and clicked on the attachment. I know that sounds pretty remedial doesn't it, but that was the entirety of my computer skills at that time. So, up popped a copy of my book, the whole book! I was startled to see the cover page with the title of, "Daddy Had to Say Goodbye" with my name in 18pt. type, I felt like I was going to have a stroke, whatever a stroke feels like. I think I was very close to it. I am not a crier at least publicly but on that day, at that moment, I publicly wept, like a child.

Only then did I realize that I had the dream and the dream had just come to fruition. For the first forty-three years of my life I didn't dare to dream, I knew better than to dream. Dreaming gets you nothing but hurt. Dreaming does nothing but bring more pain.

Dreams are for suckers and children, not for men. At least not for men my age.

So that was the beginning of my journey twelve years ago. I was a man with a stack of yellow legal pads, a pack of gel ink pens and nothing more. Today I am about to become an eight time published author. Yes, I've written eight novels all with the assistance and guidance of a loving God. I have had a lot of help along the way, without question. Today I actually own my own website, not a web page but an actual website. I would now like to inform you and this will be the first time I've mentioned anything publicly, that I have signed a contract with a voice actor to bring my books into the audio book format. Who woulda ever thunk it? I have to remind myself daily and oftentimes more than once during that day that I'm living the dream afforded me by the God of my understanding and again, the principles of Alcoholics Anonymous. So please understand that if you hear nothing else of our time together today please know, "That dreams are worth dreaming." I never dreamed that I could or would become an author. It's still hard for me to pronounce that word author. It still sounds funny and so distant. I never became an author to realize profit. I never dreamed that my writing would allow me to buy a new car. I never dreamed I could have a bank account that I didn't have to check twice a day to make sure I still had money. I never dreamed that my writing would affect people in the way it has. I never dared to dream because I couldn't take the disappointments, but I did take a risk and I developed a dream and since that day to this, I've been living that dream that I will call, "My blessing."

You all know that we're here to support a new project to bring grocery stores and other small businesses into the West End of Duluth. Or if you want to call it Lincoln Park feel free, please just support our project.

There's another reason why we're here today, or at least why I'm here. I have to announce that my current book (that is close to publication) must be my last book. I'm 74 years old and my mind and body is becoming my enemy. I have crossed the threshold into Dementia. I am no longer the man or the writer that I once was, just two short months ago. It will kill me at some point, it's the same for all of us. Going back to my childhood way of not letting people overwhelm me, (big people, rich people, mean people, all kinds of people) was when I came to the understanding that everyone poops and everyone dies, and when we do die, we will all be going into the same size hole. When I came to that realization in my youth, it was my first taste of freedom and with knowing that, it told me that I no longer need to be afraid of people, guarded yes, but no longer afraid. Today as I stand in front of you and no disrespect meant but I personally don't give a shit what people think of me. Oh I do have my values, believe me and I voice them on a very regular basis in my writings and in my everyday life because I think it's important.

Back to my book. This will be my last work because I no longer have the mental, emotional, or physical abilities to continue on. My bucket list has never changed. It's always been the same. I've never been interested in going somewhere special (other than seeing my books on a shelf at The U.S. Library of Congress) seeing something special or meeting someone special. That's never been any part of what a bucket list should be, at least for me. My bucket list falls in line with my writing and my driving spirit of, "If I can just reach one soul!" I write to help people like me, who have lived like me, with mental and emotional secrets like me. I write to help people find the same freedoms, perhaps even more freedom than I have, within themselves. I write to save lives, I write to bring people from the darkness back into the light to where they know they're valued and for them to trust that there is a place for them and that place is wherever they're standing at the moment. That's their place and they can move left, right, up or down if they so choose. In line with, "If they so choose" I'm going to ask you now to please choose to support the grocery store program in the West End of Duluth. It's not just about bringing a grocery store into the neighborhood, it's about giving young people an opportunity to realize their value. To help them perhaps for the first time to develop their own dreams from their own experience. The support has been overwhelming up to this point by several different organizations and that's wonderful. Organizations are critical to this mission but people, people are absolutely the most critical and those are the people that I'm looking at right now listening to my voice. You are the people we desperately need. We need your help, we need your support, we need your financial support, we need your emotional support, we need you to tell your friends and your family of our mission. You need to tell them that there are young people out there suffering and if we don't rescue them, they will drown in the world of extreme sadness and loneliness and in many cases these young teens will die with a syringe in their arms, lethal drugs in their bodies along with knife and bullet wounds. They will fail because we have failed them! I don't believe anyone volunteers to become a victim, I believe everyone is victimized in various ways at some point in our lives but most all recover with little measurable damage.

We need to show these young people that there's always another avenue, there's another route, just because something doesn't work, doesn't mean that it's not workable. It just needs to be refined a bit.

So the end game is, I want these children to have the tools and the belief that they can properly use those tools to succeed in life. We can't look to the police department to solve all of our lives' many ills, this is our task, yours and mine. On a side note and quite importantly, the kids in our program will receive a full ride scholarship from the University of Minnesota, College of St. Scholastica And the University of Wisconsin.

I can see by your facial expressions that several of you are quick listeners and thinkers. You just heard me mention that these students involved with our program will get full ride scholarships to three different local universities. Well if all of that is true, about the full ride scholarships, then what warrants a second scholarship program? Hear me out please. The children that we are talking about here, in most cases don't have broadband service in their home. They don't own laptops, they don't own PCs or tablets or cell phones. They are lucky just to have the lights on and hopefully heat for the brutal winters of northern Minnesota.

The scholarships that I'm asking you to support has to do with supplying these children with the proper, standard electronic equipment that your family enjoys, whether those be tablets or laptops. We expect these children to perform and compete at a Junior year, high school level but they can't possibly compete because they are hamstrung by extreme poverty. We've got to help bring them up to a par level with their fellow classmates. Understand that they have siblings behind them and these siblings have to be prepared as well. If not, we're going to fail and we will fail the entire family. That's why the request for the extra donations and remember, your authors are donating all of their books at the full retail price to this project. I hope you people will do the same.

I want to thank you all for coming this morning to support our future, our children and our country.

I will be taking a short break and I will return to sign my books and again you can pre-order my eighth and final novel, "Betrayed My Body is Killing Me" at any one of the purchase tables.

CHAPTER 22
Getting All You Can

I spoke a bit longer than I intended to and I had difficulty managing the stairs to walk off the stage. For whatever reason there was not a handrail on either side of the stairs. I felt like I was at risk of falling down the stairs. Either it was because of the way I was walking or because they just know me that well, but Heather and Amanda both bolted up to the stairs and each took my arms. I needed to lean on them to help me down the stairs and help me walk into the garden area. Just as I sat down there was a tap on the glass door. It was my buddy Ms. Tami from the bookstore with a rolling cart along with several different juices and fruits. She said, "I don't mean to interrupt but you look like you could use a pick-me-up. I'll talk to you later." She leaned over and gave me a kiss on my cheek and left.

Heather: Honey, there's some questions that Amanda would like to ask you. In all honesty, with my being a selfish brat too, I would like to hear those answers as well.

Me: Well I know I'm amongst friends, so yes, ask away, anything you'd like.

Amanda: David I don't know if you should be doing any more signings or speaking, it seemed to take an awful lot out of you.

Me: Honey I appreciate your concern but I'll decide if I'm up for it and no one else. Let's remember that these kids have one chance, all they may ever have, is this one chance in life to get on the right path. I've got day's after this event to recover.

Amanda: David, please tell me about your facebook friend, Kevin Cudbertson.

Me: Kevin is a Facebook and a personal friend of mine from the UK. He's also a good man and a good parent and obviously a good spouse. He is a highly respected, top-level rescue paramedic from Sedgwick, UK. He has trained a great number of young people just completing their education in EMS before they're given their assignments as paramedics. Kevin and I have spoken on the phone I believe on two occasions and we share a number of emails back and forth, he's just a tremendous guy.

Well it was almost a year ago that Kevin and the people he worked with were promoting a fundraising project to purchase portable defibrillators to place them in public places. Kevin's crew on his Ambulance Service were very active with their fundraising, so I sent him a case of my books, "Daddy Had to Say Goodbye" and told him to use them anyway he saw fit to help them raise funds. Well they had a fundraising auction event and they sold all of my books. One of the young people that Kevin worked with was named Leslie. Leslie had developed a heart condition of some sort that became quite serious in a very short period of time. She knew that there was little hope for her to see her next birthday. She was the one that was spearheading this whole thing about having portable defibrillators in public places. Not for her of course but for those she would have to leave behind. Need any further testimony as to what bravery and character may look like?

Well Kevin contacted me on August 10th of this year to tell me that his friend Leslie, had passed away on a Thursday. The following day, the very next day, a 17 year old boy in Sedgwick went into cardiac arrest and one of the portable defibrillators that Leslie fought so hard to put in public places was used to save that 17 year old boy's life!

Yes, I am blessed to be associated with people such as Kevin and his crew. That's why I do what I do, there's no other reason.

I know there's people like me and you always tweak your eyes somehow like "What do you mean people like me?" Simply baby doll, people like me are those that oftentimes lose their strength because they gave too much of it away, sometimes I feel that there's nothing left for me. There are times I truly do feel a void and then something like Kevin's note comes at the time that those voids are having their way with me, those times re-energized me. Yeah, I'm blessed in my experiences, I receive blessings because I make the attempt to be blessed. It's like that Canadian hockey great, I don't recall his name right now but he said something to the effect that he will miss 100% of the shots that he never takes! I believe it's Wayne Gretzky. How fucking profound is that? If you don't put yourself in the play you're not going to get any results. So I try to make people want to have results! I want to share what was so freely given to me. Simple enough babe?

Amanda: David, do you ever cry?

Me: Do you ever stop asking questions? Why do you find it important that you break me down? I no longer do that lower lip quiver stuff. I do often times, find tears of joy for others. Most of those 'joy' tears are for others that are in the process of finding their way. For me, a smile is a dry tear. How in the fuck can I not be happy when a person in AA obtains 30 days, three, six, nine months, a year and multiple years of continues sobriety. You know that living sober is just not about not drinking! As you do well know, It's about regaining self-control, self-respect, dignity, and honor. We earn the blessed opportunity to regain the trust of family and friends, if we do what is suggested in the steps of recovery. But you don't want these easy answers, you want to dig around in my guts in hopes to find that secret key to unleash the hidden and well protected emotional release buttons. You're not getting it baby, you're not getting it, listen to me when I say that I'm ok with dying. Your questions are not about me, it's about your comfort. Baby look and listen to me, if you want or need to sit on my lap, hop on. You and the people close to us know as well as my readers know of my extreme blessings and the pain from whence they came. Of course the Phoenix arising from the ashes comes to mind to most people but it wasn't that way for me, for the first several years. My early sobriety was more akin to a crow that got caught in a snow and hail storm, crashed into a tree and lost a few feathers, fell to the ground and lost a few more feathers and fucked up my foot. That storm may have kicked the shit out of me but here I stand with fewer feathers perhaps but none the less, I'm still a crow!

Sweetheart, I've cried a number of rivers and filled a few ponds without names, all before I was twenty years of age. If each tear could be turned into a pearl, I could outfit every woman in this city with a string of pearl necklaces along with matching earrings. I know that we've talked about that a bit before. Some people like to say that crying is the way of cleansing the soul. I'm okay with my soul today. All right, what's your other question?

Of course the tears of deep hearted shared love flowed for the both of us.

It reminded me of my chance meeting with Stephen King where we sat in private and he told me, "Celebrate your blessings and speak of them often."

Amanda: David, when you were talking about that cattle guard and how you've never violated anyone's private property, I saw something in your eyes that was quite different. I didn't know what it was but I believe it was some form of affirmation. Correct me if I'm wrong, what was that look I saw?

Me: Babe you try to read too much into too much. What I was trying to do is control myself from not speaking further on cattle guards. Remember, well you're pretty young maybe you don't. Back in

2014 the then, President Barack Obama was doing a press conference just a few days before the elections. He was talking about his plan to balance the budget. He mentioned that there are more than 100,000 cattle guards in Colorado on the federal payroll. Well according to the story, Obama was already frustrated with the ranchers for their protests about proposed grazing policy changes and fees. Obama wanted to fire half of the cattle guards as a cost savings. VP Biden stepped forward to suggest that they not fire all the cattle guards but instead, give them six months of retraining. Well from there, the damage control people realized the stupidity of both Obama and Biden and came up with a story that said, 'it's a long-standing joke among the politicians.' It was no joke, I watched both of those assholes in that live news conference. I so much wanted to make mention of that today but my political agenda belongs nowhere in this project so what you saw me doing was biting my tongue and chewing the inside of my cheeks as best I could, but God damn it, I so wanted to!

Amanda: I feel bad for not having Norbs sitting here with us but there's times when she gets to be a bit of high maintenance. I was questioning if you're thinking that I'm doing the right thing. I'm not even officially her sponsor. She's afraid to get a sponsor, what do I do with that?

Me: That's simple enough, tell her to get a fucking sponsor or just to leave you the fuck alone. She's working you over, don't let her get away with it. But now my lady, we've got to talk a bit about you.

Sweetheart, here's what you're doing and I'd like you to stop it. All of the time that we spent on that train you have placated me and all but bowed to my every want, word and suggestion. You needn't do that, you have a right to take your own stand on all issues, you've always had that right, Jesus Christ woman, you have swung deals with world powers and now you're going to just collapse and let me walk all over you? How am I to respect that? Stop doing that to yourself, you're worth more than that. Much more!

Amanda: David I'm sorry, I'm watching you and I guess I just have to say it, I'm watching you fail, not in what you do but I'm watching your body fail you and it just breaks my heart. I know the next time that I see you, it'll be worse for you and I know it'll be worse right up, right up until the end and it just kills me.

Me: Baby here's a lesson in life that I was taught many years ago when I was a young police officer. I had applied to be on the department's SWAT team. The only openings they had was for an alternate on the perimeter team. They already had two fully staffed entry teams so I knew I was never going to probably get to the top level and in all honesty, these people spend way too much time training which would of course take away from the other parts of my life. I wasn't willing to make that sacrifice but I still wanted to be part of the deal. The department I was with, used a forward team which is kind of a misnomer because we actually are the back team. When we go into gang controlled or rough neighborhoods it's nothing but wall-to-wall assholes and bad guys. You need to have a specialty team to protect the SWAT members. So we would stand with our backs to the suspect's house or building, whatever it was. We would face the crowd because there's always empathizers that want to make themselves look like tough guys. You want to be sure that nobody tries to embed themselves and attack your team, when they have their backs to them. That is where the term, "I got your back" comes from. Well I was almost at the end of my training and I'd already done one short, three story 'tower jump' where you kick off of a roof or window sill, swing away from the building free falling (but tethered to a rope) and crash through a glass window. It's a high-risk maneuver where you expect to get cut by glass and probably shot. It's only a last resort to rescue hostages.

    Well, just before I hooked up to earn my final certification for the team, I had to do a twenty-six story rappel in full battle dress. I was scared shitless but I acted like I always do, that nothing ever bothered me.

One of the instructors came up to me and stood almost nose-to-nose and squared up. He said, "Son, you don't have to do this, if the idea of you going off this ledge and doing a high speed, free repel down twenty-six stories doesn't scare the holy hell out of you, you don't belong here.

Now just before you hook up, make your decision, you need to clasp your ring or you can turn around and take the stairs all the way back down. There's no shame in knowing your limits."

Well, I squared my shoulders, smiled, hooked up and kicked off and I've never regretted it. Honey, If I've ever given you what you think to be the best council, let me give you this. Baby, regardless of what you do in life, don't do it unless it scares the holy hell out of you. That's where your gut value comes from. Doing what's comfortable, doing what's safe, denies you the pleasure of knowing your limits. Testing your limits is what stands you apart from all the others. Take chances and if ever you feel the chance is not worth the outcome, that's when you take the stairs and walk down those twenty-six stories. *Capiche?*

Amanda darling, you can walk away at any time. Heather can not. You having to watch me go through this process is not mandatory. I know this is painful but I want you to learn from me, fear nothing and fear no one. The reason that I take crazy risks in my writing is it's my barometer and how I measure my efforts and my success. When I start to feel a bit at risk I dive deeper, I don't step back and I will be damned if I will apologize to anyone. If I call someone a lying, cheating asshole and expose you with facts and use their real name is because I owe it to my readers. I owe it to my friends and family. If I'm going to be believable, I first must believe. How will others find their truths and their courage to follow me if I'm not believable? So you see, I'm not done giving. Of course, I can't give as quickly or perhaps even as deeply as I once did, but I'm not quitting. I won't quit until they close the lid on me and if you hear a knocking sound when they do, it's me, just fucking with everybody one last time. Baby, dry your eyes, rig-up and hook-up because we're about to kick off the top of this building!

Honey, I love you but I've gotta break away. There are some other people that I want to chat with. See you at the cocktail party tonight.

CHAPTER 23
Making The Rounds

After a warm hug I left the garden and went on a search for Norbs. She wasn't hard to find, she was like a butterfly fluttering around the room. She was engaging with guests, posing for photographs and at the same time giving direction to some of our people. It made me smile to see her still in the game. As I approached her she turned and saw me coming. She graciously excused herself from a handful of admirers and almost did the identical body embrace that Amanda had just done, but in private.

Me: You little trollip, your public is watching!

Norbs: Yes my lovely man, and I just increased your fan base! Look around you stud, there is a room full of women right now that want to cut my throat. Sick or not, you still got it! The people that read your work all fall in love with you. Women that haven't read you, are buying your books because of your loving heart. You got the goods like no other man or woman! You sure do make me wish that I was single at times, well at least for just a few minutes.

Me: Stop with that silliness, I need some of your time baby, come with me.

I stepped into the restaurant for a donut and a second carafe of coffee and led Norbs into the now unoccupied garden. I sat facing her for several moments without speaking and just looking at her. I wanted to put her on edge and slow her defenses.

Me: Norbs, let me ask you, what's on your mind, is something bugging you? I saw it earlier this morning. What is it Norbs?

Norbs: David, I am absolutely thrilled that you're going to make an audiobook. I'd like you to tell me about that because independent authors almost never have an audiobook produced, it is too damn expensive! Tell me about that please?

Me: Well sweetheart, that has been my deep desire and you know of course how I got hosed twice with supposed friends of mine. I still wasn't willing to let my dream die. I was going to find a way no matter who I had to fight, I was going to find a way, because I believe that my books make a difference in people's lives. I could show you testimonials as to my books having been credited to saving people's lives, people who were on the very edge of death, by their own hands. How could I possibly not find a way? Yes, it's still a continuation of my living and lifelong amends. Those never stop, they can never stop. So I went online to Amazon ACX and did a search for audiobook producers. I found a voice actor by the name of, "Buzz Blackburn." After reviewing several samples of other male voice actors. It was clear to me that Buzz had something special going on, he sounded natural. He had a special voice structure and edginess that I was drawn to. He reminded me of myself. As you well know I can be an edgy smartass with a level of compassion that is uncommon for most men. I was convinced that he is the voice that I want to speak on my behalf. He has a lot of experience, he's a trained professional and has done work in several different genres of voice acting. So I put on my big boy pants and I sent him an email and asked him when he would be available to take a phone call.

He answered back the next day with his phone number and a good time for him to take my call. This was back in early May. Well we got through all the specifics and the price structure was just a bit beyond my financial abilities. I would never say that I thought he was overcharging me, it's just that I don't have that kind of money. $6,000 to me is a damn lot of money that would eat six months of my Social Security payments. I just couldn't go it, but I wasn't ready to quit either, so I did the one thing that grates against my deepest values. I decided that I was going to sell off part of my gun collection, that's how much it all means to me. It must have been four months later when I said I'm now ready. Buzz said, "Great, send me a copy via email and I'll look it over and I'll decide whether or not it's something I want to be involved with." I thought, well holy shit, I have to convince this guy? I have to sell him on my book being a viable venture for him to record it? Jesus Christ, I'm paying him a huge amount of money and he still says, 'Let me decide whether or not I want to do it.' Well you know me, I won't accept no as an answer. I asked him straight up, "How do I pitch you to do my book, what do you need to know to be convinced?" Buzz asked me if I had some readers observations or reviews, well of course I started to laugh thinking, "You fuckin arrogant dummy, if that's all the smarter you are, I'm not sure if I want you to record my book!" And that's when I told him two stories, one about the young lady paramedic who text me late at night who wanted to say thank you and farewell as she was about to end her life, the other of course is the story about my friend in the UK whose fellow worker founded a fundraiser to place portable defibrillators in public places. That young lady passed away one day after a defibrillator was placed and was used on a 17 year old boy who was in cardiac arrest and survived! I stopped there and said, "Do you need anything more?" You could almost hear the smile in his voice as he said, "Give me your web address." I did, he looked at the covers of my books as we were talking. He said, "Why hasn't anyone heard of you? I want to apologize, I had no idea of your operating level, so the answer is now... yes! Yes sir, it will be my extreme pleasure to produce your book in audiobook."

We agreed on the price and he told me that as soon as the check cleared he would start the project and hopefully it'll be complete before the end of January. So that's the story.

Norbs: Well, I can't be surprised with any of that. I wanted to approach you and fund your audiobook venture but I was firmly told by some people, quite close to you, that you may be offended. David I have money, I have a lot of money, I came from money, my whole career was propped up with family money. You come along without any formal training, you live paycheck to paycheck and you sit down with a gel ink pen, hovering over a yellow legal pad for three years before your first book was published!

You're a fighter and you don't quit, if you do get knocked down you come back up swinging. You're the type of writer with a level of heart that far exceeds most any trained professional writer. In all honesty, I'm honored just to sit in your presence, there's a greatness about you David, you may not realize it in this lifetime but there will be a point in time when you will become one of the few, "Must read people" even if you just write on a bar napkin, people will want to read it!

Me: Thank you sweetie, I appreciate you saying that to me. I guess I needed to hear that from you more than anyone else. Now, how do you think the presentation is going? Norbs smiled and said, "Do you realize that you're almost sold out of all your seven book titles, how many cases did you bring in?" I said, "Four, thirty-six count cases of each title."

Norbs: You may want to call your people and have them air freight twenty-five cases of each title tonight. You're down to twenty books of each title! I smiled as I said, "Babe, I dont have people like you have people. My people do stunningly quiet magic tricks and make bad people disappear. Your people make things happen. I think that we should go with your people. You're the big gun around here, you need to call them fuckers and tell them to put them on a super jet!" Norbs took a sip of her juice and said,

"Stand by one, I'll show you how this is supposed to work."

I'll be damned, Norbs dialed up a number as she turned her phone on to speaker. Norbs talked to a lady that gushed and fell all over her, with the promise that all of those seven titles, with twenty-five cases of each book, will be loaded into an aircraft before the sun goes down. Well I guess that's the beauty of being believed, when someone believes in you to the point where they pull out their largest of 'Big Sticks' and make things happen. It would take me several days if not weeks to accomplish what she did in less than five minutes.

Me: Now sugar britches, we're going to sit right here, if it takes all night long, even if I have to miss my last presentation, my book signing and the cocktail party. We're not leaving this room even for a potty break, until you level with me. So here's the question and I expect a righteous answer. What is it that you're running from, why are you hiding behind Amanda like a little kid in the dark? There's something going on with you that you're not willing to talk about. Futhor, there's a reason why you haven't gotten an AA sponsor. I further understand that you've been avoiding AA meetings. So right here and right fucking now, you need to put it all out here and you need to do it now. I'm done soft pedaling with you. It's time to get hard, let's have it babe.

    Norbs: David, I'm so damn miserable. I don't even know where to start, so many things have changed in my life. Some good friends, actually some real good friends have become unbearably horrid. One woman that I was friends with for many, many years suddenly is making sport of me. Not to my face of course, but behind my back. I do have some loyal friends that do report to me because they think it's important that I know. But how can these people that I've known for so many years be so cruel and make fun of me because I went to treatment, because I'm an alcoholic.

David, I've even had women tell me that they didn't believe I had a drinking problem because I didn't drink any more than they did. They thought that maybe I just had a nervous breakdown and maybe I went to treatment because I was ashamed of my mental health issues.

    Me: Okay sweetie, you said everything I need to know. It's time for a few of life's lessons, that somehow have passed you by. Baby, people, most all people, will use another person to make themselves look better than you, equal to you, or maybe just try to look as normal as you.

I don't believe that you have anybody as a friend, who could have written, produced, and directed movie scripts. Look at the number of books you've penned. Most all of your friends look at you with great admiration and envy. But do they respect you? No, of course not. Even accomplished fellow authors know in their heart of hearts that they aren't and never will be your equal. You get national and International awards for your work as often as I get a newspaper delivered! How many of your fellow authors pay their press secretary six figures to solely reply to invitations that you graciously must decline for personal appearances for award ceremonies and charities? You have no equal in the literary industry.

Your supposed friends think you act superior to them, whether you do or not. Keep in mind that in their mind's eye, that they saw you fall from grace. Suddenly you're both the same size and they want more, they want to see you disappear into oblivion. On the flip side of that, they also resent you for killing their idol. I'm sure you have heard that current saying of, "Be someone that nobody ever thought you could be"?

Ain't that a bunch of bullshit! Hell girl, I have done that and people that have known me for years resent me for it! You and I are on opposite ends of the spectrum but it's the same for the both of us.

People have done this kind of shit for centuries, they will stand on your chest to make themselves appear taller. It's a simple matter of envy. Baby it's also a simple matter of, 'murder by character assassination.' Now all of the nobodies get to be somebody's at your expense.

I have an example I will give you and I hope you find this somewhat educational and entertaining. I had a friend for over fifty years. We spent some quality time drinking together almost daily in the 'Neon Moon' type of dance hall bars. We hunted and fished together all the time. I guess you could say that we were pretty good pals. I will call him Kent. When I left Minnesota as a young man, Kent and I stayed in contact and talked about every month on the phone just to shoot the shit. The times I came back for vacations we always got together for a few nights out. When I returned back to Minnesota to live, we picked up that same relationship although I no longer drank or went to bars. We were now meeting at an old Mom & Pop restaurant every Saturday morning.

Kent, on the other hand, brought his drinking game to such a great level of importance and honor, that there is a high-dollar bar/restaurant in town, that actually awarded him a brass name plate that was embedded in the bar surface at his favorite barstool as, "Customer of The Year" using his full name. How would you like to have a bar, name you as the,

"Customer of The Year?" Would that not send out some kind of a red flag, or a little message or maybe sound an alarm-bell that maybe you've got a serious fucking drinking problem? Well no, not him however.

When I returned to Minnesota to live, I wasn't here for more than a month and he insisted that he take me down to the bar to show me his brass embedded name plaque on the surface of the mahogany bar! When we walked in the bar there was a guy sitting at what's known as 'Kent's stool'. Kent asked the fellow to lean away for a moment so he could show me his brass name plate with his name and the year of him being, "The Customer of The Year."

Well that's not the total fuckery with Kent. This gets better, a lot better, if you're him that is. Well I had a concealed carry permit from Colorado which is only good here in Minnesota for thirty days. In Minnesota you have to take a two day six hour concealed carry class and qualify with a live fire 22 caliber revolver on a pistol range before you can apply to the county sheriff for a concealed carry permit.

Well I registered Heather and I for a concealed carry class. She had never fired a handgun in her life. All of my handguns were 45 caliber. I couldn't see buying a 22 caliber revolver just for the class, besides I was going to buy Heather a high quality 9mm pistol for her first pistol. I asked Kent if he had a 22 caliber revolver that we could borrow for the class. He did and he loaned me his revolver. Heather and I went shooting for two days in a row after work a few days before the class. She was an amazing natural shooter that needed very little coaching other than the standard safe gun handling procedures. I was quite proud of her natural abilities. At the end of the two day class when we had to qualify, Heather out shot most all of the other students. All during the sessions we had a group (of fourteen) 'contract' minimum security prison guards from one of the local minimum security prisons. They were there to re-qualify. Oh my God, I don't know who needs to be locked up more, them or the inmates. These guys had more war stories than any ten SuperMax prison guards. They're not armed but they had all kinds of armed encounters as civilians. These dinks cost us three hours of class time with their 'Barney Fife' bullshit. Heather and I sat there for two days without saying a word. I openly grinned towards those ass wagons as they were talking, to telegraph to them that the entire room knew that they were full of shit. The instructor was tired of their stupidity as well. The last two hours before we qualified the instructor asked if there were any other questions and of course these mouth breathers still wanted to play, 'pound my chest and amaze the panel' with the instructor. The instructor wisely asked, "Anybody here who has not spoken, have any questions or any law enforcement experience that they would like to share?" Heather put on her best Cheshire Cat grin as she said, "My husband does, he was a real cop" and softly elbowed me. The instructor almost kissed her out of pure relief. He smiled and nodded at me as I said, "Denver Metro Police, I was assigned to the Gang Unit and SWAT."

Those larger than life prison guard hero's suddenly became quiet. The instructor was openly beaming with relief and obvious joy. He asked me how often I had to draw my weapon during each shift. I smiled as I said, "I've never counted but I did wear the snaps and lining out of my holster every ten months. You could almost hear the heroes gulp. The instructor completed the next hour and a half of the class without any further interruptions. If it were up to me I would not issue these clowns a permit for a slingshot.

Back to Kent. His loaner revolver shot flawlessly and was dead on accurate. I remember when he actually got this pistol and how proud he was of it. It was a very pretty satin stainless steel with an engraved cylinder with a cougar and bear design on it. It was a beautiful work of art. This was a first generation "Ruger Bearcat" 22 caliber revolver built in 1958 and was discontinued for twenty years. The retail price on that gun was $49.50 in 1958. There have been three reproductions since the original release. Today's price for that same style of gun with a few minor upgrades is now $639!

Kent wasn't as thrilled about the attractiveness of the gun or its collectibility as he was thrilled with the fact that he paid only $30 for it. He bought it from a guy in a bar who was on his financial ass and needed gas money to get to work. That gun was Kent's pride and joy, not the fact that he's got a beautiful collectible gun but it was his trophy that represented the fact that he got to fuck a friend. Which made him better than his broke ass friend. Are you starting to get it yet sweetheart?

So Kent loaned the gun to Heather and I to qualify with. The night we completed the concealed carry class and qualified, we drove home to find my nephew was sitting in his car in our driveway. He asked if we would like to go to dinner with him. My nephew lives about 100 plus miles away and has to come to this area once a month for National Guard Duty. Every time he does come here we take him out for a meal as he has three little kids at home and not a lot of money. He's a good kid and I enjoy his company. I ran my shooting range bag (with Kent's gun in it) into the house. I didn't want to leave that in the vehicle in the parking lot of a restaurant. I set the bag up on the counter in the kitchen and off we went to the restaurant. We were gone for just a tick over an hour. When we got back we realized that our house had been burglarized. There were lights on in all the rooms and I could see dresser drawers open in our bedroom at the end of the hall. As I drew my weapon, I pushed Heather to the floor in the corner of the kitchen. We have three bedrooms and two full baths down the hall on that level. I loudly announced my presence and the fact that I was armed and if they didn't call out and I found them that I would kill them. I dialed 911 on our house phone so police dispatch could record my final warning to the bad guys to call out or suffer the consequences. That and of course our address would pop up on their caller ID so they didn't fuck up the address while sending the cavalry.

    I told police dispatch that we had just walked into our home and found we had been burglarized and the suspects may still be in the house and I was armed and was going to sweep the house. The dispatcher was going nuts with saying shit like, "Leave the house, don't look for them, don't shoot anybody, get out of the house!" I remember having a huge grin as I hung up on her, I had just established probable cause to blow those mother fuckers cleanly out of their socks, with my 45 with two extra eight round magazines in my shoulder holster. What I didn't realize was that the dispatcher read my call out and warning to the bad guys as a threat that I was going to shoot some people. We had bumper to bumper squad cars lining both sides of the avenue. There were several city squads, county squads and state patrol units along with Border Patrol and Homeland Security. I heard several cars pull up and that unmistakable, single thumb push to latch their doors but not slam them.

The cops ran a K-9 thru and did a search. They were gone, gone with all of Heathers jewelry and the guns in the shooting bag.

The uniform police called in the crime lab to process the crime scene and then asked us for descriptions of the jewelry and gun inventory as well as their value. Heather is intelligent enough not to just give answers off-the-cuff, because they become facts in police reports and then the insurance companies will use that to shove it up your ass when it's time to pay for your loss. They did ask me about the three guns we lost including Kent's and if I had the serial numbers. I did and gave them the serial numbers. One of the young investigators asked to see my Kimber 45acp still in my shoulder holster. I said, "No, this is not part of the crime scene do your job or get the fuck out of my house, I know god damn well what your trying to do. The senior investigator sent the newbie out of the room. I told her that one of the three guns stolen was not mine but was on loan from a friend. She asked me to call Kent and ask him if he had the serial numbers recorded. I called him and he said he did not have the serial numbers recorded as it was a private sale and the guy he bought it from was a stranger. That was quite different from the story he told me. It was clear to me that Kent knew he had bought a stolen gun.

Nonetheless, Kent loaned me that gun in good faith and I felt that I had an obligation to replace that firearm. I looked online and found that a first generation revolver like his, was now selling for about $400 and probably not in as good a condition as his. I didn't have the cash at the time because I had just paid my editor and pre-paid for two hundred of my latest books. I knew I had to replace it but I couldn't just hand him the money at the time. I was the one that lost it. I was the one that needed to replace it.

A few days later our outdoor shooting range was having their annual banquet and we already had tickets. It's always a well done dinner, banquet. It's to honor the volunteers over the course of the year and the board of directors for keeping the shooting club open and well maintained. One of the things they do to support their youth fishing and shooting programs is they buy several firearms at deeply discounted prices and sell ten dollar tickets for a raffle for each gun. There are always several handguns, shotguns and rifles up for raffle. The winners take their guns home that night. Well, we went to the banquet and we actually won a Remginton 30:06 "Youth rifle." A youth rifle has a shorter barrel, stock and forearm. It just so happens that my buddy Kent (who lent us that 22 revolver) has a daughter who I think is quite frail and might be 14 or 15 years old. She loves to sit in the enclosed and heated deer stand with dad. Kent has told me in the past that the rifle she uses to hunt with is too big for her and he was thinking about having the stock and barrel cut down to better fit her.

I called my buddy Kent the next day and asked him over for coffee. He came over and I showed him the rifle that we won the night before. He thought it would be perfect for his daughter. I smiled and said, This is yours if you wish to square my debt with the loss of your 22 revolver. Well he looked at me like I just stepped off a spacecraft, he started nodding his head like a bobblehead. Followed of course by his trademark shit eating grin, which told me he was very happy to get to fuck me over. That's not the end of the story however, oh no! I was glad to retire the debt I owed him. One of the few things I'm not is a cheat, so we shook hands and he went home with a brand new Remington scoped 30:06 deer hunting rifle for his daughter and then it started. Word got back to me in a rather short fashion, that my dear friend Kent, from my young adult years, was bragging to his friends about what a dumb fuck I am because I gave him a brand new Remington, scoped deer hunting rifle valued over $700. Of course he made it $900 because he had to be even cooler, to get a new scoped rifle for a $30 pistol that he fucked somebody else out of.

Yep isn't that cute! He just couldn't say, "My friend who is a very honorable man, gave me this $700 rifle to make-up for the loss of my revolver knowing full well that I only paid $30 for the pistol that was stolen in their home burglary." Maybe he would go another notch further and say this is what honorable people do but no, not this kookfuck! No he had to brag about how he got over on me, he got to brag how he hornswoggled me. So yeah, he was standing on another man's chest in the attempt to make himself appear taller. Baby it's Universal, people are fuckers and there's nothing we can do about it but avoid them and for us not to become fuckers like them.

Norbs: David I just have one more question, actually it's a comment. I know that you've donated all of your books to the Minnesota Department of Health for the visual and physically impaired to be recorded and enjoyed by their clients free of charge, I don't quite understand how that works, how does that work?

Me: Well I think you might find this interesting, as an author I cannot submit my own books that I wrote directly to that organization. My books can only be received by a registered member of services. Now understand that I donate my books to them and I don't get payment or any residuals of any kind. They use volunteers to voice record my books and again those are all free including postage to both the vision and physically impaired. What I found was sad and actually embarrassing and I had this conversation with Buzz not too long ago. Buzz asked me about that very same thing, what was sad is that my second book, "Flesh Of a Fraud" has a lot of hard language, should we say words like the word, fuck. Of course, I see those types of words as sentence enhancers, they drive home a point where it seems that no other word would work, at least not for me. Remember now, I'm not a trained professional, I'm just a writer. So my friend Jerry smuggled me that tape of that book to listen to with his recorder provided by the State of Minnesota. So I listened to it and I don't know if it was recorded around the Christmas holiday or if a number of people were sickly. It was, of course, during the early days of covid. Whatever the reason, that book, that one book was recorded by six different people, two of them were women. There was this one lady who had to be quite elderly by the sound of her voice and her diction. Well here's this poor little thing, that might have only whispered the word shit under her breath when she was absolutely sure that nobody else could hear her, is suddenly saying the word fuck out loud for the entire world to hear. I was so embarrassed for her that I contacted the state and requested her contact information so I could directly apologize to her. They refused my request.

The readers do have to read all sentences and words verbatim. I could almost sense her struggling with it but she persevered and pushed through. You would think that I would have learned something from that, but of course I didn't. Bless her heart and all the people that volunteer to read books for the visually and physically impaired. I think that it's a beautiful program but as a writer, I could not submit my books directly to the state. It has to be sponsored by a registered member of the Department of Health. I get that whole thing about not allowing the actual author to submit their books because oftentimes people use that as a marketing tool which has never been my intention in any way, shape or form.

Well so there we have it babe. Some people won't let you be kind, regardless of your intentions. Now my lovely friend, you have taken up a great deal of my valuable time and as you well know, there ain't nothin for nothin. I am not going to speak this evening, you are going to speak on my behalf and I will of course, still be there and I will sign my books. You are simply just going to announce that my voice is pretty much given-out for the day and then you do your magic. And no my love, *YOU* will …. and no one else but you! *Capiche?*

CHAPTER 24
As the Sun Sets

Amanda: David can we go up to the "Eagle's Nest?" Mother and I have a special favor to ask of you. We'll have to have it in the conference call. Mother's feeling a bit under the weather. She doesn't feel like flying. Can we do that?

Me: Only if you hook my arm and walk me to the elevators. Yeah baby, we can do that, there's always time for sweet sister Jane. Dial her up.

Me: Hello sweetheart, I understand that you're not feeling well, have you talked to your doctor?

Jane: Oh I'm just finer than frog's hair, just a bit of the sniffles and I think I need to slow down a little bit, I've been going too hard for too long.

Me: Well no shit, all you've done is save the world on several occasions. Yeah I can see where you might be a bit fatigued, what can I do for you baby?

Jane: David this is the hardest question I've ever had to put in front of anyone but I feel it necessary, please forgive me for being so forward. David, there is someone that would like to interview you. Someone of some rather great fame. I know that you've done interviews on national and international radio shows and podcasts but you've never done anything for television, so where people can put a face to a name.

David, I think you owe it to yourself to go public, but certainly not for myself or our family. And yes sweetheart, I've been reading what you've been writing as many of us have. What I'm hoping to do is capture the man before his end of life. David, you and I are both very direct, so let's just cut right to it. I'm afraid as you are, that you are running out of time. You made me realize how precious time is and how little bit of time we all actually have. I want to capture you as you are today. That person that wants to interview you is a very dear friend of mine and she gets you. I know that a lot of people don't get you for all the wrong reasons of course and that one reason is always the same as you've taught me about, *'fear.'* False Evidence Appearing Real. I know of course this is quite presumptuous of me but that person along with a film crew are in the "Bridal Suite" awaiting you. David, people have to know who you are and what you've done.It would be a terrible crime against all mankind not to know who David J. Brown was and pardon me for using that word 'was'. David honey, the people that know you, see you as a National Treasure that has yet to be unearthed. What I hope to do David is to dispel people's negative opinions of you. We have both witnessed (time after time) people guessing what this person meant or what their goals were and it just goes on and on. I want you to tell them who you are and let the chips fall where they may.

    Me: Well hell yeah babe I don't give a shit I'll be dead anyway. Hell, I tell the truth when I'm alive and the truth doesn't frighten me. The lies to support the next lie is what frightens me. So honey, I have to guess that they're what, waiting for me with makeup and hair people and all that other bullshit. What am I going to wear? Who's going to dress me? Is she going to be scantily clad? Is she beautiful?

    Jane: I'm sure she is, my darling, you're burning daylight and you're burning my money. I'm paying for this production and I want results!

    Me: You darling little hard-ass, now you too are putting demands on my time just because you paid for this? Honey, if you were here right now I would want to spank you. Yes babe, I'll do it. I just need to brush my teeth and we'll go visit with these nice people who want to what, figure me out and just what makes David J. Brown tick? It should be cute, I think I'm going to have a lot of fun with this. I love you babe, gotta go, my public awaits.

As we stepped out into the hallway, there sat Heather with Paul. They both looked a little apprehensive. Heather came to her feet and said, "Baby you don't have to do this if you're not up for it. As much as we both love Jane, if it's not what you want, I'll tell Jane. I love you more, I'm not going to sacrifice you for the public that you've never even known."

Paul: David, I have to affirm what Heather just said, you are under no obligation to go through any of this but if you choose to, I think it would be the most wonderful parting gift a person could ever give, it's your call Buddy Boy.

Me: Well it sounds like I'm going to get a new wardrobe so that's a plus. Gonna get my hair washed and styled and probably a close shave and other stuff like that? Yeah I can do this, it might even be fun, I do need a distraction.

The three of us rode the elevator down two floors to the bridal suite. Other than my "Eagles Nest" this is the largest of all the guest rooms in the hotel.

As we walked into the room there was a temporary makeup booth with several light bars along with a hair joint, whatever the fuck they call those things. They actually had a pretty damn nice set-up considering everything is temporary and it all came off a truck an hour ago. I was quite impressed. There were four lovely ladies lined up as though they were in line for an inspection, wearing crisp starched maroon short dresses which were well tailored with sparkling nylons and matching high heels, like you might see in a Las Vegas dance review show.

Of course they had to wash my hair which I had washed less than two hours ago but yeah ladies, go ahead. I think I'll ask them to do Heather's hair when they're done with me. Next came a lovely young lady with gorgeous legs, shimmering lipstick and a straight edge razor. I sat statue still for her of course and kept my snide comments to myself. Next came the makeup people who surrounded me like we were in a football huddle. Lastly, here comes this young toothy grin gal with the pinkest gums and whitest teeth with a whole cart of finger nail type implements. I said, "No dice baby, I trim my own nails, I file them smooth on the edges and on the top surface because I get those crazy ridges on my nails as my gift for aging to this advanced age. We're not going to buff my nails and we sure as hell are not going to lay polish upon my nails. You my sweetness, go sit over there and I will just wink at you okay, cuz I think you're awful cute.

Then here she came with her entourage, yes she is a well known nationally and probably even internationally as an actress and reporter. She introduced herself to me with a warm handshake and one of those celebrity brushing side-cheek kisses. Which I thought was a bit classy but I wasn't going to trust her, not at all.

Me: So I understand that you want to interview me and record my final words? That's quite interesting. I do want your absolute guarantee (and just so you know, I have people who know other people) I don't think I need to go any further with that now do I? I want your personal and professional guarantee that you will not air any part of this until after six months after I have passed. This is about giving Heather and my friends time to grieve and time to heal. If we can agree to this, we can start right now, if not you and your people can pack your shit and get the fuck out. What say you babe?

Sally: Well they told me about you and yes you did not disappoint. I get it David, I get every bit of it and yes, I will properly show the respect and honor you as to your wishes. I don't have a lot of questions (strange as it may sound) we've got an awful lot of video footage and background already. We've already cataloged snippets of you speaking on several different occasions and locations. We have your entire presentation that you gave to the Greater Chicago community leaders, which I have to say was brilliant. I do have one question and that is, David, why do you so grossly undersell yourself, let me go further, you all but fight away fame and recognition, tell me why that is?

Me: Thank you, that's quite easy, I don't even know if we need to roll any cameras but I'll simply tell you this. The thought of success terrifies me. Now let me explain. Honey I have an ego as large as the entire great outdoors. Once again I need to repeat for my sake probably more than yours. I am an alcoholic and as an alcoholic and as most alcoholics, I have a hidden pride if you will. Yep, I'll start thinking that I'm some kind of a big deal with money and fame and I will be magically insulated from my alcoholism because I will have money. Suddenly a drink will sound mighty attractive to me to celebrate my big dealness and I will lose my life, in a very short period of time. Let's go sit wherever you have all your lights and people set up and get to it. Before we do, you have to know that I am a free man and well over twenty-one. Where that should take you, is to understand that nobody owns me. I'm under no obligation to anyone, I'm going to give you my safe word. I'm going to give it to you just once and my safe word (if you want to continue) is, "PASS." If you try to push me, pressure me, prod me or back door me in any way, outside of my boundaries we will be done and I will walk and you'll be left to answer. Wouldn't that be fun, I call the ball and this is my show, take heed my lovely. Now you are a very seductive woman, you're absolutely gorgeous without question. The way you posture and hold yourself is all about you getting what you want from me. That shit don't fly with me babe, I don't mind just looking you square in the eye with saying, "Honey, I've had better" but that's not about you and me, it's about you. If your skirt was any shorter it would be called underwear. That's cute, but again that shit don't fly and that dog won't hunt. Still love me babe?

Sally: Fair enough Mr. Brown, may I call you David?

Me: Me, well of course you may. All right, now that we're done with that bullshit let's get to it. My gut tells me that you want more than the story, you want to create a story around the story, that's what you do, that's what you type of people do. Well honey here's the deal with me. This story is my story, I tell my story my way, whatever you do after I'm dead and gone is entirely up to you. You may want to remember that there's a lot of people out here to protect me and my image, so if you want to take on those powers, have at it. And yes, let me make this clear to you. I am a novelist, a novelist is someone who, as you should well know, writes fiction. You, as I, are both protected by the First Amendment and I smell your angle. I can not be held liable as I write about myself. The difference between us is that nobody pays me to be me. I'm ready, first question please.

Sally: David, you have personally experienced situations from your youth and adult life that any lesser person would have rolled-up in a blanket and turned out the lights. Why not you?

Me: At a young age I learned to be a fighter to survive, I was not given a choice. I had to fight or be the kid rolling-up in that blanket, turning out the lights. I see that you're coming in soft, I'm a big boy, there is little left for me to fear. Bring it fast, hard and dirty!

Sally: I have never in my private life or career ever presented this type of question to anyone. Some people have questions as to you being an extreme empath. You want it fast, hard and dirty, (your words) so here it is. When you were a paramedic did you help terminal people reach their end a bit sooner than expected?

Me: Now, I'm actually starting to like you. I had a number of patients who died in my arms or laying on a gurney next to me on the way to the hospital. So let's get right to it with the sugar plums dancing in your head. Am I a serial killer? Do you think I murdered those people to end their suffering?

Yes many of my patients suffered greatly, did I assist them in any way? That's a hard no. I'm no Dr. Kevorkian but do I support assisted suicides?

I will answer that with a question for you. How long must a person suffer who is not able to care for themselves, not able to communicate or eat or drink? How long do they have to have an IV bag as their only source of food intake? Who is being served by us keeping them alive? I will tell you who. Their family, the pharmaceutical company's, the hospitals and nursing homes all receive a rather handsome return in keeping a shell of a human being alive. Are you okay with that?

Sally: I have never thought of things in this way. That is a heavy burden to consider. You are right, without you even saying it, in telling me that I have no right, nor does anyone else have the right to challenge you on your level of medical care. I am convinced that you are no killer, let's move away from this topic?

Me: Not so fast, there are crazy people in the medical care business that are investigated on a regular basis with many being arrested and incarcerated. Abusive family members fall into "Munchausen syndrome by proxy" which is derived from them abusing their children for the parents' attention. We live in a sick society which I have little hope for.

Sally: Is there anything you want your readers, friends or family to know about you and your life?

Me: I have fought my demons all of my life to help others fight theirs. My demons were on the cusp of winning several times and it continues still today. My rage is alive and well, yet today. You have been somewhat on point with your suspicions.

I don't mind telling you that I have had a kill list for many, many years. Keep in mind sweetheart that I worked in emergency services for almost thirty years. I had to deal with child molesters, rapists, killers and a world full of assorted shit heads. If I had a short time to live, I wouldn't go after them. I would go after the people who allowed them to walk free. I have to be careful with these liberal assholes and their proposed red flag laws. But I would definitely do some damage. But remember that I have creative immunity due to my being a registered and published novelist.

Sally: I would like everyone to shut your equipment down and leave the room now. Do it now please! I need to talk with David in private.

I knew that silence was in order now. I somehow struck a chord deep within Sally and she needed a few minutes of silence to allow her to process it, whatever 'it' was. I could see Sally start to wilt with the deeper she drifted into her hidden memories. Her perfect posture was all but forgotten as she started to curl-up like a house cat in her chair. My guess? She may have been molested as a young child or is a rape survivor, ether way she was about to let it out and I was the only one for her at the moment. I briefly thought of calling Heather or Amanda but I didn't want to break the spirit of the moment. I would have to work without a net. I said a brief prayer in asking God to guide me, as Sally began to sob.

I knew it was time for me to sit stone-still as though I am not even in the room. This is Sally's time. Sally sat as though she was in a trance and perhaps she was. My only fear was that she might bolt for a window, I slowly set my feet to sprint to stop her if she did, as I watched her tears run down her cheeks and off her chin unchecked. She didn't try to wipe her tears, she let them run onto her dress.

I lost track of time, I don't know how long this had been going on but I felt a fatigue start to overtake me. I knew that I needed to let this play out but I was fading quickly.

Me: Sally, I need you to come back to me. Tell me of what's been running through your gut and mind. I think that we need to move around a bit. I need coffee and you might need a stiff drink. On your feet honey.

I got to my feet and walked to the service bar. I poured a very tall water glass almost full of some kind of expensive looking Scotch. Sally had a sly smile as I handed her the scotch with her saying, "Word has it that you always know exactly what a woman needs and when, I most definitely concur!"

Me: I think we need some sunshine and a bit of a stroll. You game?

Sally: You know damn well I'm game. The same as all the other women who walk into your life. Your beautiful, loving soft eyes draw us all like moths to a flame. Your edgy danger also flashes behind your tenderness. You would be a hell of an actor.

Yes David, you hooked me but you didn't try to reel me in, you let me struggle with my hidden truths until the sting wore off to where I want to talk about them now. I have been fibbing you a bit. David I am a heavily experienced professional, I do a great deal of research on my subjects long before I do the interviews. I have a staff that does nothing but validate my findings. Because of obvious time constraints, I have been running at warp speed. I have interviewed several of the hotel employees, all the people that were principles in your first book signings and presentations and a few of your AA and local facebook friends. What surprised me the most was that almost no one knows of your current health condition. That sir, speaks loudly of your humility.

Me: Shut up with that shit, you're trying to shift away from your breakthrough by focusing on me. You took up my time and now you must take my lead.

What snared you during my rant about my kill list and reduced you to a pool of blubbering tears? When you curled deep into that chair I saw your panties, you need to buy longer dresses. Get to it god damn it!

Sally: Your eyes told me that you already knew. I felt ashamed that you knew of my secrets when I spent all of my life trying to bury them. David, my life, my entire life has been a lie. I've had two wonderful husbands but I couldn't speak to them about these things but something tells me that I'm safe with you. You said you had the time, I think now is the time for me. I'm not sure where to start so I'll just start with my father who molested me when I was a young child. He did it almost every night. My mother was a wino and went to bed by 8:30 if she wasn't still in the bars. Dad would tuck me in most every night. He would pull down my pajama bottoms, look at me and then made me roll over. He made an ugly smile as he rubbed my bottom. That's when it started, it got worse as time went on. I fully knew that my mother knew what he was doing to me but she was so busy chasing other men and preening in the mirror for hours to stop him. I guess you could just call her a bar whore, she was nothing more than that, she was certainly no mother. She couldn't boil water. She didn't care about us kids. Most of our meals consisted of and from the frozen section of grocery store goods. I was raised on pot pies, pizzas and hotdogs.

Well my dad fancied himself as the ultimate salesman. He hustled everything and everyone. I never really knew what his job was. He worked for some kind of company selling advertising. I think Billboards mostly but he would get other advertising jobs that he would go sell to the newspapers, radio and the TV stations as an independent. He was always on the hustle, always looking for his next dime. He had this thing about him thinking that he was a world champion Walleye fisherman. He would join local fishing tournaments sponsored by small-town Chambers of Commerce, bait shops, guide services and fishing lodges.He had an old boat but it was lettered like it was a NASCAR car. I think he was one of the first ones to do that so he sold advertising on his boat and he held himself up as a top tournament fisherman. The other real tournament fisherman made fun of him. They called him 'mud flaps' because if he could figure out a way to sell advertising on mud flaps he would attach them to the boat.

Well, my dad didn't catch many fish, he just wasn't able to be the fisherman he thought he was. He couldn't focus because he was too busy trying to figure out another way to make a quick buck. My dad took me to the three day fishing tournaments. My mom insisted that he take me but never my other two sister's. It was just me and that's when he molested me the most. He used the tournaments as a cover for him to get me alone into a motel room, to do the filthy things he did to me. The local tournament fisherman in our club had some great fishing skills. One of the things they did at night at a competition was they made their own flies and lures. They would bet on who could catch the first, biggest and most fish on the next day. One of the ways I could get away from my dad was to go to their motel rooms when they were making lures at night. They taught me how to tie flies, how to carve balsa lures and all different kinds of topwater and diver lures. I got pretty good at it. I was really good at painting them. I made them look almost lifelike. It was a lot of fun for me and then it started. I actually found my place, my comfort and my safety with those other men. Isn't that a bitch when you have to go to all but strangers to feel safe because of what your own father does to you? David, I was married to two wonderful men but I couldn't keep them because I couldn't be intimate with them. Whenever they touched me, I felt my father's hand, whenever we made love I thought it was my father and I would vomit and get violently ill which is not conducive to a good marriage, now is it? So yes he ruined me for other men. He stole my childhood away from me and my adult years as well. He still has power over me in my mind. He is still alive, he's in a nursing home. I'm looking forward to the day he dies. It probably won't give me any relief but at least he will be gone. I want to get back to the other fishermen; they were all like uncle's to me. They were really sweet and patient. Our local guys didn't have many sponsors, not like the big guys do so they had patches made which read, "Sally's lures, fly high and dig deep." I was their sponsor, although I never had any money to pay them anything but I made lures for them and they started selling lures for me. One of the guys worked for a company where they made packaging. They designed packaging for my lures, so at the fishing tournaments I had a little table with the overhead umbrella and I would sell my lures. When our local guys won a tournament they would always say. "I caught these fish with 'Sally's Lures' and a lot of people would rush over to my table and buy all of my lures. I became pretty popular at the tournaments. I spent most all of my summer days making lures. I told everyone that I wanted to buy a boat of my own and become the first lady professional fisherman. They thought that was great, but the truth David, the hard cold truth was that I was saving my money in hopes that I could hire a hitman. I wanted someone to kill my dad.

In the first few minutes of our interview and when you were speaking of a hit list is when it struck me, the deepest part of me! I wish I would have known you back then, you would have been the man without question. I'm glad of course that I didn't know you then because you and I would end up in prison of course. I had to be ever vigilant to protect my sisters from my dad. Sometimes I would actually, I know this sounds sick but I would actually try to entice my dad to get him away from my sister's. I had to protect them, well finally my mother ran off with some guy and ended up in another part of the country. She never said goodbye, nothing, she was just gone one day. I didn't miss her at all. I hate her because she knew what my dad was doing to me and she didn't care because he let her do what she wanted to do. Everything she did had to do with alcohol and men.

As I got a bit older and entered into junior high school, my dad suddenly started to be nice to me. He wasn't always pawing me as much and he was not always trying to rape me. David, I know I'm minimizing this but that's kind of where I was living in my head. I knew the truth, my dad was afraid that there were people in junior high school, teachers and counselors that I could go to with my problems and that frightened him. He was afraid that I would expose him but even as young as I was I could see that if I were to tell what he did to me that he would go to prison and me and my sisters would have to go to an orphanage. I couldn't do that to my little sisters so I just told him one day, no more! You can never do this to me again, if you do I will go to the school guidance counselor and tell them all about what you've been doing to me and you will go to jail for the rest of your life.

Sally slid herself out of her chair and laid on the floor face down with her arms under her and cried. I knew there was nothing more I could do for her. I went into the bedroom and got her a pillow and pulled a blanket and the comforter off the bed. I covered her and went back to my room to freshen up for the afternoon events. As I left Sally's room I had the thought to call one or a couple of the girls to come to be with her but then again she just had a breakthrough. She needed to taste it, she needed to digest it, it was her time to be free.

I didn't realize how early in the day it still was. I cleaned up a bit and called for one of the Bills from the security team. I asked him to meet us in the lobby in 20 minutes with a car out front. I then called Sally and said, "Honey, be ready in 20 minutes, wear jeans or slacks. I'm tired of looking at your underwear, we're going for a ride.

Twenty minutes later as I came off the elevator there sat Sally in one of those high back lobby chairs. She looked surprisingly calm. As I approached her she said, "We are going somewhere? Now you get to schedule my activities?" I smiled as I said, "Girl, you sure had a quick recovery. Yeah, we're going somewhere."

One of the bills was standing near the front door. I reached down to take Sally's hand to walk her to the door. I gave the driver the address where I wanted to go. Of course there were three cars and not just one, all three security cars were all different colors this time. When we pulled up to the front of Kohl's Sally said, This is not my type of shopping store. I grinned with thinking, perfect this is fucking perfect!

I took Sally over to the woman section where they had discounted women's long wool coats. She just looked at me and shook her head and she asked what the fuck are you doing?

Me: Sally gal, we're going to buy you a new coat. Oh lookie here, this might be the one! As I walked over to a coat that was at least 10 gallons larger than she could wear, I think it was probably a size 28 and it was an ugly son of a bitch. It was pink with a black and green houndstooth pattern. I smiled as I asked, "You want to try it on honey, before I have them wrap it up for you?

Sally: David, I know you're sick but you're also fucked in the head! What do you think you're doing?

Me: Baby, here's a life lesson that I want you to never let go of. You have taken responsibility for what happened to you in your childhood, you somehow blamed yourself, which is not uncommon for many survivors. You carry a heavy shame that doesn't fit or belong to you just like this coat. That's what you are, you are a survivor, you can no longer be a victim, you now must be a survivor and you must emotionaly and spiritually thrive because survivor is only one step up from victim, so you have to become a thriver, if that's even a fucking word. I don't know but here's the deal, you assumed a responsibility for your abuse that you had no control over, you were just a little kid, there's nothing you could do, you were a hostage and you were a captive but not anymore! That's what this coat is all about, you won, it's your trophy! Come over here I want you to put this on you, please humor me. Over here in front of the mirror, put this fucker on.

Sally wouldn't put her arms in the sleeves so I draped it over her shoulder as I said, "How's that look?" Sally started laughing and it grew to a deep belly laugh.

Sally: It looks like a large zoo animal could probably wear this but not a human! I'm drowning in this ridiculous looking thing!

Me: Good baby, now here's the lesson, listen tight and listen hard. I am buying this for you. I want you to put this in your coat closet at home right in the front. I don't ever want you to close the door to that closet. Every time you walk by the closet you'll see this coat and what this coat signifies is that it doesn't belong to you. It doesn't fit you, it was never designed for you, you have been wearing a deep scar that doesn't belong to you. This coat will represent the scars, the many scars that don't belong to you, you didn't earn them and you're not at fault. This coat hanging in your closet will tell you that you're free today and for all the days to follow. *Capiche*

Sally: I accept but let me ask you, Why do you have to always go so deep with everything? I mean it all makes sense, it's beautiful and yes I'll take it and I'll put it in my closet with the door open, so I see it every time I walk by. How do you come up with this stuff, nobody else thinks this way other than you.

    Me: Maybe they should. But I'm buying you this coat. Yep, that's my gift to you. Still love me babe?

CHAPTER 25
I Knew He Was There

No, I didn't see, smell or feel his presence but I knew he was there. I wasn't going to look for him, I was going to let him find me. Sometimes you have to let yourself be the bait and when they think that they finally have you trapped, is when they will make a mistake. I was willing to risk that he would expose himself before I pounced.

I knew that he was slipping through the crowd completely undetected. But he had one major "tell" much like a poor poker player. It wasn't him per say, it was his shadows. His shadows were even apparent in the darkest of the dark of nights. I knew that I would find him by watching who was watching his shadows. If I wasnt so damn tired I would have made a game of it. I was short on energy and even shorter on patience.

I had finished my book signings (and yes the book orders had arrived, right at sunset) and did a fair amount of glad handing and posing for photographs. I called the hotel front desk and told the clerk to send me the security manager and three of his people.

They were in front of me in two minutes, I gave them their instructions and told them to wait for my signal at the water fountain next to the express elevators. I sent the security manager to go to his office and to que-up the full "Crows Nest" security systems and report any heat signatures or movement. I called Amanda and told her that I needed three of her people at the same location and to wait for my signal. I called the front desk again and told him to send the entire housekeeping staff to the express elevators and wait along with the rest and to bring a full laundry cart of master suite linens along with two empty laundry carts.

Five minutes later and I was standing outside enjoying a cigarette as eighteen stories above me, people were nothing but a flurry of movement. I called Tim, the former doorman and told him that I was taking back my suite for an indefinite period of time, perhaps even for ever.

It was time I return to the ballroom, stick out my foot and trip the shadow and hard ride him to the ground.

Me: You slummin it Sport?

Paul: Not until just now!

We had a soft handshake and a hug.

Me: Shake my hand like a man, you limp wristed asshole! Where the hell is your mini-you, Gregory?

Paul: You opted out asshole. We operate on a need to know basis and you Skippy, don't need to know. You are out of the loop and you need to stay there. How do I ask you how you are doing, you staying sober?

Me: Cute you dick head. Haven't drank all day for the last 31 years of days. But it has crossed my mind as of late. So what's up with you slimming around my city. You broke the dog chain off the porch to run free or maybe you didn't like the reports that you've been getting from your troup of spy ladies? Had to see for yourself did you?

I would have done one of those ballet pirouette thingies for him but I'd end up on my ass.

Me: Yes I'm a bit diminished, but I can still fuck you up in three different languages.

Paul: I have little doubt that you could. I didn't come here to fight you, I came here to support you. You still put on one hell of a front but you might want to hike up your skirt lil miss, your slip is starting to show. Can I buy you a cup of coffee my friend?

We went to the garden and Paul called for coffee and donuts. The cocktail party was in full swing in the ballroom and had spilled over into the lobby. The garden was glass enclosed and of course locked. Several party goers were trying to peek in and a few thought they just might want to join us. The overly served were met with walls of rippling flesh with cold, hard, steel under their sport coats.

Me: Ok doctor, now that you can see that the patient is up and taking nourishment shall we move on to your confession. Don't try to bullfuck me ole son, I've been at this game a long damn time.

Paul: What the fuck are you doing with my security and housekeeping staff and why are they in the (Your former diggs) top suites? I own this joint and you have my people racing around like you own this shack and they are your people, you asshole!

Me: Do you enjoy trying to out think yourself? Sport, there are two kinds of loyalty in this world. The kind you buy and the kind you earn. You want to slide your chips up against mine? I'm taking my property back, I think it will be a nice place to die.

But for right now, the suite is being emptied of Tim's and his family's stuff for this weekend. You and your lovely daughter will be in, "The Birds nest." You both have some serious shit to work through. You think that you let her down and you are trying to balance your shame with your rage, she feels stupid, unworthy and lost. Neither of you ever thought that you could fuck up so badly. Buddy Boy, life ain't always fair, especially when it involves affairs of the heart. One of your own life's mottos is, "Trust but verify."

Yes, I understand you had your best people on it, people that you hand picked and have trusted for years. You and your entire family walked into the, "perfect storm."

This is not the time to dissect the internals and how the breaches occurred. What matters, what can only matter, is that we care for our wounded. Keep in mind that the blast pattern is deep and wide. I'm sure the Bills are also on the casualty list, let's not lose sight of them either. Oh and yes, I am proud of you for not wacking that cock-bite. I'm proud of myself too! I am now ready to hear your confession, my son.

Paul: No wonder people fucking hate you! I hate how you know me so well. David, as always you are right. My security intelligence system broke down when I trusted and needed it the most. I have created a spreadsheet of words, terms and phrases to cover my self-disgust but what hurts the most, is that I can't fix it and I can't erase it. I thought I had this whole sobriety thing covered but in the last few weeks a drink sounds damn good to me too. How do you avoid the, "Fuck-its?" Jesus Christ, David, I can't get away from myself. Fuck, I'm sitting with a man with a death sentence hanging over his head, you are faceing body changes daily, if not hourly and all you do is sit here, just like you are now, with a grin on your face. Now I hate myself even more. How the fuck can I be so self-absord and selfish? What the fuck is wrong with me?

Me: Do you really want an answer? Of course you don't, at least my type of answer. Buckle-up buddy boy, here it comes. You're all so used to being in charge, you all have people, you have people who have people, you are affluent and your wealth has insulated you. Real life, everyday life for most people, is confusing and uncomfortable for you. So fucking what, you weren't able to protect Amanda from herself. Now we are back to that heart and love stuff that you can't wrap your head around. Amanda fell in love, Amanda married that man and was looking forward to a long life of pure bliss. Yes, Robert was deceitful. How was anyone to know that Robert preferred men over women? Do you know what all that shit is really all about?

News Flash buddy boy, your pain is simply about your bruised EGO!

Yes....EGO in capital letters.

This guy is a master con-man. For him it was about the money, the high dollar clothing, the exclusive restaurants, slamming down the finest wines, the concert hall premium seats and visiting exotic south sea locations. Yes he took you guys and he probably would still be at it if Amanda wouldn't have walked in on him. Even with that, he still owned her, he was so ballsey that he thought he could move his steady boyfriend in with them. Sadly, none of that is all that uncommon these days. People use people and when they think they got all they could get, they move on to the next target.

That type of usery is an actual lifestyle for many. We all get used to it and at some point, the question that begs to be asked in these matters is two fold. What's in it for me and is it worth it? Is it time that I shut the door or kick the fucker closed?

CHAPTER 26
The Final Holdout

Yes, she will be the last one, she must be, I am exhausted. She has the look that makes me nervous because I know that she is deeply hurting. I don't know if I'll be able to reach her. I don't know if I have anything left to give her but I have to give her my time, at least my time. Cat has been sidestepping me for the last week and I allowed it. I could see that she was deeply affected by my condition. I wanted to spend some time with her, I just didn't know how to talk with her but I know there's something deeply unsettling behind all this. We have hardly even had one hug in all the time she's been here. I could see that she was hanging on my every word. She's watching, she watches every move I make. I don't know if she's trying to lock me into her memories of the man who she once knew or if she's trying to process the impending loss of the man she once knew. Either way today is a day that I must give her

her turn, like any other unsettled business, I struck out to find Cat.

Me: Baby we have jointly been avoiding each other, you know where I sit, and know where you sit, we are very well connected to what's in our hearts. We are going to go to your room now, just you and me and no one else. It's now our time sweetheart.

Cat: David, I don't even know what to say to you! How do I lend comfort to a man that has given me so much? Given all of us so much, how do I encapsulate any part of what you've done for me?

Me: Baby you just did, so tell me about what's going on in that gorgeous little body of yours?

Cat: David, my parents are only six years younger than you but yet I have been seeing some of the same, I don't know if you'd call them symptoms or behaviors. I don't know what to call anything, it's just things are going upside down so quickly for them! I noticed in both my mother and my father that they are less than they once were. They of course had to slow down and some of this might have to do with both of my parents being martial arts sensei's and stunt artists. All of those many years of being struck and striking, breaking boards and all the other things that we do for the studios have caught up to them. They look to be worn out but I also notice as you've talked about, they both have problems with balance. Like you, they don't walk in a straight line either. They slightly but noticeably lean to the side as they walk. Oftentimes they won't walk in front of me, if they're on their feet when I walk into a room they sit down quickly and they don't move until after I leave the room. Also like you, they know that their body and brain is changing.

Me: Sweetie you're talking to the wrong person, you need to sit with Heather. She's been my witness of my continuing illness and changes. She watches it develop every day, sometimes even every hour. I'm not going to diagnose your parents or anyone else for that matter and I suggest you stay the fuck away from all of the medical online bullshit and talk to your family physician. Do they have what I have, has theirs come on sooner than mine? Hell I don't know what I have other than,'Frontotemporal Dementia' sometimes known as 'Lewy Body Dementia'. For me one of the hardest things to process is knowing that I am becoming a completely different person. Everything changes, just so you know, Dementia is also called, "The Long Goodbye."

In my case, I have a rapidly shrinking brain which is what I'm entertaining today. It is untreatable and can not be reversed. My brain is slowly dying. I will eventually forget who my loved ones are and become less of myself. They say that I can eventually become bed ridden with me being unable to move and unable to eat or drink or talk. Many people don't know what it's like to have a loved one who is fighting a battle against dementia but understand this baby, it's not just about me it's just not about your parents it's also about you and your siblings and your extended family. Everyone suffers to some degree when a loved one steps into the arena of Dementia. There's no coming back, there's no treatment, there is no such thing as better days ahead. Everyday becomes more difficult. I'm not concerned about me. I'm concerned about Heather, she's going to have to survive this shit. Did I do anything to deserve having this condition? I guess I could take responsibility but it doesn't matter at this point, but does she deserve all the heartache that comes with it and before you ask, I'll answer your question. No, I have not and I will not consider suicide. Some people may believe that by taking their own life they will save their loved ones' suffering by watching them disintegrate into nothing more than dust, suicide may be viewed as a loving and honorable gesture, in some cases, but not for me.

Remember my dear, that I am the, "Never quit on yourself guy." How in the fuck can I hold myself up as a man of truth if I'm lying all the time. This is just one of those deals, like most all things in life, you have to take it on the chin. It is what it is and ain't nobody going to be able to change it but what we can change however, is the way we approach it. I have already written out my final wishes and I think you've read in this current book I'm writing. I want to be put away, I don't want Heather to have to look at me, day in and day out with living on the edge, always wondering when that day will come and what she's going to do.

As you also know I've given away a bunch of my shit and I have something for you set aside that Heather will give to you when my final day ends. And yes, I do fully expect to have strippers at my service. I expect you to drop a twenty into their G strings if you don't have $20 I'll leave that with your package. Yeah honey, my heart hurts for my friends too. There are times that I wish I was never engaged with any of you, and yes even Heather for that matter. That way I would have no one to say goodbye to but then again, I would have no one that ever loved me. No one's ever cared for me the way you people do. You all gave me the life I live today, through your love, understanding and acceptance. Besides, what kind of guy can get away with squeezing other women's body parts with their wives nod of approval? That nod of approval comes only from trust, she knows what I'm about, you guys all know what I'm about. No, I'm no predator of any kind, all I've ever tried to do is trap people into looking at their own realities and making a plan and implementing the changes for them to live free.

Regrets are one of the things we can never change, for me I have no regrets. I've made all the necessary amends, at least I believe I have, to all of those I've harmed. If I haven't been able to reach them I make living amends with simply practicing decency and kindness to everyone. It has everything to do with the life I live because today, I'm free.

I know that you've met my dear friends, Erik and Christine Bomey. Yeah there's some fine, fine people. No airs about them, what you see is what you get and what you get is priceless. Regarding the topic of true friendships, let me tell you about this. You're not the only one sweetheart that looks at me the way you've been looking. Erik and Christine try their very most not to look at me like you are now. They can't help it because they too can see me starting to diminish or maybe they've seen it for some time, I don't know. It's nothing they want to talk about at this point, I fully know that they are trying to protect me. It's not about their discomfort, their only true concerns are my comfort. On New Year's Day, Eric and I went shooting at our Gun Club. I had a new (to me) but gently loved and used pistol from that asshole (good friend) Craig Lawrey (my favorite gun dealer) who is going to cater my funeral with his world famous catsup sandwiches. Lucky for me, Craig was in a bit of a financial pinch with gun shows being canceled and people not having money because of the sudden high cost of living. Guns are now considered once again, an item of luxury rather than of necessity. People just aren't buying guns or attending gun shows like they did just six short months ago. I have to back up just a bit, I had a bitter blowout with Smith & Wesson gun manufacturers, one of the most successful gun makers in the world, but like everything else in the last four years they too have drastically changed. The customer service people are nothing but assholes in my opinion, they did their damndest to insult and berate me, to avoid them having to admit that they have a problem with the structure quality of their aluminum handguns. If they admit it and if they replace my $2,000 gun as I requested they might be held liable in the future for injury to a person using those particular guns. So replacing my gun would be an admission on their part that they have substandard handguns in the marketplace. If they had to do a recall, it would cost them gazillions of dollars. They would obviously pay someone off who gets injured from the use of those particular guns rather than do a recall and keep everyone safe. That's the story across the board of Corporate America today. This shit wouldn't have gone on six or seven years ago, I've lost all faith in Smith & Wesson firearms. As a matter-of-fact, I sold off all of my Smith & Wesson pistols. I won't have one in my home and I will never shoot one again, so now I slowly have to replace my favorite handguns which of course are no longer my favorites. I have decided that I need to use the money to afford my first audiobook. Baby that's a $6,000 hit and that's just for one book. I have eight books that will come to $48,000 to have my audiobooks recorded and there's absolutely zero, none, nada guarantee of my ever selling any of them. I'm not in the position to take those kinds of risks especially now that I'm at the twilight's end of my life. I don't know what the fuck you call it but I'm not laying down and no one's going to put me down. So yeah I'm going to keep buying guns until I can no longer buy guns. I'm giving away a lot of stuff but I won't give away my guns. This last gun that I just got from Craig will go to Eric, the rest belongs to Heather. Okay I'm done now, on to you my little lovely and I know there's something behind those eyes of yours, let's have it baby.

Cat: Well David, I don't even know how to approach this, nobody knows how to approach this kind of shit.

Me: Just put it out there and we will work through it.

Cat: I think we have all been asking ourselves what would we do if we had this problem that you do? If I knew that I only had twenty-four hours left to live, or one week or a month to live, would I do anything different? What amazes us all, is that you are just so calm and cavalier about this whole thing. I don't think I could hold up, I don't think I could have people around me. I would just want to close and lock the door and sit with my favorite blanket over me. But not you, nope that's not you at all. How do you maintain that? Is there going to be a time where you're going to just close that door?

Me: You know baby, that's not a crazy question, you needn't be afraid to ask it. On the way home from shooting with Eric we had very much this type of conversation and his concern was that I was going to off myself, trying to save Heather from the pains of watching me slowly disintegrate. I assured him that that's not something I will ever entertain. Eric knows me well enough to have that concern and I appreciate his honesty. If you want someone to be direct with you, go talk to Eric, he'll tell you the truth you never even knew existed and those truths will be about you. It's like he is my understudy in knowing his and your truths. As a friend he is at the top of my list.

So let's get back to your question. What would I do differently? Some people say well hell, I go rob a bank! What the fuck are you going to do with the money, you've got only 24 hours to live! If you're going to rob a bank either you're going to get shot or caught and your last few hours on this earth you will be processed into a County Jail or a morgue. If I had a week to live, if I had a month to live, I could tell you what my fantasy is and I've entertained this fantasy most all of my life. If I was given a death sentence of let's say 90 days before I'm called forward I think what I would do is that I would go on a hunt and I would kill every fucken sexual predator that I've ever come across both as a paramedic and as a police officer, if I had my way. Oftentimes you needn't look far from the family tree to find a sexual predator, there are relatives or neighbors who view children as soft targets. So these sick bastards of course befriend a young child, some people call it grooming. I don't know what the fuck you call it but they molest children within the family structure and there's a reason for that. I believe there is no viable reason, just their twisted motives. These predators understand that the family doesn't want to be bothered with that kind of stuff so they overlook it. How many times have adults had to warn small children that if Grandpa or Uncle or Cousin wants you to sit on his lap or to touch them, come and tell me."

My question is why arn't these fuckers already in jail or dead! It's all about protecting the family image, that's all it's about. What would the neighbors think, what would the people from church think, what would the people at work think if they found out that I not only knew but overlooked my relatives or husband molesting our daughters or our sons? Again, it's all about protecting the family image. I have seen women who have been sexually molested by their fathers, as a matter of fact I've had two relationships with women like that, and you know what, they're not right, they somehow I think that they're responsible for what their father did to them. The dirty family secret gets buried and hidden and never spoken of. As that young female matures, she brings that shame and guilt which doesn't belong to her, forward into adult situations. They bring it forward into marriages and what happens? Everything gets broken, why, because intimacy is terrifying for them the trust in men has been broken. This child, now a woman, can no longer believe that they're safe, no matter how convincing the spouse might be, no matter how loving, patient and caring they might be. There will always be that bit and not always a small bit of mistrust. I had to walk away from both of those relationships. Not that I didn't care for these women, it's that I knew the truth and that truth is, I can't make it go away, I can't pretend it didn't happen and I further can't pretend that hasn't affected her nor can I pretend that it doesn't affect me and our relationship. Without massive therapy these people will be broken for their lifetime, all because the family needed to overlook those behaviors to protect the family image. How fucking sick is that? Okay I'm done with that, what else sweetheart, what is it you want to take from me and install into your own life?

Cat: David you have taught me so much about trust, you are the epitome of what trust should look like. You ask no one for nothing unless it's for someone else. You give to all and you have no agendas. You're just a guy that wants to be a good guy to help people. David, you have already given me the gift, I got to witness you. I got to witness you being you, you doing you. I never knew there was anyone like you. Yes I do live in a rather small circle in this world. You have reaffirmed my trust in mankind not all of course, I'm nobody's fool but I know there's more of you out there and it makes my heart glow. That's what you've done for me David, you've made my heart glow and I'll forever be in your debt.

Me: Be careful sweetie, I might call that debt due. Hell I might want you to build a fucking statue of me! I love you sweetheart, you're a wonderful woman and even a more wonderful person. There's nothing better than looking at a person like you and feeling the love and knowing that when it's time for me to go that I've lived a good life.

DAVID J. BROWN

THE END

To contact the author David J. Brown
please email: davidjbrown@gmail.com

To order David's other seven novels
Please visit David's website at:
davidjbrownbooks.com

1 Daddy Had to Say Goodbye

2 Flesh of A Fraud

3 Harvest Season

4 Altered Egos

5 Brothers of The Tattered Cloth

6 The Judicial System Is Guilty: The Raping of Lady Justice

7 Betrayed My Body Is Killing Me

Other books: #BELIKEED

To submit requests for David to speak at your upcoming events: Dbrown624@gmail.com

Watch for David's eight novels to be released in audiobooks throughout 2023.

Printed in the United States of America

Made in the USA
Monee, IL
24 August 2023

41498996R00193